BONES UNDER THE ICE

BONES UNDER THE ICE

A JHONNI LAURENT MYSTERY

MARY ANN MILLER

OCEANVIEW PUBLISHING

SARASOTA, FLORIDA

ISBN 978-1-60809-607-7

Published in the United States of America by Oceanview Publishing

Sarasota, Florida

www.oceanviewpub.com

10 9 8 7 6 5 4 3 2

To my family and friends
Dreams really do come true

BONES UNDER THE ICE

CHAPTER ONE

SHERIFF JHONNI LAURENT half-strode, half-slid down the huge pile of snow, her breath streaming out in a white plume. A February blizzard had blown through northern Indiana the night before. The gusting winds had now died, but the late morning temperature was plummeting. She glared at the pesky reporter perched at the bottom of the hill, pelting questions.

"What's going on? What'd you find?" Ralph Howard shouted. "When can I take pictures? My deadline's in two hours."

"Your deadline is not my concern," she snapped back. "The internet does not get to inform next-of-kin."

"The kid who found the body saw a hand sticking up in the pile of snow," Ralph Howard persisted. "Can you determine the sex or age of the victim? I need to get a few shots. I'll hold off publication until this afternoon."

"Absolutely not. I have no idea what's underneath that mountain of snow or how long it's going to take to extract the body. Get back and stay back." Laurent pointed to the parking lot. She waited until he trudged back to his car, slammed the door, and crawled out of Webster Park's snow-covered parking lot. As far as Laurent was concerned, freedom of the press didn't start until after next-of-kin notification. And that was part of *her* job.

Tucking her long braid inside her fleece-lined jacket, Laurent climbed the pile of snow, knelt once again, the ice-crusted snow cracking under her knees. She was glad she had worn the extra layer of snow gear. She'd need the warmth and moisture protection today. Laurent leaned forward and peered at the slender frozen hand—wrist broken, fingertips resting on the icy ground. Squinting against the glare, she noted the hand was blue, not black, which meant the victim had died before severe frostbite set in. She had seen this before. Frozen extremities. Fingers, toes, top of the ears, tip of the nose—all blackened with frostbite. *Old man Dawson lost both pinky fingers and the tip of his right ear rescuing a baby calf and its mother in the last blizzard.*

Was there an entire body encased in the snow and ice? Laurent brushed away more snow until the frozen limb was exposed to the elbow. The victim wore a white, puffy coat and purple nail polish. Female.

Laurent swallowed and blinked away tears before they froze. In the small farming community of Field's Crossing, Indiana, there wouldn't be a lot of women wearing purple nail polish and certainly no one over the age of forty, possibly even thirty. So young. This was going to hurt. The family, the community, herself. And to make matters worse, today was February 2. A day she dreaded. A reminder of her failure. Exactly thirty years ago she'd given up her baby girl for adoption.

Laurent rose to her feet, head pounding. She had a nasty cold. Her head hurt and she couldn't breathe through her nose. Every time she swallowed, shards of glass stabbed her in the throat. February in Indiana. Everyone had a cold.

She slid her sunglasses down from her forehead, stomped to her SUV, and grabbed the radio, one foot perched on the running board. "Dispatch. Get a hold of Caleb Martin. I don't care what he's doing or where he's at. I want to talk to him. Send Greene and Dak out to

Webster Park. Tell them to bring hand trowels, ice picks, buckets, something to kneel on, and the camera. Also, advise Henry Linville we'll need to use his refrigerator box to thaw a body."

"Ten-four, Sheriff."

"Tell Ingram he's going to have to handle everything else until we can extract the body. Call me immediately if anyone reports a missing person. Contact Starr at the village office and get her started on the welfare safety checks. Make a list of everyone who doesn't answer. After Ingram deals with the fender benders, have him start knocking on doors. Greene and Dak should be able to give him a hand this afternoon."

Laurent grabbed her silver Yeti from the cupholder, slammed the SUV door closed, and strode to the group of parents gathered next to an overturned picnic table. She estimated thirty children had been sledding in the park while ten adults huddled in a circle sipping coffee and chatting. She would need to be careful with what she said.

She took a sip of hot tea from the Yeti and set it in the snow next to her foot before pulling out her notebook. "Thanks for waiting, everyone. I need to get some information. First, who found the hand?"

"We did." Two red-cheeked boys stepped out of the crowd, their mothers' hands on their shoulders.

"I like your Spider-Man skullcap." Laurent slid a gloved hand into her pocket and rocked back on her heels. "What's your name?"

"Danny Gibson. My mom got it for me because I got all As and Bs on my report card."

She lifted a hand for a high five and then nodded at the other boy hopping from foot to foot. "What's your name? You have Batman snow pants. Awesome."

"Tyler Hayes. Batman can beat Spider-Man every time." He punched Danny in the arm.

"Can you tell me what happened?"

"We were racing down the hill," Danny said. "I got flipped over. I thought it was a rock, so we climbed back up to dig it out, except it wasn't a rock."

"I beat him down the hill," Tyler said.

"Did not."

"Did too."

"Doesn't count."

Laurent picked up her thermos and sipped her hot tea and tried to hide her smile. Boys. Always trying to one-up each other. "When did you get here?"

"We'd have been here earlier, but Mom said we had to wait for Field Street to be plowed all the way to the park," Danny said.

Danny's mom's breath whooshed out in a long stream. "We got here around ten, and even then, none of the side streets were plowed. What's going on? Do you know who it is?"

"I'll know more in a few hours. Were you the first ones to arrive?"

Four heads nodded.

"Did you see anyone leaving the park when you got here?"

Four heads shook.

"How long is it going to take to dig it out? Is it just an arm or is there a whole body buried under all that snow?" Danny asked. "Can we watch?"

"Please, Sheriff. This is so sick," Tyler said.

"I'm sorry, boys, but no one can watch. I'm not sure what we're going to find." Laurent raised her voice. "Folks, I want everyone to go home. No sledding at Webster Park until I say so. Build a snow fort in your front yard. Have a snowball fight with the neighbors. If I catch anyone out here, I'll ask Principal Li to assign detention."

Laurent finished her hot tea as kids and parents piled their sleds into minivans and pickup trucks, then she walked to the SUV, her feet squeaking on the snow, and slid behind the wheel. Her heart ached and her eyes blurred. She had been a deputy sheriff for fifteen years before being elected sheriff and had never recovered the body of a child. Grabbing a tissue, she blew her nose. Pulling nasal spray out of her pocket, she inhaled. As she waited for the cold medicine to take effect, she popped two sinus headache pills, smeared Vaseline under her sore nose, and rested her forehead on the steering wheel. Tomorrow was her day off, and she'd been looking forward to staying in her flannel pajamas, fuzzy slippers, and robe all day, binge-watching her favorite Netflix series, *The Great British Baking Show*. Not anymore.

Finally able to breathe through her nose, she pulled her headband down over her ears, flipped up the hood of her parka, and switched into snowmobiling gloves. Sliding out of the front seat, she popped open the trunk and grabbed four stakes and a hammer and paced off twenty steps in all directions around the frozen limb, her back to the hand. As she pounded the stakes into the frozen ground, ice chips flying, Laurent wondered how long the body had been encased in the snow and ice and how long it was going to take to dig out. What did the snow and cold do to the body? And what kind of parents didn't know where their daughter was?

Giving the last stake one more whack, Laurent piled snow around the bottom of it and paused to catch her breath. The entire recovery area had been trampled by sleds and boots and debris. If there were any clues as to why the body was buried here, they'd be hidden under the snow or would have been carried farther down the hill by the sleds.

Hearing the crunch of tires on the snow, Laurent glanced toward the park entrance. Caleb Martin, Public Works Director, was heading toward her in his orange county pickup—plow in front.

"What can I help you with, Sheriff?" Caleb asked as he pulled alongside the SUV and rolled down his window.

"There's a body frozen under the snow pile. I need to retrieve it and place it in storage and to collect anything that doesn't belong with snow and ice. Can you bring me a sheet of plywood to slide her onto?"

"*Her*?" One of Caleb's eyebrows rose. He left the engine running, climbed out, and slammed the door.

"Purple nail polish and a white coat," Laurent said. "I don't suppose you keep track of where all this snow comes from? Maybe you have a wager on who can build the highest pile of snow the fastest so we can tell who built this particular mountain."

"Wish I would have thought of that. The boys would've bet on it. I've got all the plows and dump trucks working, and we're moving snow as fast as we can. But this might help—we've only cleared Field Street and Leeson Street, so all the snow will be from those two areas."

Laurent tipped her sunglasses down and stared at him, her five-foot, ten-inch frame dwarfed by Caleb's over six-foot one. "That's two miles of snow. Who's driving right now? Can you walk me through the process?"

"The quad-county area has twenty-four snowplow drivers or dump truck drivers. Most of them are in Field's Crossing, but there's at least one plow and one truck in every county. I can't be in four places the morning after a heavy snowfall," Caleb said.

"I'll have to talk to all of the drivers assigned to Field's Crossing."

The sheriff and the road commissioner stopped outside the staked-out area, the yellow tape fluttering in the slight wind, the arm and broken wrist exposed.

"How many years have the dump trucks been dumping the excess snow in the park so kids can sled down the hill?" Laurent said.

"We used to toboggan here. Who'd have thought that someday I'd be building this pile."

Wind blew Laurent's hood off, exposing her wind-burned cheeks to the cold air. She was glad her teary eyes were hidden under her sunglasses. The snow swirled at her feet as she stood shoulder to shoulder with Caleb in quiet silence, the enormity of the task in front of her temporarily robbing her of speech. She shivered. The high temp today was going to be thirty degrees, and with the wind feel lower. The cold rarely bothered her, but being outside for the next several hours was going to take all of her strength. Mentally and physically.

Caleb cleared his throat. "Do you want me to help dig her out? I've got shovels in the back of my truck."

"Thanks for the offer, but Greene and Dak are on their way. I'd like to use the back of your truck to transport her to Henry Linville's. He's agreed to store the body until it thaws."

"That old hearse shouldn't be on the roads. Let me empty out the back." Caleb walked to his truck. "Before I go, I'll plow out the parking lot, the entrance, and one lane on Webster Street. Back in an hour."

"I know today's going to be a busy one for you. When you get a minute, would you email that list to me?"

* * *

"Do you recognize her?" Laurent asked.

Deputies Mike Greene and Dak Aikens joined Laurent and the three officers knelt on both sides of the body, sifting snow handful by handful. After Caleb Martin left, she'd given herself a mental shake and banished all thoughts of what lay ahead. Right now, she needed to focus on retrieving the body without further damage and making sure she and her deputies collected any potential evidence. She was assuming this was an accident, but if it wasn't . . . She shook her head. Thinking negative thoughts got her nowhere. There was nothing to indicate this wasn't an accident—some kind of terrible, awful accident.

"No. I don't know who she is." Dak rose to his feet, snapped more pictures, and then ducked outside the yellow tape, aiming for a wider angle. "If we did, it would be easier to figure out why she's here. There are no other vehicles in the parking lot. Did she walk or was she dropped off?"

"I'm betting she's a townie," Greene said.

Laurent shifted six inches to the right. "You're probably right. God, this ground is cold. Knee pads would be nice."

Deputy Mike Greene was a few years older than Laurent and had been with the sheriff's office for thirty years. She barely beat him four years ago in the election for sheriff, and he made no attempt to hide his bitterness. Now he was running against her again. The election was a month away, and the stress brought on by the thought of another campaign battle tightened her shoulder blades and threatened a back spasm. She sat back on her heels and rolled her shoulders, face tilted to the weak morning sun.

"Do you think we can get a print off the hand?" Dak asked.

"If we try to move the fingers, they'll snap like pretzel sticks. We'll have to wait until she thaws." Laurent brushed more snow off the victim's face. "How long has she been here, do you think? She's frozen solid and partially attached to the ice on the ground. This didn't happen this morning. I think she's been here for at least a day, maybe two. I wonder if Caleb did any plowing on Wednesday night before the blizzard. Was she scooped up by one of the snowplows and dumped in the park? Truckload after truckload of snow piling on top of her? Or was she already here, walking through the park, and somehow got buried under a snow drift?"

"I don't know her, but teenagers are dumb enough to go out in a blizzard." Deputy Mike Greene stood and kicked a pile of snow, throwing up a cloud of white. His corn-colored hair stuck straight out from under his headband. "Why in the hell can't people die when it's warm and sunny? Winter in Indiana sucks."

"Farm kids are smarter than that and their parents would've had them home and battening down the hatches, but I'm with you. I think she's from town." Dak stood outside the yellow tape. "Done with that round of pictures. Now what?"

The three officers had chipped around the buried victim until a large chunk of snow and ice with the entire body embedded broke loose. The young girl lay with her knees tucked under her chin, right hand propped up, the broken wrist stiff. Tiny ice crystals had formed in the corners of her eyes, and her eyelashes were frozen to her cheeks. The long bangs were brittle. A pink skullcap was perched on the back of her head—part of it frozen into the ice. A scarf was wrapped around her neck, a few strands of hair caught in the teeth of the coat zipper, and her ripped blue jeans were tucked into ankle-high Rockport boots, the laces loosened.

"She looks like she's sleeping," Laurent said. "Like she had no idea what was happening."

"How can you fall asleep outside when there's a blizzard raging?" Greene snorted.

"Sleeping pills."

"Suicide?" Dak's large gloved hands balled up.

"Please, dear God, no." Laurent scooped up a handful of snow, packed it into a snowball, and hurled it. "We're not jumping to any conclusions. First, we need to find out who she is. I'm going to search for a cell phone. It may be somewhere in the snow, but let's hope it's in her pocket."

Laurent slid her hand into the pocket of the white coat. No phone. She patted the pant leg of the torn jeans. No phone. She brushed a strand of the victim's hair, the brittle pink breaking into several pieces.

She held up a hand. "I'm waiting. I don't want to break any bones or snap off any more hair searching for a cell phone that may or may not be on her person. We've done everything we can for now." She pushed to her feet, the warmth of her breath creating a cloud of white in the frigid air.

"I hate to state the obvious, but she's got no signs of frostbite," Dak said. "Even through the camera lens, I didn't see any. But, look at this." He handed the camera to Laurent.

She thumbed through several shots, raised both eyebrows at the observant deputy, and crossed over to the girl's head. Bending over, she peered closely at the side of the head. "Shit. I see what you mean." She handed the camera back to Dak. "The autopsy will determine the cause of death. For now, we're going to treat this as an unfortunate accident. We're not going to speculate and rile up the community with talk of suicide or murder. That round indentation in the side of her head could be anything."

"You think she was killed?" Greene said. "That's crazy. She's a stupid high school girl who got caught where she shouldn't be and paid the price. For all we know, that's a birth defect." The belligerent deputy stamped his feet and muttered under his breath.

Laurent glared at her deputy. "Let Dr. Creighton do his job. Keep your opinion to yourself until he can perform the autopsy."

"How are we going to move the body?" Dak asked.

"Caleb Martin's bringing a sheet of plywood. We'll slide her on and he'll drive her to Henry Linville's to thaw." A horn sounded from the park entrance, and Laurent waved the road commissioner over. "Here he is now."

Caleb rolled down the window. "Where do you want the plywood?"

"By her feet. If we lift the slab an inch or so, we can slide her onto the plywood. We shouldn't break anything." She massaged her knees.

"Have you been kneeling in the snow since I left?" Caleb asked. "That was two hours ago."

"Getting old is a bitch. My knees are screaming at me. And I stopped feeling my toes an hour ago." She slid her hands under the frozen body. "Greene and Caleb, take the bottom. Dak, you and I are going to lift the top."

Caleb knelt next to Laurent. "No. No. No. I can't do this."

"Don't look at her." Laurent glanced at him.

Under his wind-burned cheeks, Caleb's face was white, his breathing rapid.

"You don't understand. I know her. It's Stephanie Gattison. My brother's girlfriend." He scrambled backward like a crab.

"Easy, Caleb." Laurent crouched next to him, handing him a tissue, putting a gloved hand on his back.

"Take your time."

Caleb blew his nose and wiped both eyes. Stuffing the used Kleenex in his pocket, he shoved to his feet and stumbled.

Dak caught him. "Easy, big guy. Hold on to me. Let's go sit in the sheriff's car."

"Let me crank up the heat." Laurent slid behind the wheel of her police SUV, started it, and clicked the heat on high.

Caleb walked unsteadily to the SUV and slid onto the back seat. "When I was here before," he began, "all I saw was a hand. I didn't know it was Stephanie."

Laurent handed him a bottle of water.

"I think Stephanie really liked Dylan."

"You're positive it's her?" Laurent asked. "Do you know her parents? Where they live?"

"Yes, it's her. Owen and Theresa. Out on Bees Creek."

Laurent stood next to the open rear passenger door. "Caleb, please don't talk to anyone until after I inform next-of-kin. I don't want

Owen and Theresa Gattison to find out their daughter is dead through social media. Do you understand?"

"Yes, ma'am."

"Who should I call to drive your truck?"

"John Cook."

"Give me the keys to your pickup." Laurent slid the truck keys into her pant leg pocket, sealing the Velcro. "After John drives the body over to Linville's Funeral Home, I'll drop you off at your office. Don't call your brother until I've talked to him."

* * *

After John Cook inched out of Webster Park with the frozen body strapped to a sheet of plywood in the bed of the orange county pickup, Laurent dismissed Dak and Greene, climbed into the SUV, and directed the heating vents onto her knees. Pulling off her headband and gloves, she wiped her nose with a tissue.

"How long have you known Stephanie?" She twisted in the front seat to face Caleb.

"Stephanie and Dylan have been dating for a year now. Every month she changed that streak of color in her hair. This month it was pink. And her nail polish. She liked bright colors." Caleb's eyes were closed, his hands bunched into fists.

Laurent put the SUV in gear and eased onto Webster Street. "I'm going to drop you off at your office. I'll radio your secretary when I leave the Gattisons. Until then, please don't say anything. You know how gossip spreads in this town."

"I know how to keep my mouth shut."

"Can you plow out Bees Creek Road as far as the Gattison driveway?" Laurent glanced in her rearview mirror. "I'm sorry. I know this has been a shock for you. Why don't you go home? I'll have someone else plow out Bees Creek."

"Call John Cook. He's the closest plow." Caleb leaned his head against the back of the seat. "It's going to be hell at home."

A few minutes later, Laurent watched as Caleb climbed out of the SUV and stumbled up the stairs to the township office. She popped a Tums, swung behind the county offices, and headed toward Bees Creek Road, her right hand on the bottom of the steering wheel, the knuckles on her left hand knocking on the driver's-side window, following the slow-moving plow.

Twice in her career, she'd had to inform next-of-kin. Both of the deceased had been elderly and the death somewhat of a relief, mixed with sorrow. Today was different. A young woman had died. Laurent's throat swelled as she cranked the heat up higher. Between being outside in the bitter weather for the last few hours, finding a deceased young female, and the fact it was thirty years ago today she lost her daughter to adoption, Laurent was chilled to the bone, inside and out. She knew a lot of the farmers in the quad-county area but didn't know Owen or Theresa Gattison. Was Stephanie an only child? The emptiness of losing a child. The snow-covered road blurred in front of her, and she dabbed at her eyes. She had a job to do.

CHAPTER TWO

"SHERIFF, COME IN. Get out of that miserable cold." Theresa Gattison held the mudroom door open, one aged-spotted hand holding a dish towel, the other hand fighting the outside wind. "You wouldn't know where Stephanie is? We've been trying to contact her all morning. You know how bad cell phone coverage is after a snowstorm. It's nonexistent. Let me get Owen. Hang your coat in the mudroom. Would you like some coffee?"

Laurent pulled off her gloves, palms sweaty, heart thudding against her police vest, mouth dry. "No coffee, thank you. May I sit down?"

The farmhouse kitchen was quiet, except for the scrape of chairs on the linoleum floor and the ticking of the grandfather clock in the hallway.

Laurent waited until Owen sat down and stirred cream into his coffee. Gray stubble covered both of his cheeks and his chin, and deep forehead wrinkles stretched from the top of his bushy eyebrows to his receding hairline.

"When did you last hear from your daughter?"

"Wednesday. Have you seen her?" Theresa stood behind her husband's chair.

"I'm sorry to tell you, but I found your daughter this morning in Webster Park. She was buried under a pile of snow, frozen to death."

Theresa clutched the back of the kitchen chair, one hand covering her mouth, tears forming. "How do you know it's her?" she managed.

"Caleb Martin identified her."

Theresa grabbed the chair next to Owen and slumped into it. "Nooooo!" Her breath came out in a half-scream as her husband turned and grasped her hands.

"Stephanie's dead?" Owen asked. "You're saying Stephanie is dead?"

Laurent nodded. "It took us over two hours to chip away the ice and snow. That's when Caleb identified her."

Theresa leaned back against the chair and closed her eyes. "Where's my baby girl?" Her voice was barely above a whisper. "Where's Stephanie? What happened?"

"Henry Linville's."

Tears streamed down Theresa's splotchy face, the end of her nose turning a dull red. Her lips pressed together, a visible shudder running through her thin body.

Owen sat next to his shaking wife as his gaze made contact with Laurent. Tears ran down his face as he wrapped his arm around his wife's shoulders, tucked her head under his chin, and grasped her left hand, intertwining their fingers.

Laurent stared at her feet and picked a nonexistent strand of hair off her pants. There was nothing she could say to ease the pain and raw emotion. Nothing. So, she waited and listened to the sounds of someone else's grief. To tell a mother and father their child was dead . . .

She twisted her small pearl earring. She retied her boots. Finally, after the grandfather clock chimed the quarter hour and then the half hour, Laurent rose. "Take all the time you need. I have a few questions, but I can come back."

"Wait." Owen cleared his throat and wiped both eyes with the heels of his hands. "I told her to come straight home. She knew there was a blizzard on the way. Why'd she go to the park?"

"All I can tell you so far is that a couple of kids sledding at Webster Park found her under a pile of snow this morning around eleven. It took my deputies and myself a few hours to completely clear the snow off. Do you think you can answer a few questions?" Laurent asked.

Both Gattisons nodded. Theresa wiped her face on her sleeve, grabbed a bottle of all-purpose cleaner from under the kitchen sink, and squirted a clean cooktop, tears dripping and mingling with the disinfectant.

"What can you tell me about Stephanie? What kind of vehicle did she drive?"

"An old pickup. Looking at it, you'd feel like you needed a tetanus shot." As Theresa scrubbed furiously, Owen settled in to talk, a box of Kleenex on the table in front of him, his weathered hands clasped together.

"Where's the pickup now?"

"It's not at the park?"

Laurent shook her head. And sneezed.

"It could be at the water tower. Stephanie and Dylan often met there after school."

"I'll drive out and check. What's the license plate?" Laurent jotted down the number. "Is there any other place the truck might be?"

"You can check the township office where Caleb works," Owen said. "Sometimes she met Dylan there after work."

"You might check Caleb's house, too," Theresa said. "And the high school." She finished cleaning the already spotless cooktop and removed another bottle. Stainless-steel cleaner. She squirted the refrigerator, both hands shaking.

"What time did she usually get home?" Laurent wiped her nose with a tissue.

"Six. She was always in time to help with dinner."

"When she didn't come home on Wednesday after school, what did you think?"

"We assumed she was riding out the storm in town with either Claire Cahill or with Dylan at Caleb's office or house," Theresa said.

"Who's Claire?"

"Stephanie's best friend."

"You didn't call?"

"We lost cell phone coverage and the landline went out when the wind hit," Owen said. "Around four on Wednesday afternoon. The weather hits us out here on the west fifteen minutes earlier than the rest of town. By the time we realized we'd lost coverage, we couldn't reach her."

"So, your last contact with her was Wednesday morning. Did she say anything about her after-school plans?"

"She was supposed to work at the village offices that afternoon," Theresa said. "I called Starr Walters and asked her to send Stephanie home early, and she said she would. She was closing the village office at four due to the weather."

"What were her hours there?"

"Monday, Wednesday, and Friday afternoons three until five," Owen said. "Scanning some old files. She said it was the most boring job in the world. No wonder they gave it to a teenager. A first grader could have done it." His voice cracked, and he laid his head on his arms.

Theresa stepped behind her husband and rubbed his shaking shoulders. "Stephanie worked hard at everything. She was up at five feeding the chickens, collecting eggs, and grabbing breakfast before she drove to school. She worked at Beaumon's as a cashier all day Saturday and Sunday. She didn't spend a lot of time with her friends."

"Social media has changed relationships. Being in the actual presence of friends isn't necessary these days. I'm not a fan." Laurent picked up her gloves and headband and cleared her throat. "The first thing I'm going to do is locate her vehicle. I'm so sorry. Stephanie is with

Henry Linville now, and he'll be taking care of her for a few days. He's a good man to talk to."

Quietly closing the mudroom door behind her and stepping into the cold evening, Laurent caught the burst of another sob from the farmhouse kitchen and glanced back through a window. Theresa sat on her husband's lap, the couple's arms wrapped tightly around each other, both crying, rocking back and forth. Her throat tightened as she bent into the wind and trudged to her SUV.

As she crept out of the Gattison farm yard, Laurent drove with her elbows, blowing her nose and wiping her eyes. Parking the SUV at the end of the Gattison driveway, she took another round of cold medicine while waiting for the defroster to clear the windshield. Theresa and Owen wouldn't sleep well tonight. Or tomorrow. Or ever. In her mind's eye, Stephanie's pale hand waved at her. Sleeping was going to be difficult for her, too, and might be even harder after she interviewed Dylan Martin.

CHAPTER THREE

"I didn't kill her," Dylan Martin said.

"Why don't we all take a minute and calm down. No one is accusing you of doing anything wrong." Laurent's throat was on fire, and she popped a cold lozenge before pulling out a kitchen chair.

"Don't lie to me." Emmit Martin chewed his tobacco furiously, leaned over the kitchen sink, and spat, the yellowish-brown spittle disappearing down the drain.

Dylan sat on a chair in the middle of the kitchen, tears leaking out of his red eyes while Caleb hovered in the doorway with their mother, Jane.

The Martin farmhouse kitchen was warm, the door to the mudroom shut, keeping out the cold night air. Light spilled in from the hallway and family room, where Laurent saw an old German shepherd curled up in the corner of the couch, brown eyes watchful.

"Let's review your last encounter with Stephanie. When was your last contact with her?"

"She texted me during lunch on Wednesday." Dylan shifted his chair to sit across the table from Laurent. He picked at a scab on the back of his hand.

"May I read it?" Laurent jotted Dylan's cell phone number and Stephanie's number into her notebook. *"Meet me at the water tower right after school,"* the text read.

"When cell phone coverage is restored, will you forward that text to me?"

Dylan nodded. His white face had lost its streakiness, and his breathing was steadier, but his shoulders were hunched, his chin trembling.

"You both knew there was a blizzard in the forecast," Laurent said. "What was so important it couldn't wait until after the storm?"

"She was accepted to Indiana University and got a scholarship."

"That's good news, but let me warn you—omitting information is the same as lying in the eyes of the police."

Dylan's gaze dropped to the kitchen floor.

Emmit leaned against the kitchen sink, arms folded across his chest.

"She was pregnant," Dylan said.

"I assume you're the father," Laurent said.

"As far as I know."

"Stephanie had another boyfriend?" Laurent asked.

"No."

"Was she cheating on you?"

"I don't think so."

"Why do you think that she may have been sleeping with someone else?" Laurent asked.

"She accused me of sleeping with Brittany; and so I accused her of hooking up with her old boyfriend."

"Did you sleep with Brittany?"

"Yes," Dylan whispered. A tear trickled down the side of his nose, and he wiped it away with his sleeve. "But I didn't kill Steph."

"Brittany's last name and phone number?"

"Hansen." Laurent waited as Dylan scrolled through his phone. "317-123-4567."

Laurent flipped to a new page in her notebook. "Before we make a timeline for Wednesday, let me make note of who's here. Emmit and

Jane Martin, Caleb Martin, Dylan Martin, and myself. Now, Dylan, start with your route to the water tower."

"Eighth period ends at two thirty-five," Dylan said. "I went to my locker, got my backpack, and left. I turned out of the school parking lot, right on Field Street, and left on the gravel road. There's only one road to the water tower."

"You didn't stop anywhere for food? Something to drink?"

"I went through the McDonald's drive-thru," he said. "Big Mac, large fries, large Coke."

"Go on," Laurent prodded.

"I ate in the car. I got there and parked and waited."

"You were the first one to arrive? What time did you get there?"

"Three. I was a little surprised she wasn't there," he said. "She's got a lead foot, and she was driving on a ticket."

"Was there anyone else at the water tower?"

Dylan shook his head.

"Did you pass anyone on the gravel road?"

"No."

"What time did Stephanie arrive?" Laurent leaned back in the kitchen chair. With Emmit scowling at his son, there would be no lying from Dylan. She didn't know what would happen after she left.

"I don't know. Long enough for me to finish eating. Little after three. I saw her turn onto the gravel road, snow flying behind her. She didn't know how to go slow." Dylan's hands dangled off the end of the armrests, his gaze on the floor.

"Then what happened?"

"We got out of our trucks."

"She didn't get in your truck? You didn't get in her truck?"

"I know the weather sucked," he said, "but her truck was old and smelly and didn't have any heat, and she hated McDonald's. Called them the artery-clogging corporation. She thought there was a conspiracy between McDonald's and the AMA. Get people to eat the crappiest food and twenty years from now there'll be a rash of heart disease and diabetes and God knows what else."

"A conspiracy between the AMA and McDonald's—interesting theory," Laurent said. "So, the two of you are standing in the snow and cold and wind. Then what?"

"She told me she was pregnant."

"And what was your reaction?"

"I swore. I threw a few snowballs. Kicked the tires on my Jeep. Pounded the hood."

"Did you hit her?"

"No. No. No. I'd never hit a girl. I accused her of trying to trap me into marriage. She said she didn't need an asshole for a husband." Dylan raised his head, his sad eyes looking at Laurent. "I'm not an asshole."

"But you were angry with her."

"She said she screwed up and forgot to take her pill and missed a day."

"Then what happened?"

"I suggested she go to a clinic and get it taken care of, and then she threw a snowball at me and screamed what kind of bastard am I. I'm not a bastard. I'm eighteen, and I don't want to get married and have a kid and be a farmer." Tears flowed down both sides of Dylan's face as he laid his head in his arms on the kitchen table and cried.

In her peripheral vision, Laurent saw the frown on Emmit's forehead deepen and his hands clench.

Does Dylan realize he just stabbed his father in the heart? "Who left first?"

"I did."

"Was she in her pickup when you left?"

"Yes."

"You didn't wait for Stephanie to leave, even though you knew the weather was getting bad?"

"I was pissed. You have no idea how much I wish I'd waited. She might still be alive and I wouldn't be talking to you."

"Selfishness always comes back to bite you," Emmit snapped.

"Where'd you go after you left the water tower?" Laurent asked.

"My brother's office," Dylan said. "I knew he'd hole up there, and I didn't want to get stuck at the farm with no TV or cell phone. The power always comes on faster in town."

"What route did you take to Caleb's office?"

"Same, except I turned right on Field Street. That's when I passed Theo. He clipped my side mirror. It should be in the middle of the intersection." Dylan sat up straight, his eyes wide. "Ask him. He'll know it was me."

"Theo who?"

"Theo Tillman. He works at Beaumon's Hardware and plows snow for Caleb. Him and his old man live in that run-down piece of shit house over on East Road."

"What time did you arrive at Caleb's office?"

"Around four thirty."

"Who was there?" Laurent asked.

"Caleb. Maggie, his secretary, was getting ready to leave."

"What did you and your brother talk about?"

"His obsession with the Weather Channel. My obsession with ESPN. School." Dylan rolled his eyes. "The stuff brothers talk about."

"Did you tell him about your conversation with Stephanie?"

"Yes."

"What did he say?" she asked.

"Am I sure I'm the father. Call Mom. Tell her you're staying with me. Dad's going to kill you. All that."

"I notice you're still alive. Then what?"

"I put in a couple of frozen pizzas. We drank a few beers. Watched TV. Caleb talked to Uncle Vern. Twice. We lost power. Waited for the generator to kick in. Went to bed."

"What did your uncle want?" Laurent tugged at the collar of her turtleneck. She was sweating. *Am I getting a fever?*

"Said he saw lights at the water tower. Must have been Theo's headlights."

"Why do you think that?"

"That's where he smokes his weed. He's a pothead."

"Both Theo and Stephanie worked at Beaumon's. Did they get along?"

"Theo was pissed at Stephanie because she caught him stealing money at Beaumon's and reported it." Dylan's eyebrows raised. "I bet he killed Steph."

Emmit pushed away from the sink. "If that pothead is responsible for this . . ." His fists clenched and unclenched.

Jane gasped. "Emmit, don't get started on that old feud."

"I'm going to fire his ass," Caleb snapped.

Laurent held up a hand. "You think Theo killed your girlfriend because she caught him stealing money from the hardware store?"

Dylan shoved to his feet. "I don't know. I'm just saying he's an idiot. Maybe something snapped in that little pea brain of his. Maybe he's lost too many brain cells."

"You've never smoked?" Laurent asked.

"Caleb's got asthma and allergies; smoke of any kind sets him off. Sometimes he has to go to the ER for a breathing treatment. I've seen him struggle to breathe. I wouldn't do that to him. No one in the family would." Dylan gripped the back of a kitchen chair. "Stephanie was alive when I left. I swear. Ask Theo if he can swear she was alive when he left."

Laurent closed her notebook. Darkness had blanketed the country-side before she arrived at the Martin farm, and it was now after eleven at night. She was exhausted. It was clear to her the entire Martin family was in a state of shock and anger and denial. She pushed her chair back and rose, every bone in her fifty-two-year-old body aching.

"What happens next?" Emmit asked. "Are you going to arrest Dylan?"

"I'm not going to arrest Dylan." She smiled wearily as she glanced at the teenage boy.

Dylan slid into a chair as Jane and Caleb sagged against the hallway doorframe.

Emmit cleared his throat. "Thank you."

"No need to thank me. I have to verify Dylan's story so I may have more questions for you later, but we're done for now." She shrugged into her jacket and slipped her notebook and pen into a pocket.

"How are Owen and Theresa?" The dish towel in Jane's hands was twisted into a knot and her thin shoulders were bowed.

Emmit cleared his throat. "Me and Owen been best friends since kindergarten. I hate to think what he's going through."

"You know them better than I do, but I doubt they'll sleep much tonight. If you can get through, I think a phone call would be appreciated."

*　*　*

Spotting the four pole lights ringing her circular drive, Laurent ex-haled, her breath fogging up the windshield as the SUV's tires crunched on the new snow. Four years ago, she'd purchased the decay-ing farmstead on the outskirts of town and demolished the milking barn, leaving the equipment barn, silo, three-car garage, and the farm-house. The paint on the farmhouse was worn to a dingy gray, and black shutters lay rotting on the ground or hung by a single nail.

Weeds and small trees grew out of the dirt-filled gutters, and half of the chimney bricks were missing. The farmhouse had sat vacant for a decade, and the mice had taken over the first and second floors, the raccoons the attic. Laurent loved every inch of her fixer-upper. Vermin and all.

Before moving in, all of the plumbing, electrical, insulation, and drywall was removed, replaced, and brought up to code. In the kitchen, workers discovered the pipe for the exhaust fan above the stove had been hammered shut and the gas line for the oven ran behind the refrigerator, the conduit lying on the floor. An outdoor spigot was found in a dining room wall, and a family of skunks had been chased away from under the rotting front porch, the odor lingering for days.

After closing the door connecting the garage to the mudroom, Laurent hung her parka on a hook, dropped her keys into a ceramic bowl, and turned on every light on the first floor.

Midnight. She had no appetite.

Unlocking the door to her converted music room, she tucked a box of tissues under one arm. Half-burned cinnamon candles dotted the bookshelves and tables. She didn't have the strength to play her cello tonight, so she plopped onto the padded seat below the bay window and hugged a throw pillow to her chest. An eighteen-year-old high school senior frozen to death in Webster Park. Nothing in Laurent's twenty-year career prepared her for the anguish of losing someone so young.

The tears started at the back of her throat and there was no stopping them. Her grief had been building since midmorning, when she first brushed snow off Stephanie's face and then listened to Owen and Theresa grieve for their daughter. Now, in the comfort of her music room, she released the pressure in her chest. Tonight, instead of battling her memories, she let the pain flow along with the tears.

CHAPTER FOUR

"Put the shotgun down." Laurent stared at the black barrel of the gun pointed at her chest, a rush of adrenaline flooding her entire body. The rumors about Vern Martin being crazy were true. She'd located Stephanie's pickup at the water tower across the road from Vern Martin's cabin and followed a shoveled path straight to his back door.

"Gun's goin' nowhere 'til you tell me why you're here."

"I pulled a body out of the snow yesterday."

"What's that got to do with me?"

"Why'd you shovel a path to the deceased's truck?" Laurent asked.

"Shit." Vern's shotgun lowered and he took a step back. "Who was it?"

"Stephanie Gattison."

"Owen's girl?"

Laurent nodded. She released the breath she'd been holding and her hand inched closer to the weapon at her side. "Why are you answering the door with a loaded shotgun? Do you want to spend the rest of your life in prison?"

"I'm not that far from hell right now." Vern took several steps back and disappeared into his cabin.

"Lock up that shotgun." Laurent tugged off her glove and rested her hand on the butt of her gun.

Vern reappeared, hands empty, eyes sad. "Shotgun's locked up."

"Do you always greet people that way?" Laurent glared at Vern, raising her voice to cover the fact that Vern had scared the shit out of her.

"Other than Emmit and Caleb, you're the only person to knock on my door in the last few years."

"What? No door-to-door salesmen?"

Something in Vern Martin's eyes changed. Gone was the fire and fury of the man with the shotgun. His shoulders bowed as he waved her inside. "You're letting all the heat out. Get in here."

Laurent knocked the snow off her boots and stepped into the mudroom. Ten propane gas tanks were stacked to the left and built-in shelving held canned goods, toilet paper, paper towels, and boxes of Kleenexes. Winter coats and sweatshirts hung on a row of hooks on the back wall, and a bench sat below the outerwear. Tucked under the bench stood a pair of winter boots dripping into a boot tray, and next to the tray sat a worn backpack. She folded her sunglasses and slid them into a pocket. "When did you shovel the path to Stephanie's truck?"

"Yesterday morning."

"Why?"

"Wednesday afternoon 'fore the blizzard hit, I saw four sets of headlights at the water tower, but only three left. There had to be one more vehicle over there. I had to make sure no one waited out the storm. I was afraid I was gonna find a dead body."

"Why didn't you check on Wednesday afternoon?" she asked.

"I don't have a rope or carabiner that long and, with the wind and snow kicking up, I was afraid I'd get over there and not be able to get back. You were here when Ray Butler died twenty feet from his back door because of a winter storm. I didn't want Emmit to find me like that."

Laurent tilted her head. "Fair enough. How were you able to see the headlights?"

"I got eyes."

"You must have extraordinary eyesight," she said.

"Same as you."

"What'd you mean?"

"All those shooting contests and marksman's trophies you've won. You, me, and Jim Cotter are the best shots in the quad-county area. You got eyes like mine."

"Point taken." She glanced at the puddle she had created. "Sorry about the mess."

"That's why it's called a mudroom."

Laurent wasn't expecting the wry sense of humor, and Vern wasn't evading any of her questions, but still, she kept a safe distance between them. His shotgun might be on the other side of the kitchen wall and, as far as she could tell, he had a quick temper. "Keep going."

"The blizzard got here. The damn snow was blowing sideways, and I couldn't see two feet out my window. I called Caleb. He offered to come out, but I said no. I'm fine by myself. I was hoping to God whoever left the truck got a ride home with one of them other cars. I sure as hell didn't want Caleb driving out here to look."

"Why'd you call?"

Vern shrugged. "Knew I was gonna lose the phone line. Wanted someone to know I was out here. Alive. Emmit would've been busy bringing in the cows. That's why I called Caleb. If something happened to me, who knows how long that truck would've sat there. Maybe with a dead body. I don't know. Seemed like I ought to tell somebody."

"You told Caleb there was a truck stuck at the water tower. Which window faces the water tower?" Laurent asked.

"Kitchen."

"May I take a look?" Laurent took four steps to the kitchen window and peered out. Her SUV was clearly visible as was the top half of Stephanie's pickup. "Perfect sight line." Keeping her gaze on Vern, she backed up into the mudroom. "When did you lose cell phone service?"

"I don't own one of those goddamn things. I got a landline. Must have been right after five."

"I noticed you shoveled around the entire vehicle. Did you open either door?"

"I had to make sure no one was in there and I tried to start it. No gas."

"Then what?" she asked.

"I walked home."

"Did you touch anything in the pickup?"

He shook his head. "I had my gloves on."

"Did you take anything?"

"No."

"Before the blizzard hit, what were you able to see at the water tower?" Laurent asked.

"I saw Dylan's Jeep. Then I saw Owen's old truck. Then Dylan's Jeep left. Then there was another bucket of bolts, and then there was another car."

"Dylan's Jeep, the pickup that's still there, and two other vehicles," Laurent said. "What time on Wednesday?"

"Between four and five."

"The first vehicle to arrive was your nephew, Dylan?"

"Yes, but he left and then the bucket of bolts left, and then the last car left. The pickup never moved."

"Could you see the drivers of the other vehicles?"

"I saw a pink hat get in the pickup that's still parked there."

"Your nephew leaves and you see Stephanie's pink hat get back in her vehicle, but you can't see the drivers of the other two vehicles. Why couldn't you see the other two drivers?" Laurent was skeptical. She knew she had excellent eyesight, but she hadn't known Vern did.

By his own admission, he should have been able to see the drivers of the other two cars. If they existed.

"It was whiteout conditions by then. Snow blowing sideways. Couldn't see a damn thing."

"Then what'd you do?" Laurent unzipped her coat. The tiny cabin was well heated and a trickle of sweat slid down her back. She had woken up with a low-grade fever to go along with her cold.

"I locked up, turned on the TV, made dinner, and settled in for the next two days. Lost TV the first night. Got a lot of reading done."

"Let me get this straight. You can see your nephew and Stephanie's pink hat, but you can't see the other two drivers?"

"You think I'm lying."

"I'm gathering information," she said. "How well do you know the Gattison family?"

"Just because I don't make myself known in town doesn't mean I don't know anyone. I know everyone in the quad-county area. Born here, grew up here, still live here. And Owen and Emmit have been inseparable since kindergarten." Vern scuffed the kitchen floor. "How did Owen's girl die?"

"I have no cause of death at the moment."

"You think Dylan killed her." Vern's fists were clenched at his sides, eyes narrowed. The angry man who had greeted her with the shotgun was back.

"She was found at Webster Park. Her truck is here. How'd she get there? Did you move her body?"

"No one was in the truck."

"What about Wednesday afternoon? Before the blizzard?"

"You think Dylan killed his girlfriend and ran over here and we dumped the girl in the park?"

"And Caleb dumped snow on the body early Saturday morning before any of the other drivers or plows were out," she said. "The timing fits."

"Get out."

Laurent rolled her shoulder blades to relieve a twitching sensation as she traipsed back across the two-lane blacktop, counting her steps. *Is Vern going to shoot me in the back?* She kept her head up and her footsteps even and remembered to breathe. She needed to talk with the old guys at the Skillet restaurant. How dangerous was Vern? Greeting her with a loaded shotgun? The man was a loose cannon—literally.

The distance from Vern's cabin to Stephanie's truck was five hundred yards. Almost one-third of a mile. The blizzard dumped five-and-a-half feet of snow on the open prairie—at certain points, higher. The stamina required to dig a five-hundred-yard path, five-and-a-half-feet deep, was immense. How many fifty-year-old men would do that? How many fifty-year-old men could do that?

Snow was piled high on both sides of Vern's back door, and a path had been shoveled to the barn. Tire tracks in Vern's driveway stopped short of the barn. The man hadn't driven anywhere, but someone drove out to see him after the blizzard. Laurent made a mental note to ask Vern who visited him while she and her deputies had been digging out the frozen body. With no phone service, she was betting Emmit had driven over to check on his brother.

What had Vern and Emmit talked about? Despite telling Caleb not to talk to anyone, she was assuming he had spoken with Dylan. The question was—when Emmit had driven out to check on Vern, did he know about Stephanie and his son's involvement? Did Vern say something about the pickup at the water tower? He acted like he didn't know whose truck it was, but, according to his own admission, he'd been born here and lived his entire life in the quad-county area. Were the two brothers hiding something?

The Martin family was mixed up in this somehow. Caleb knew Stephanie was pregnant when he identified her at the park on Saturday morning. And then there was his reaction. She didn't think he faked the puking. Maybe he hadn't expected the body to be found. Maybe the sight of the frozen body triggered guilt. Whatever the reason, she needed to interview Caleb. And the family's reaction to Dylan's claim that Theo killed Stephanie had startled her. All she knew of the century-old feud was that Emmit and Neal's grandfathers had started it.

Sliding behind the wheel of her police SUV, Laurent chugged a bottle of water and popped another cough drop. If Stephanie's pickup had run out of gas and the teenager gotten a ride to the gas station, would she have tried to walk back to the water tower? Maybe she lost her sense of direction. Laurent thought that highly unlikely. Farm kids were born with a sense of direction.

She pushed these thoughts away, pulled on her gloves, and wrapped her scarf around her nose and mouth. The blizzard might have passed, but the air was ice cold. A line of gray clouds touched the flat horizon. She had an hour, maybe two, before the next round of precipitation arrived.

Sticking a dozen evidence bags and tags in her pocket and slinging the camera around her neck, she trudged through the shoveled path around the deceased's vehicle. Opening the passenger-side door, she snapped pictures of the interior. She rolled up two blankets and placed them in a garbage bag. Laurent was positive the crime lab would find Stephanie's hair, but what else might be hidden in the blanket? It was too cold to fingerprint the truck. She left the floor mats but took everything inside the glove compartment and behind the bench seat.

Vehicle registration, insurance card, flashlight, Kleenex, rope, small toolbox, jumper cables, candy wrapper, backpack, and purse.

Slamming the passenger door, Laurent wrapped yellow crime scene tape through the handle and tied a knot. She stomped around the rear of the truck, hit an ice patch buried under the snow, and fell to one knee. Swearing under her breath, she grabbed the bumper and pushed to her feet as the first drop of sleet hit her cheek.

The gray clouds were here.

CHAPTER FIVE

"I'M GLAD SHE'S dead, but I didn't kill the bitch." Theo Tillman's dirty blond hair hung down on both sides of his fat face, and beady eyes darted around the conference room. "I haven't seen her in days."

"No one said she was killed." Laurent knew the local rumor mill had decided it was an accident. A careless teenager not realizing how dangerous her situation was. Why would Theo think she was killed?

"It's all over town."

"What is?"

"Her hand was cut off and a snowplow dumped her body at the park," Theo said.

"You've lived in Field's Crossing long enough to know not to believe everything you hear." Laurent set her Yeti of hot tea on the conference room table and pulled out a chair.

She had watched from her third-floor office as Theo walked through the parking lot. Baggy pants, holey tennis shoes, coat flapping open. The bottom button on his shirt was undone, and a roll of flab poked out. Theo was a large young man with big hands and hadn't showered recently.

Despite her stuffy nose, she caught a whiff of his body odor as he walked past and had left the conference room door cracked open. "How long have you been driving a snowplow for the village?"

"Three years. I didn't dump her in the park. You really oughta be talking to Dylan. Or Caleb. Dylan's not old enough to drive a plow, but he could've shot her and his brother dumped her."

"A conspiracy between brothers."

"Yeah. That's it."

"Why do you think she was shot?"

"Just sayin'."

Laurent jotted a note to herself. "What's your relationship with Dylan?"

"There's no relationship."

"Friends? Acquaintances?"

Theo snorted. "I wouldn't waste my breath to say hello."

"Caleb?"

"Asshole. Why are you asking about the Martin brothers?" Theo wound several strands of hair around a finger, tightened it, and let it spring loose, a line of sweat appearing on his upper lip.

"You proposed the conspiracy theory. How do you know Dylan? He's several years younger than you." Laurent clicked her pen.

"Cuz he's Caleb's little brother and he was banging the bitch, so he came into Beaumon's a lot."

"And Caleb?"

"Caleb and me were in the same class at school. Graduated in 2009."

"What classes did you have together?" she asked.

"I don't remember."

"Ever have an argument with him?"

"No."

"Never?" Laurent raised an eyebrow.

"I asked his sister out once. His twin, Morgan."

"What happened?"

"She said no."

"That's all?" Laurent asked.

"Yes. That's all. It was a long time ago."

"And now Caleb is your boss when it comes to plowing snow."

"He sucks at it."

"Why do you say that?" Laurent asked.

"Everyone knew the blizzard was coming. He didn't salt or plow what he could have before the storm hit. No. He sits in his office. He did no preparation for the storm. I ran for the road commissioner job, but they gave it to Caleb. His dad bought off the old guys." Theo smacked his hand on the conference room table, spittle flying.

"Sounds like you don't like him."

The chip on Theo's shoulder wasn't a chip, but a boulder. The Martin family didn't like Theo, and it was apparent Theo didn't like anyone in the Martin family. The century-old feud was alive and well.

"I hate his fucking guts."

"Does that extend to Dylan?"

"Damn straight it does."

"Other than plowing snow for the village, you work at Beaumon's? What's your position?" Laurent asked.

"I do everything."

"Please be specific."

Theo rolled his eyes. "I'm a cashier. I do returns. I drive a forklift. I stock shelves. I'm all over that store."

"Did you ever have contact with Stephanie at Beaumon's?"

"Duh."

"What does that mean?" Laurent narrowed her eyes. She was fed up with Theo's attitude. Every word was laced with contempt or disdain.

"Of course we had contact."

"Tell me about your last interaction with Stephanie at Beaumon's."

"I didn't steal the money if that's what you're getting at." He cracked his knuckles. "I was transferring money from one of the registers to the vault in the back. I forgot to put it in a transfer bag, and I stuck it in my apron. She saw me and thought I was stealing." He cracked the knuckles on the other hand.

"Go on." Laurent hoped Beaumon's had security surveillance and it wasn't erased every day.

Dylan's story and Theo's were different. She sipped her tea. Theo wouldn't look her in the eye. *What is he nervous about?*

"The store manager walked by and caught us arguing."

"What'd he do?" she asked.

"I gave him the money in my apron and he said he'd put it in the safe."

"Were there repercussions?"

"I'm on probation for a month because I didn't follow proper procedures." He air-quoted "proper procedures" with his fingers.

Laurent noted the derision in the gesture. "What does that mean?"

"I can't handle money or work at returns or a cash register for a month. They've got me unloading semis in receiving on second shift."

"That's hard work. Where were you on Wednesday afternoon before the blizzard struck?"

"Beaumon's closed early. I left around four."

"Where'd you go?"

"Home."

"Directly home?" Laurent pulled out a tissue and wiped her nose.

Theo's breath was as bad as his body odor. "I might've driven to the water tower. I don't remember."

"What's at the water tower?"

"Nothing."

"But yet you went there," she said.

"Says who?"

Laurent raised an eyebrow at the sweating young man.

"Can I get in trouble for saying I smoke weed?" Clear fluid leaked out of Theo's nose, and he wiped it on his sleeve.

"No."

"I drove out to the water tower and smoked a joint before going home to my old man."

"What time was this?"

Theo shrugged. "Four fifteen, four thirty."

"Anyone else at the water tower?"

"Stephanie was sitting in her truck, crying."

"What'd you do?" Laurent jotted a note.

If Theo and Dylan were telling the truth, then Theo was the last person to see Stephanie alive. And if the teenage girl's death wasn't an accident, Theo had just implicated himself. She wondered if he knew what he had said.

"I knocked on her window and she told me to go fuck myself and leave her alone, so I did."

"What else did you say to her?"

"I told her I thought Dylan was sleeping with big-boobs Brittany. She gave me the finger." Theo smirked.

"You didn't talk to Dylan that day?"

"That asshole owes me. He hit me in the middle of Field Street and the Five-and-Twenty. Busted my side mirror."

"Did you pass anyone else on the way back into town other than Dylan?"

"It was snowing like hell," Theo said. "I didn't see anybody else."

"Then what'd you do? Where'd you go?"

"I drove home. My old man yelled at me the minute I walked through the door."

"About what?"

"Where have I been? Don't I know there's a blizzard coming? He treats me like I'm ten." Theo rolled his eyes.

"Is there anything else you'd like to add or clarify?"

"Dylan and Stephanie were boyfriend/girlfriend."

"Dylan and Caleb mentioned that, although I'm not sure why the Martins would want Stephanie to die. What do you think?" Laurent tossed her pen on the yellow legal pad and leaned back.

Theo shoved his dirty blond hair behind his ear. "Stephanie must have had something on them or someone in the family. Maybe that crazy old uncle of theirs lost his marbles. Saw headlights at the water tower and thought an alien ship had landed. Demented old fool probably thought she was an alien and shot her."

*   *   *

Laurent climbed the stairs to her office, refilled her hot tea, and watched Theo squeeze into his pickup and rattle out of the parking lot. His driver's-side mirror was missing, and the junker wore two different size rear tires. A screwdriver was jammed between the door panel and the passenger-side window, keeping the window in a permanently closed position. She had found the third vehicle. Bucket of bolts. That's what Vern called it, and he was right.

"What'd the pothead have to say?" Deputy Mike Greene's desk was the closest to her office door. Her reelection opponent was fifty-six years old and cynical and bitter. He had alienated most of the other deputies when he asked them not to show up to work the first day Laurent was sheriff. She didn't think any of her staff wanted Greene elected as sheriff.

"He despises everyone in the Martin family and thinks the deceased was shot." She blew on her tea. "Even though we know he's a pothead, please don't refer to him that way."

"The truth is the truth. He'd be behind bars for a long time if I was sheriff. Did you get anything out of him?"

"Not much except he hates the Martins."

"His dad would've made sure Theo despised the Martins. Neal and Emmit go way back."

"I'm planning to drop by the Skillet and see if I can get more history on the feud."

Greene snorted. "Those two old geezers probably started it. What did Theo have to say about the Gattison girl?"

"He floated a conspiracy theory between brothers. Dylan killed her and Caleb dumped her in the park and covered her up with snow."

"It fits, but he could be saying that because he hates them. Theo doesn't have a lot of brain cells."

"Then there's the alien theory." She pulled her mouse pad toward her and looked at her reelection opponent. "He thinks Vern saw an alien ship land at the water tower and thought Stephanie was an alien and shot her."

"You gotta give him credit for imagination," Greene said. "What are you going to do next?"

"I need to verify a few things while I wait for Dr. Creighton to issue a death certificate and cause of death. For now, we're treating this as an accidental death."

Laurent watched as the lanky deputy settled into his desk chair and pulled out his cell phone. She knew Greene was going to watch her like a hawk and hope she tripped up on this investigation. Anything to give him an edge in the election next month. He was probably on the phone with his best friend, Ralph Howard, the pesky reporter from *The Crossing*, the quad-counties' only printed newspaper. She dropped into her chair behind her desk. She wouldn't put it past Greene to drop hints or misquote her or leak information. *Asshole.*

Deputy Dak Aikens tapped on the window and waved a piece of paper. "Got a minute? Caleb dropped off his list of snowplow drivers. You've got wrinkles in your forehead. What's the matter?"

"I've always got wrinkles in my forehead. Earned every damn one of them," she said. "I talked to Maggie Bailey at the county office, and she confirms both Dylan and Caleb were there at four thirty on Wednesday afternoon, which puts a hole in Theo's conspiracy theory unless they left the township offices after that."

"When did we lose landline and cell phone coverage?" Dak asked.

"Owen said they lost the landline around four, and they're west of us. Cell phones were out by five."

Dak shaved and shined his bald head, sported no body fat that Laurent could see, and was her favorite deputy. The former sheriff, Glen Atkins, hired him five years ago, making Dak the first African American deputy sheriff in the quad-counties.

"The only way the Martin conspiracy works is if Vern is involved, and that old coot doesn't carry a cell phone." The chair creaked as Dak settled his large, muscled body in front of her desk.

"Dylan said Vern called Caleb twice on Wednesday between four and five and said there were headlights at the water tower. I verified the calls. Three and four minutes," she said. "Vern's landline went down at 5:02."

"Enough time to explain and cover up a death, accidental or not."

"I agree. So, Vern and Caleb talked before 5:02. Theo says Stephanie was alive at four thirty." She laced her fingers behind her head. "What happened between four thirty and 5:02?"

Dak arched one eyebrow.

"Stephanie's truck ran out of gas. I tried to start it. Gas gauge read empty. There were two blankets, two bottles of water, and six Hershey chocolate bars. It looked like she had settled in to wait out the storm until the fourth vehicle came along. Maybe the fourth vehicle dropped her at the gas station and she tried to walk back to her pickup with a full gas can."

"We didn't find a gas can, but, with all the snow and wind, a gas can, full or empty, could be in the next county." Dak crossed one ankle over his knee. "There's no way a farm girl tried to walk two miles with a full gas can in a blizzard. I don't care what Greene thinks of high school kids."

"I'm wondering why Theo thinks the victim was shot. He specifically said he didn't kill her, not once, but twice. Are we going to find a bullet hole?"

"God, I hope not."

Laurent rolled her chair back. "I'm having lunch with Starr. She was Stephanie's boss at the village. Tomorrow, I'm viewing the exterior of the body. Henry thinks he should be able to cut away the clothing and Dr. Creighton can conduct an external exam. Then we'll be able to rule out foul play."

"Let's hope so or things are going to get ugly, especially if Neal and Emmit get their backs up."

"And you know they will."

* * *

Laurent loved the Skillet. The restaurant was owned by a farmer's son, who sold his inheritance, bought the old diner in town, and razed it, keeping only the name. The diner opened at five thirty every morning, except Sundays, and the first two pots of coffee were emptied within fifteen minutes. The Skillet was the local watering hole for Field's Crossing's senior citizens, retired farmers, and veterans. On any given morning, at any given time, there would be ten to fifteen elderly people sitting, chatting, and drinking their share of coffee. The working locals ate breakfast and left.

Laurent opened the door and inhaled the aroma of fresh-baked bread, the house specialty. Toasted and served with every meal. She sent a silent thanks to the makers of nasal spray as her stomach rumbled and her mouth watered.

The restaurant was half-full, but Laurent spotted her best friend, Starr Walters, in the middle of the room, menus unopened on the table. "Have you been waiting long?"

"Two minutes. How's your cold? I ordered hot tea for you." Laurent loved Starr's armful of bracelets and colorful muumuus. The two women met when Laurent answered a domestic disturbance call at Starr's residence and discovered the large woman had hit her husband over the head with a frying pan because he cheated on her. As the two women waited for the ambulance to transport the unconscious man to the hospital, Starr asked if Laurent was going to arrest her for domestic abuse. "Only if he presses charges," she had answered. Laurent never knew how Starr convinced her ex-husband not to press charges, but she was pretty sure the seared memory of an outraged Starr holding a cast iron skillet had something to do with the ex's decision.

"I feel like shit. Hurts to talk, low-grade fever, and my ass is dragging. You sure you want to be in the same room as me? You might catch it." Laurent squeezed lemon into her hot tea.

Starr scoffed. "I'll fight it with booze."

After they'd ordered, Laurent sipped her hot tea, leaned back, and sighed. "That felt good all the way down. I didn't realize Stephanie worked for you."

"I hired her in September right after school started. Sweet girl. Big dreams. She was saving every penny so she could go to college." Starr dabbed at her eyes with her napkin, the bracelets jangling as they slid to her elbow.

"Did you know she was pregnant?"

"Damnit. Who's the father?" Starr asked.

"Dylan Martin."

"Fuckin' A."

"When was the last time you saw her?"

Laurent was used to her best friend's coarse language. Starr's opinions were always laced with a swear word. Or two. Sometimes she wondered if Starr were to stop swearing if she would know any other words or be able to complete a sentence. Fortunately, Starr toned it down in public, and Laurent was grateful for that.

"Monday afternoon. I told her I was keeping an eye on the weather and I'd call her about Wednesday. Weather reports are becoming more and more reliable, and the Weather Channel's been predicting this blizzard for the last five fucking days."

"When did you call her?"

"I texted her at two thirty. Right before school let out. Her mom called earlier in the day asking to let Stephanie out of work. I told Theresa I'd send Stephanie home immediately."

"Did she show up?"

"Never saw her that day, and she didn't return my text."

"Would you forward that text to me? What time did you leave?" Laurent asked.

"I closed the village offices at four and changed the message on the answering machine and forwarded all calls to your office," Starr said. "The last person I talked to was ass-wipe lawyer Jim Cotter, and he was putting on his coat and leaving, too. He said he'd lock the office doors but leave the main entrance open."

"What was Stephanie's job?" Laurent asked.

"The village trustees got the shit scared out of them when the fire in Alexander County burned up the county's records, so they allocated money in this year's budget to hire someone to scan in all of the old documents. They also authorized a separate laptop for the job."

Both women sat back as the waitress placed Starr's Cobb salad and Laurent's chicken noodle soup and toasted white bread in front of them.

Laurent blew on the hot soup. "Anything else about Stephanie or last Wednesday?"

"Nothing that I can think of. When will Henry have her ready?"

"It'll be at least a week. Who knew she was going to the water tower?"

"Probably Dylan, friends at school, her parents, coworkers at Beaumon's, anybody with a phone. Why do you ask?"

"I'm searching for a fourth vehicle. I've confirmed Stephanie's truck, Dylan's Jeep, and Theo's pickup were at the water tower before the blizzard struck. Dylan and Theo both say they left Stephanie crying in her car. Vern Martin says there was another vehicle."

"How reliable is that old bastard?"

"He greeted me with a loaded shotgun."

"I thought that old fucker was getting better." Starr laid her fork down and leaned back. "How are you doing? Saturday had to be the mother of all days."

"Finding a teenage girl frozen to death on the same day I gave up my daughter for adoption, thirty years apart, sucked. Big-time. I woke up depressed and then the day got worse. By the time I left the Martin farmhouse, I barely had enough energy to drive home, take off my coat, and collapse. I don't remember a worse day."

*　*　*

After dropping Starr off at the village hall, Laurent headed to Cook's gas station mini-mart. She pulled open the door, the overhead cowbell clanking.

John Cook's head popped up over the counter. "How's it going, Sheriff? How ya holding up in this godawful weather? I understand we're in for more nasty stuff, not that this isn't bad. It's been a long time since I've had to wear two sets of long underwear to keep me warm. But that could be old age talking. Too bad about Stephanie. Do you know what happened yet? That poor girl. She was in here a couple of times a month. Nice kid. The entire town is talking about it. You should hear the old guys at the Skillet. They've been arguing for days. 'Course, they remember when Ray Butler died twenty feet from his back door. You got a cold? You don't look so good."

Laurent held up a hand. John Cook would talk anyone's ear off if they let him. "This cold is kicking my butt, but I wanted to ask if you saw Stephanie Wednesday afternoon before you closed up?"

"Nope."

"When did you last see her?"

"Probably a week to ten days ago. If you want, I can check. She always used her debit card. I've probably got it on file somewhere."

"That's what my investigation shows," Laurent said. "She filled up on January twenty-first for thirty-seven fifty-three. About a week before she died. I wanted to confirm it with you."

"Wednesday was a busy day. Everybody filling up. I ran out of cases of water."

"What time did you close on Wednesday?"

"I shut down between four and four thirty. When you can't see through your store front window, it's time. Nobody's coming," Cook said.

"Would Stephanie have been able to pump gas if you're not here?"

John Cook shook his head. "Against the law. And I shut off the pumps."

"The next nearest gas station is at the other end of Field Street."

"That's right. Not a whole lotta competition this part of town."

"Did you see either Dylan or Theo on Wednesday?" Laurent asked.

"I never see Dylan. Emmit's got a pump at the farm. Easier to fill all his equipment. Theo comes in every week. Pays cash. Never completely fills up. I've seen him count the money in his pocket before pumping gas. Seems to me money is tight at the Tillman household."

"You're the closest retailer to Vern Martin. How often do you see him?" Laurent placed two granola bars on the counter and pulled out her wallet.

"He fills up about every two weeks. Pays cash, just like Theo. He really ought to get rid of that beat-up old truck. Must have a million miles on it."

"Can vehicles even drive that many miles?"

"Just sayin'. That truck is at least twenty years old. I can't remember seeing Vern drive anything else."

"How do you think he's doing?"

"Fit as a fiddle. Spends the whole day chopping wood, shoveling snow, skiing around the lake. Emmit has him planting in the spring in the far fields. Reads a lot. You might ask the librarian. He might talk to her more than me. I can't get ten words out of him. Yeah, yeah, I know. It would help if I didn't talk so much." He scanned the granola bars. "Can I get you anything else?"

"Large hot chocolate to go."

CHAPTER SIX

"Heard you found a body at Webster Park." Glen Atkins and his chocolate lab, Duke, filled the doorway of Laurent's office.

The former sheriff had grown stoop-shouldered in the last few years as arthritis crept up his spine and crippled his knees. Laurent wondered how long it would be before Glen needed a walker, or worse, a wheelchair. It would hurt to see him that way.

"Technically, two fifth-grade boys found the body." Laurent walked around her desk and crouched to scratch Duke's ears. Ten years ago, Glen had rescued the chocolate lab from a car fire and, after recovering from burns, Duke could be seen riding shotgun with Glen or lying on the carpet in Glen's office. Now, the old dog's muzzle was gray, and he was in an advanced state of hip dysplasia.

The winter sun streamed through the windows in Laurent's office, catching stripes of dust drifting in the air, eventually landing on the dark-gray carpet. Her office was quiet, the squad room empty, except for the department secretary. The oval clock she inherited when her parents died hung in the middle of the side wall, surrounded on both sides with bookcases filled with department manuals collecting dust. The intertwined dangling vines of two golden pothos lay along the tops of the bookcases. In the corner sat a music stand, where Laurent draped her scarf, headband, and gloves.

"How are you, Glen? And yes, I have a cold. Everyone keeps reminding me."

"I've already had my winter cold, but some days I don't think these old bones will ever be warm again. Duke and I should have driven south before the blizzard. What in the hell's wrong with me? I say I'm tired of the winters and the snow and yet I still live here. I'm even thinking of getting a snowblower. Took me all damn day to get out from under the blizzard."

"You should've called Caleb. You know he'd plow you out."

Old-timers. Gotta do it the hard way.

Part of her admired that. The other part was grateful for snowblowers. "Don't kid yourself. You're not going anywhere. You're attached at the heart just like the rest of us. I'm heading over to Henry's to see how the body is thawing. Want to ride along?"

"God, yes." Glen pointed to the carpet. "Stay." Duke circled the carpet, closed his eyes, and, with a soft sigh, settled in the sunshine. "There are times when I wish I was a dog. I'd like to bask in the sun and take a nap."

Ten minutes later, Laurent knocked on the back door of the only funeral home in the quad-counties of north central Indiana. The white brick building had two porticos, one in the front and one on the side. Large empty urns sat on either side of the main entrance, and white lights circled the fluted pillars of the overhang.

"Come in. Come in. Get out of the cold," Henry said.

Laurent had never seen Henry in anything but a black suit, white shirt, and boring tie. She wondered if he owned any other clothing. What did he sleep in? The thought tugged the corners of her mouth up.

Laurent and Glen knocked the snow off their boots and hung their jackets on hooks by the back door. Laurent stripped off her vest and flannel shirt, leaving only her turtleneck. In her experience, funeral homes were always too warm.

"I set the locker at thirty-eight degrees Fahrenheit so the body would defrost slowly," Henry said. "I assume you don't want the exterior thawed and the organs frozen like a Butterball turkey."

"I'd also like to collect what's left over after the snow and ice melt," Laurent said. "I need to determine whether a snowplow scooped her up, dumped her into a truck, and then deposited the body at Webster Park or if she was at Webster Park already and the snow dumped on her. Basically, I want to make sure her death's an accident."

"Let's pull her out."

The two sheriffs stood in the hallway outside the refrigerated lockers as the funeral director donned a mask, gloves, and gown. Henry steered a gurney out of cold storage and into the embalming room. The empty room was warm, the bitter astringent smell of embalming fluid absent.

"It's been three days since I dropped her off. Has she thawed at all?" Laurent asked.

"I believe so," Henry said. "As you can see, I placed her on her back and the arm sticking up has thawed enough so I laid it across her stomach. There's been a constant drip, and her hands and feet seem to be thawed, but that's all. Most of her limbs are partially frozen. If we try to move them, they'll break."

Laurent crossed the room so she was on the body's left side and peered at the high school senior. There was the streak of pink hair Caleb mentioned and the purple nail polish Stephanie's mother had confirmed. The girl's face had softened, and mascara from the frozen eyelids had thawed, running down both sides and into her blonde hair.

"Can we brush off more snow and ice?" Laurent had been hoping more of the body would have thawed, but Henry's analogy of a Butterball turkey seemed correct.

"Gently, don't tear," Henry said. "See the ripped jeans? The ice has frozen the leg to the threads."

"I'm going to unzip her coat." Laurent snapped on latex gloves. With two fingers on her left hand, she held the edge of the coat at the top of the zipper and, with her other hand, pulled down. And parted the coat. The pink plaid shirt was stiff and unbuttoned, revealing a spaghetti strap T-shirt peeking through. She opened the coat wider and frowned. "Her chest cavity seems caved in."

"It looks to me as though the entire body cavity is depressed from the sternum down to the pelvic area," Glen said. "Henry?"

"From my angle at her feet, it looks like she has a 'V' running down the middle," Henry said.

"Does anything else look out of place to you?" Laurent glanced at the wrinkled forehead on the funeral director's face.

"Her head isn't settled, but that could be due to the fact her neck is still frozen."

The pink skullcap slid off the girl's head and lay soaking wet next to her ear.

"I'd like to move her scarf off her neck and drape the ends over the sides of the gurney so it can drain," she said.

"Let me get some clamps."

Gently, Laurent brushed a few strands of hair from the girl's forehead. Nothing broke off in her hand today. "So young. Why her? Why now? How does something like this happen? I haven't slept well since I found her."

"You've got a lot more sleepless nights ahead of you. The older I get, the more difficult the answers are. Aging isn't for the faint of heart." Glen reached over and squeezed Laurent's arm. "Other than the sleepless nights and yearly winter cold, how are you holding up?"

"Stephanie's death hits close to home. When I gave up my daughter for adoption, it hurt worse than death. Now, I'm not so sure." Only two people in Field's Crossing knew about Laurent's past—Starr and Glen. And she wanted to keep it that way. No one else needed to know the special circumstances of that horrific night. When Glen offered her a job with the sheriff's office, she had felt obligated to inform him. After all, there was a police report on file from thirty years ago. He deserved to know. She had told Starr during a ladies' night out and too much wine.

The two sheriffs stood on opposite sides of the gurney as the door opened and Henry wheeled in a stainless-steel cart with tools. "I brought a few other things we might need."

Using clamps, Laurent and Glen lifted the frozen scarf away from the neck and hung the ends off the gurney.

"I don't think she was strangled." Laurent bent over and peered at Stephanie's neck. White, unmarred, no bruising, no discoloration.

"I don't see anything unusual other than the depressed body cavity and the weight of the snow may have done that," Henry said. "Why don't we prop her on her side and look at the back side?"

"Are we going to break any bones?"

"Let me get some towels and line one side of the gurney. We won't be able to do a full turn, more like a gentle prop."

A puddle formed under the gurney as the warmer room temperature melted snow and ice. Laurent slid a gloved hand under the girl's shoulder while Glen steadied the body at the hip. It was like sliding a hand into ice water. She shivered.

The funeral director moved to the head of the gurney, and his hands cradled the sides of her face. "What else can I do for you?"

"Can we shine more light on her head?" With one gloved finger, Laurent traced the outline of the deceased's skull. She did it again. "Something's not right."

"Let me comb out her hair," Henry said. "Then I'll lift it off her head and neck." The funeral director's touch was gentle, reverent, the wide-toothed comb gliding through the wet hair. "I've been in the funeral home business for twenty-five years. Do you know that if your spouse dies, you're called a widow or widower? If your parents die, you're called an orphan. But there's no word for a parent who loses a child."

"That thought never occurred to me." Glen cleared his throat.

"Amen." Laurent pulled a tissue out of her pocket.

Henry's gentle actions and thoughtful observation brought tears to her eyes.

The funeral director slid a long-necked lamp to the head of the gurney and adjusted it, strong light bearing down on the girl's head. He lifted the wet pink and blonde hair.

Laurent bent over until her nose was level with the gurney and stared at the scalp. Gently parting the hair, she saw two round dents in the skull, each one-half inch deep.

"Do you see what I see?" She looked at Henry.

"That's why her head wasn't settled. Those two dents aren't normal."

*   *   *

"Have you ever dealt with a murder?" Laurent handed her former boss a Diet Coke from her mini-fridge before sitting behind her desk. Picking up the remote control to her Bose speakers, she scrolled and clicked. *Moonlight Sonata* by Beethoven flowed.

Glen dropped into the chair in front of his old desk. "One. I really didn't have to solve it. I asked a few questions and the guilty party started crying about how sorry he was and how he didn't mean to do it and how he'd never do it again. Murder is rare out here."

"She didn't hit herself in the head. The dents were round, like a ball peen hammer. Considering how solid the core of Stephanie's body is, I think she died on Wednesday. Either way, I've lost several days of investigation, to say nothing of the fact there's no evidence. Dr. Creighton's going to stop by when he's done at the hospital and give me a prelim."

"I had the same thought. Unfortunately, there have to be hundreds, if not thousands, of hammers in the quad-county area. The village of Field's Crossing probably owns a few dozen. There's one in that old toolbox sitting in the storage room."

"If the murder weapon is a hammer, then using the murder weapon to find the killer is going to be tough," she said. "Who hit Stephanie in the head and then left the body in the park for the dump trucks to pile snow on? The murderer has to be local. Everyone knows the excess snow is piled in Webster Park."

"Was she dead or did she suffocate?" Glen said. "I'd start with her friends, but interview them one at a time. Intimidate them. Scare the crap out of them."

"Don't like high school kids?"

"Not really." He sipped his Diet Coke. "I know you like kids. Every year on the first day of school, I found you parked at the school campus talking with the teachers and the kids, all ages. You started at the high school, then you went to the middle school, and you ended up the day at the grade school. Besides that, I know you volunteer with the music department."

"Nothing gets by you." She leaned forward and put her elbows on her desk. "Dylan Martin was the deceased's boyfriend, and he admitted to getting her pregnant. According to him, however, Theo Tillman was the last person to see the victim alive, and when I talked to Theo, he said he left Stephanie sitting in her truck, crying on Wednesday afternoon."

"Crap. Just what we need is another Martin-Tillman incident. They're worse than the Hatfields and McCoys."

"What's the history of the feud?"

"How long you got?" Glen crossed one ankle over the other and laced his fingers across a slight potbelly. "It started with Emmit and Neal's granddads. Emmit's granddad bought the land where the Martins live now and built the farmhouse. Turtle River flows through the east side of the property down to Turtle Lake. Neal's granddad bought the land directly west of Turtle Lake. Then Prohibition hit. 1920. The Tillman family gave up on farming and became bootleggers and rumrunners."

"What's the difference?"

"Bootlegging is transporting liquor over land, rum-running is the same except over water."

"Got it. So the Tillmans did both."

"Tried to. Granddad Martin wouldn't let Granddad Tillman use the river that cut through his property, and Tillman couldn't complain because what he was doing was completely illegal. One night, Granddad Martin shot up Tillman's barrels of Kentucky whiskey. Tillman lost the entire shipment. Set him back some. Tillman then tried to bribe Martin and that went nowhere. He was forced to cross Turtle Lake and ship by land, north to Detroit."

"He still made money."

"Tons. But he was shortsighted. He must've thought Prohibition would never end. He sold some of his property on the north side to old man Perry, who sold it to Granddad Martin, which pissed off Granddad Tillman. Then the stock market crashed."

"That shouldn't have hurt Tillman. Prohibition didn't end until the midthirties," Laurent said.

"Nineteen thirty-three. Tillman's bootlegging business goes under. He's got about five hundred acres of land, but no crops, no livestock, and, after a few years, he's outta money. Never saved a dime."

"He brought all this on himself."

"Yes, he did. But what Granddad Martin did next was what cemented the feud."

Laurent raised her eyebrows. This was all new to her. "What'd he do? Where'd you hear all this?"

"My old man. In exchange for food and milk, some livestock, and seed to replant, Granddad Tillman signed over one hundred acres to Granddad Martin. The land next to Turtle Lake, which left Tillman's livestock dependent on rainfall and a well. There's a lot of folks who feel the Martin family was fair—gave Tillman a new lease on life after a decade of bootlegging and breaking the law. And then there's others who said Granddad Martin could have taken other property, not the lake. Either way, Tillman was now under Martin's thumb. At least that's the way he felt."

"And Granddad Martin felt Tillman should be grateful to be alive. Him and his whole family," Laurent said.

"You got it. Neal still feels like Emmit's got the upper hand, which he does. The Martin family's decisions have always been based on acquiring land and making it profitable. The Tillmans have always looked to make a quick buck, not work too hard, cheat the system. Granddad Tillman left the remaining four hundred acres to Neal's father, who left it to Neal."

"What about Emmit's dad and Neal's dad? Any bad blood there?"

"Neal's dad planted a pot farm."

"Another get-rich-quick scheme."

"Raking in the dough until he had to spend a few years in prison."

"What a dumbass." Laurent snorted.

"Emmit's dad's the one who spilled the beans. The guy who was sheriff before me put Neal's dad behind bars. Neal was too young to run the farm, so things went into the crapper."

Laurent propped her elbows on her desk. "And now Neal's a regular at Gray Fox Casino and Emmit's butt is in the saddle of a tractor

every day. Theo's a pot smoker, and all three Martin kids are successful. A vet, a road commissioner, and Dylan on his way to college. As
long as he didn't kill his girlfriend. No one in the Tillman family
wants to work hard and earn their keep, and it's the exact opposite in
the Martin family. No wonder they despise one another. They're
polar opposites."

The current sheriff and the former sheriff were quiet. Outside, the
wind picked up and the window in Laurent's office rattled.

"Do you think Neal's in financial difficulty?" Laurent asked.

"Probably."

"That doesn't help."

"Spring planting's right around the corner. If Neal didn't profit
enough from last year's harvest, he'll be begging at the bank. Again.
I've thrown his ass in jail more times than I can remember, and he's
always crying about the same thing. He's got no money and the Martins got it all." Glen pushed to his feet. "Well, call me if you need help
with the investigation. I've got nothin' but time on my hands. What
did CSU say?"

"They're swamped and, since the body is still frozen, they won't
drive out. Essentially, I'm on my own, but, trust me, I'll give you a call
as I muddle through."

"How are you getting along with Mike Greene?"

If Glen Atkins hadn't endorsed her four years ago, Laurent
doubted she would have won the election. The farming community
was very traditional, and she was grateful for her former boss's support. Since the election, Greene had been a less than ideal employee.
Twice in the last three-and-a-half years, she had conducted a repri-
mand review with him.

"He hasn't been too bad. He waits until I'm out of the office before
he bad-mouths me."

"I hired him when he was twenty-four, thinking a hometown boy would be a good liaison and have some insight on the area. He's been a disappointment. Watch out for him. His best friend is snake-in-the-grass Ralph Howard. The two grew up next door to each other." Glen shrugged into his jacket. "When are you going to start campaigning for reelection?"

"I was hoping never. I had a brief moment of hope the other day when Greene said he was sick of the Indiana winters and was retiring to Arizona. I'd pull every string I have to get him early retirement."

"He's not going anywhere until he gets to be sheriff. You need to get started. He wants your job. He had a few unkind words for me when I endorsed you four years ago. Don't underestimate him. He's got the ears of the press and, since the Howard family owns the paper, they can say whatever they want. Truth be damned." Glen opened the door and snapped his fingers. "Let's go, Duke."

Laurent watched Glen limp out of her office and stop to speak with the secretary, who still had treats for Duke in her desk. She knew he was headed to the Skillet to chat with old friends. She had learned a great deal under Sheriff Glen Atkins, and if the retired sheriff's arthritic knees and back hadn't gotten so bad, he'd still be sheriff.

She closed her door. This was her first murder investigation and her top priority was to interview Stephanie's friends, which meant accessing her phone records. The phone was missing. It wasn't in the pickup truck at the water tower, and they hadn't found a cell phone at the crime scene. After realizing the implications of the dents in the skull, Laurent searched all of the victim's clothing at the funeral home. No cell phone. She couldn't subpoena the phone records until Creighton declared the teenager's death a homicide, so she'd have to ask Dylan who Stephanie's friends were and talk to the principal at the high school.

She narrowed her eyes and drummed her fingers on the desk. A murder one month before the next election. The timing sucked. Ralph was going to enjoy poking at her in *The Crossing*. She had two days, maybe three, before everyone in Field's Crossing knew Stephanie had been murdered. Fingers would point to Dylan and Theo. And the town would line up on both sides.

CHAPTER SEVEN

"IT's NOT TRUE. Please say it's not true." Stephanie's best friend, Claire Cahill, met Laurent at the front door, her parents hovering in the foyer behind the teenage girl. "It's true." Claire burst into tears, sinking onto the bottom step of the staircase, her mother sitting next to her, arm around the sobbing girl's shoulders.

"I'm afraid so." Laurent stepped inside the cluttered hallway, trying not to trip on the boots and shoes spilling out of the tray.

"Come on back." Mr. Cahill led the way. "Can I get you something to drink, Sheriff? My wife makes the best hot chocolate in Field's Crossing."

"I love hot chocolate." Following Claire's father through the hallway, Laurent laid her gloves, notebook, and pen on the kitchen table and hung her jacket on the chair before sitting with her back to the bay window. With the sun streaming in, the kitchen was toasty warm. She waited as Claire and her mom settled into chairs opposite her. "How long have you known Stephanie?"

"All my life. Well, it seems like all my life. We were in middle school together. Middle school sucks. We hated it and couldn't wait to go to high school." Claire's pink nose piercing sparkled in the sunshine.

"Best friends are special. Do you remember the first time you met Stephanie?" Laurent nodded her thanks as Mr. Cahill placed a steaming mug of hot chocolate in front of her.

"I found her crying in the bathroom. This jerk in our class dumped her, and I told her he wasn't worth her tears."

"What did she say to that?"

"She got up off the bathroom floor and said, 'You're right. I'm Stephanie.'"

"That's a wonderful memory. You're both seniors this year?" Laurent sipped the hot chocolate, its warmth soothing her sore throat.

"And now she's not going to graduate. We were going to have a sleepover the night before prom and spend the day getting ready, and on senior skip day, we were going to Indiana Dunes."

"For graduation you might organize a memorial for her. A slideshow with her favorite music, something like that. I know it's old-fashioned, but I'm sure Principal Yoshida would be supportive of some kind gesture." Laurent clicked her pen. "Do you think you can answer a few questions for me?"

Claire's eyes brightened. "Our playlists are the same. I'll do that."

"When was your last contact with Stephanie?"

"Wednesday morning for like two minutes. Our lockers are next to each other. I waited for the warning bell, but she was running late, and we didn't have time to talk."

"Did this happen a lot?" Laurent asked.

"Kinda. She's got chores in the morning and sometimes she hit the snooze button more than once. Getting up in the morning sucks, especially when it's still dark outside. I wish winter lasted for a month. Thanksgiving to Christmas."

"The cold and darkness affects all of us," Laurent said. "I know all I wanna do is sit in my jammies and watch TV all day. What was her mood on Wednesday?"

"She looked tired, but she hadn't put any makeup on yet, so maybe that's why."

"When was the next time you saw her?"

"I didn't. We don't have any classes together this semester, and she didn't stop by her locker after school. I figured she wanted to get home and help her folks get ready for the storm."

"Who else is in your circle of friends?" Laurent asked.

"No one, really. We're pretty tight. She worked two part-time jobs and on the farm. She knew everyone. She's lived in Field's Crossing her whole life and was looking forward to getting out and meeting new people. Not the same old faces every day. We both were."

"Can you tell me about her relationship with Dylan?" Laurent asked.

"I think she thought she was in love with him, but she wasn't."

"Did she say that?"

"I'm her BFF. I know it."

Laurent raised her eyebrows over the mug of hot chocolate. Before knocking on the door, she'd sat in her SUV in the Cahill driveway for a couple of minutes debating whether or not to mention the pregnancy. Would Stephanie have told her best friend first?

"They weren't going to like, make it through the winter, like maybe not even to prom."

"Why do you think that? I thought you were making plans for prom."

Claire looked at her hands and twisted a ring around her finger. "Dylan was cheating on her."

"How do you know that?"

"My little sister is friends with Brittany's little sister, and she said she saw them making out in Dylan's Jeep." Claire sniffed. "Like I would ever let my best friend stay with a cheating bastard."

"Do you think Dylan was going to dump her?"

"For sure. That's been his pattern ever since high school started, except with Stephanie. Go out with a girl for a few months and then dump her. Lots of guys do that."

"Did Stephanie tell you she was pregnant?"

"No way. Not by that asshole." Claire burst into sobs. "Oh my God. Steph, no."

"Are you sure?" Mrs. Cahill asked.

"I'm afraid so," Laurent said. "We'll run a DNA test as soon as we can, but Dylan admitted it."

"That little shit." Mr. Cahill's face went red, and he slapped the kitchen table.

Laurent had been expecting a tearful response, but Claire's comment about Dylan's apparent attitude toward women pissed her off. She had dealt with more than one irresponsible teenage boy. Or college boy. The attitude that only the female had to deal with the pregnancy problem irritated her even more. It takes two.

"Did Dylan ever hurt Stephanie?" Laurent asked.

"Like hit her? No way. Steph would have smacked him back."

"Did Stephanie cheat on Dylan?"

"What? No. How could you ask that?"

"There are a lot of questions I have to ask that I don't like asking." Laurent flipped a page in her notebook. "Let's talk about her part-time jobs. How did she like working at Beaumon's Hardware?"

"It's a cashier job. Everybody's got to do it sometime. Steph never complained. She didn't like it, but she didn't hate it."

"What did she say about Theo Tillman?"

"Fat slob. Lazy butt. Thief. Liar. She knew he was gonna steal the money. She said his face was bright red when Mr. Kessel walked over."

"Did Theo threaten her in any way?" Laurent asked.

"Theo's a sneak and a pothead. Steph would have kicked his ass, too."

"What about her job at the village?"

"Hated it."

"Why'd she stay?"

"She needed the money to pay for college. Her folks weren't going to be able to help with tuition, and she didn't want to graduate owing thousands of dollars."

"Is there anything else you'd like to add?" Laurent asked.

"There was a rumor last year Dylan got another girl pregnant and made her get rid of it," Claire said. "Steph wouldn't have done anything like that."

"Even if Dylan pressured her?"

Claire hesitated. "Kinda depends if Steph's dad or Dylan's dad found out. They're both farmers. I can't see either of them letting Steph get rid of it."

Laurent stood and wound her scarf around her neck before shrugging into her parka and pulling out her long black braid. "I'm sorry for your loss. I wish I had known her. She sounds like my type of woman."

*   *   *

Laurent laid her scarf, gloves, and headband on the music stand in the corner of her office. Unwrapping a throat lozenge, she tossed the crinkly paper into the garbage can and wandered to the window and looked out on the white landscape. The rear of the police station faced west and her third-floor window overlooked the police parking lot and Sycamore Street. Beyond Sycamore Street lay a residential area, the rooftops covered with snow.

One of the first things she had learned about her farmhouse was it needed a new roof. The snow on the roof melted her first winter, which meant heat was escaping. The other thing she discovered was that she had a sensitivity to cleaning products. When she first started cleaning the farmhouse, she armed herself with bleach, Windex, Lysol, and gloves. She had to drive back to Beaumon's to buy a mask, and even then, her nose itched and she sneezed. A lot.

Standing at the window of her office, looking out over the homes, she noticed there were no barren patches on the rooftops. The residents of downtown Field's Crossing were safe and warm. As the cough drop numbed the back of her throat, Laurent thought about the deceased. Dylan didn't want to marry Stephanie. He'd said so, even if she was pregnant. And he was cheating on her. Dylan was definitely a person of interest, but why kill her? Emmit and Owen were best friends their entire lives, according to Vern. Claire said if either of the two farmers found out, there'd be no getting rid of the baby. Dylan must have known this. Caleb, too.

Scenario number one. Caleb or Dylan drove the fourth vehicle and, after the township's secretary left, either one or both of them returned to the water tower, hit Stephanie over the head, and dumped her body in the park, where she froze to death. Laurent leaned over her desk and jotted a note. She needed to check what vehicles were registered to the Martin family.

Assuming she believed Vern. He was the only one claiming to have seen four vehicles, but he could be lying. Covering up for his nephew. Nephews. What did he and Caleb discuss over the phone? She would have loved to listen in on that conversation. Which Vern would have shown up? The angry, belligerent man with the shotgun or the sad-eyed one who mourned the loss of a young life? Vern admitted to shoveling a path to the victim's pickup on Saturday morning. The question was—did she believe his answer? And she found she did. He had nothing else to do and John Cook said Vern was as fit as a fiddle. For now, she was going to believe the Martin family. All of her past interactions with Emmit and Jane told her they were good folk. Honest, reliable, hardworking. When Emmit endorsed her four years ago, he looked her in the eye and told her, "Beat the shit out of him." She was narrowly elected.

Scenario number two was very similar to scenario number one. Only the names changed. Theo killed Stephanie. He admitted to being at the water tower at four thirty and leaving Stephanie crying in her pickup. He admitted to smoking pot while he was there. Maybe something in Theo snapped. Stephanie provoked him at Beaumon's. She reported him for stealing from a cash register. Being called a thief might make someone snap, and Theo was a big bottleful of resentment and anger and the last one to see Stephanie alive. Except for the fourth vehicle. Theo said he passed no one on his way back into town and there was no other way to reach the water tower.

Both Tillmans drove snowplows. Either one of them could have covered up the body. Laurent added a note to ask Caleb's secretary for the clock-in times of the drivers for Saturday morning. She'd have to ask Caleb if there was any way a driver could get the keys to the plows and dump trucks if Caleb wasn't there. She added the Tillman family to her DMV notes.

Laurent leaned her forehead against the cold windowpane. Would Stephanie's murder incite the century-old feud between the Martins and the Tillmans? Who would benefit from that?

Laurent circled her office and returned to stare out the window again. She didn't want Theo to be right—a conspiracy between brothers. Simply put, she liked the Martin family more than the Tillman family. But murder required objectivity.

And she had to give credit to Theo for the alien theory. It took imagination to come up with that idea. But, for all of Theo's resentment and anger, he had said something that echoed in her thoughts. Stephanie had something on someone. What did the teenager know and what made it worth killing for?

Laurent dropped into her chair and played with her pearl earring. Last night she had dreamed of a pale hand waving at her and awoke to find her pillow wet with tears. Unable to sleep, she flopped onto her back and stared at the ceiling until the weak morning sunlight crept into her bedroom. The echoes and pains of the past chilled her, and she turned up the electric blanket, not wanting to get out of bed. The young girl's death on the same day she had given her daughter up for adoption thirty years ago awakened feelings she had long since forgotten. Or suppressed.

And even though her aunt had assured her it was for the best, Laurent remembered thinking best for who? Was her daughter better off with an adoptive family? What if a family member was mean or abusive to her daughter? No one knew where life was going to take them. Circumstances changed people. Laurent had cried silently in bed, tears dripping onto the already-damp pillow, a desperate prayer in her heart. *Keep my daughter safe.*

CHAPTER EIGHT

"FARMERS BANK WON'T loan you any more money," Bob Kane said. "You haven't been able to bring the loan current, and we're not going to chase bad money with more bad money."

"I swear I'll pay everything off after this year's harvest." Neal Tillman fingered the hole in his coat pocket and sat up straighter in the leather wingback chair.

He hated banks. Bankers. The constant need for more money. Even the banker's office annoyed him. Plush forest-green carpet, enormous mahogany desk, gold-framed pictures with politicians.

"That's what you told me last year. The bank has strict guidelines on how much money we can lend out. It's a loan-to-value ratio. For farmland it's eighty percent. Your outstanding debt exceeds the LVR. If your land is valued at one hundred thousand dollars, the amount of the loan cannot exceed eighty thousand dollars." The CEO of Farmers Bank leaned back and steepled his fingers.

"But you'll loan money to Emmit."

"I can't discuss other situations," Kane said.

"That's because he inherited his farm and bought his brother's farm when Vern went crazy and their old man paid off the loans before he died. You know my old man was a cheat. Spent a few years behind bars. I didn't stand a chance."

"I also know if you'd stay out of Gray Fox Casino, you'd have a better chance in repaying your loans."

"Who told you that?" Neal narrowed his eyes. Right after his wife left him, he became a regular at the casino. Until they cut him off. He stayed away for a long time, but the lure of quick, easy money versus the backbreaking life of a farmer sent him stumbling back. All he needed was one big hit and he would be set for life.

"I've lived in Field's Crossing all my life, just like you. You know the rumor mill starts at the Skillet."

"What you're saying is a man can't have a hobby and get money from you."

"You can have all the hobbies you want, but not ones that put your farm at risk."

"What do you want me to do?" Neal asked. "Build model airplanes? Fuck you. I'll go to Birmingham and see a smart banker at First Federal. Someone who's not such a tight-ass." He shoved his chair back, gave the finger to the CEO, and slammed the office door, rattling the windows on both sides.

*　　*　　*

"How'd it go at the bank?" Theo whisked a dozen eggs in a dented bowl. A pound of bacon sizzled in a frying pan on an old gas stove, and a four-slice toaster sat on the worn countertop. Only one slot in the toaster worked.

"Bastards won't loan me a penny. I went to all of the banks in the quad-counties and not one of them would lift a finger to help me. That asshole in Birmingham threatened to call his loan due this November." Neal dropped his baseball hat on the kitchen table and rubbed one hand over his grizzly face. "We havin' breakfast for dinner again? Don't you know how to cook anything but bacon and eggs?"

"The freezer died over the summer so there's no beef or pork, and the root cellar's been empty since Mom left. What in the hell do you want me to cook? Eggs are free, bread's cheap, and I can steal bacon."

"You're gonna have to steal a lot more if we're gonna keep the farm."

"Cash is gonna be scarce. The Gattison bitch caught me taking money from a register a couple weeks ago and told Kessel. I've been demoted. I can't go anywhere near the store's cash for the next month." Theo flipped the bacon.

"You dumb sonofabitch. I outta take my belt to you."

"Try it." Theo turned, tongs in hand, to face his father. "Touch me, old man, and you'll be the one in the hospital."

"Motherfucker. I'm going to Gray Fox."

"Go on. Lose money we don't have. At least my addiction makes me feel good."

*   *   *

Neal jabbed the buttons on the slot machine. Nothing. He fed in four more quarters. Jabbed again. He had no idea how much money he lost today. He'd never make enough from this year's crop. Corn and soy beans had taken a hit. Prices were down. Tariffs were up. The Chinese were buying from Canada. He didn't dare go to the craps table or the Texas Hold 'Em table. *Kane and his fuckin' bank are gonna take my farm.*

"The slots are tough today."

Tillman glanced at the man perched on the stool next to him. His bucket of quarters was lower than Neal's. "You got that right. I've been coming here for three years. Never won more than five hundred bucks."

"Noel Smith."

The two men shook hands.

"Whad'ya do when you're not here?" Noel asked.

"I'm a farmer. Fat lot of good it does me."

"What do you mean? I thought all farmers were rich farmers."

"The big farmers are the rich farmers. If you own or lease less than a thousand acres, you gotta fight them too. They can take a lower price on crops and livestock because they've got more. Power of numbers."

"That sucks."

Neal fed four more quarters into the slot machine. Eight quarters. Twelve quarters. Five dollars gone in a minute. Gray Fox Casino greedily swallowed Neal's money as fast as he gulped the free watered-down drinks.

"Do you own or lease your land?" Noel asked.

"Mortgaged to the hilt."

"Selling isn't an option?"

"Selling only pays off the goddamned bank, and I'm not old enough to retire. And if I did, I'd spend all my money here and be broke in five years. Then what am I gonna do?"

"What if you leased the land you owned and farmed someone else's land?" Noel asked.

"Too much work."

"Well, at least you're financially stable right now."

"I wish." Drinking loosened Neal's tongue. "I've stretched my credit to the max. I went to five banks to get a loan to extend me until next spring and all of them turned me down. Bastards. They'll loan the Martins all the money they want. But me. No way."

"Martins?"

"Richest farmers in north central Indiana. They own the most land in the quad-counties. They've got the bankers under their thumbs."

"It sounds like you don't like the Martins or bankers."

"I hate the assholes. All of them." Neal shoved more quarters into the slot machine and jabbed viciously.

"What are you going to do?"

"No fucking idea."

"Maybe I can help. I work for Renewable Farm Energy. Farmers lease out land for a windmill farm and rake in the cash."

"How much?"

CHAPTER NINE

"WHERE'S THE GAS can?" Owen's callused fingers poked at the inventoried items on the conference room table. In the days since Laurent told Owen and Theresa about the death of their daughter, Owen aged ten years. The wrinkles in his forehead deepened and he shuffled, rather than walked, as though the energy needed to pick up his feet was too great.

"We didn't find a gas can."

"I always kept a gallon in the bed of the pickup," Owen said. "Stephanie didn't like to put gas in the truck and was always running out. She'd have loved an electric vehicle."

"That might explain why she was in the park. Would she have tried to walk into town and buy gas and gotten turned around? Headed east to the park instead of west to the water tower? When I was out at the water tower, I wasn't able to start her pickup, and the gas gauge read empty."

"Teenagers think they're immortal. I'd like to say no, she wouldn't have tried to walk two miles into town to get gas right before a blizzard, but I ain't sure."

"Stephanie's truck was towed to Cook's Auto Body. After Dr. Creighton issues the death certificate, I'll call and you can pick it up."

"Got no use for it now," Owen said. "My boy Tom'll never drive. We tried a few years back and ended up in the ditch more times than I care to remember."

"Do you know where Stephanie's cell phone is?"

"Laying in the snow somewhere."

"I'll check the water tower and Webster Park. If I find it, I'll let you know." Laurent hesitated. "How are you and Theresa doing?"

"Poorly. Awake half the night. Crying all the time. Don't know what to do with ourselves. Jane and Emmit been by every day and sit a spell with us, but they got chores, just like the rest of us. I'll be glad when spring gets here. Get out in the field, planting, keeping busy. Not enough to do in the winter. Already cleaned the barn. Thinking of doing it again, just to keep moving. Tire myself out so I can sleep some. Theresa keeps cleaning the kitchen. Over and over. Gonna wear out the finish on those appliances. You can see your face in the fridge."

"Send her over to my house. Fingerprints and dust bunnies and cobwebs everywhere," Laurent said. "I'm sorry you're feeling bad. I wish I could help."

"Ain't nothin' you can do, Sheriff, but I appreciate you asking."

Laurent opened the conference room door and escorted Owen to the main entrance of the police station and watched as he held onto the railing, descending the steps, back bowed.

She climbed the two flights of stairs to her office. The lethargy of her cold was still dragging her down, and she hoped in a couple more days she'd have more energy. Tomorrow was the full autopsy. She had kept the temporary cause of death to herself. The dents in Stephanie's head rendered the teenager unconscious, the chest caved in from the weight of the snow.

* * *

"How long have you been plowing snow for the village?" After Owen left, Laurent spent the rest of the morning interviewing the snowplow drivers in Field's Crossing.

Jay Cook, owner of Cook's Auto Body Shop and brother to talkative John Cook from the mini-mart/gas station, perched on the edge of the chair in front of her desk. His fingers were stained and his overalls smelled of oil.

"Ten years or so," Jay said. "Business gets slow in the winter, and plowing brings in a few extra bucks, although, with the blizzard, I'm plum full up."

"You plowed snow before Caleb was elected road commissioner. What's changed since he took over?"

"Not a damn thing. He's using the same routes and patterns from ten years ago. I say, if it ain't broke, don't fix it. He's been trying to get some of the younger fellas to get certified to drive the big equipment, but he didn't use anyone new this last time around."

"Can a driver get keys to the plows or dump trucks without Caleb? Where are the keys kept? Who has access to them?" Laurent picked up her pen and pulled her notepad closer.

"Maggie's got them in a lockbox in the bottom drawer of her desk. She's got a key to the box and so does Caleb. As far as I know, no one can git the keys without one of them two knowing."

"What time did you start on Saturday morning?"

"Five a.m. Sun wasn't up yet. All of us got over to the township office the night before so we were ready to go, except Theo and Neal. Caleb was up before everybody, but that's 'cause he's gotta plow out Maggie so she can handle the radios."

"When did the Tillmans show up?"

"I don't know. The rest of us were already on the road. You'd have to ask Caleb. Theo's a terrible driver. Hits more mailboxes than anybody. Caleb has him plowing out the county roads, especially after last winter."

"What happened last winter?"

"Theo turned a corner too soon and took out a stoplight. Caleb said it cost his department five thousand dollars to get it fixed. Asshole tore out the moorings and everything. Cracked the sidewalk. I'm surprised Caleb keeps him on."

"Did you see anyone on the roads on Saturday morning?"

"Ain't nobody out. People in town know to wait for us to go through and make the roads passable," Jay said. "They lay in supplies and got nowhere to go. The kids are the antsy ones. They wanna get out to Webster Park and go sledding. I heard it was a kid who found the hand sticking up in the snow."

She nodded. "How does snowplowing work? I've never really paid attention."

"Field Street is plowed first. Always," he said. "Since there was so much snow, Caleb parked the dump trucks every two blocks. We push the snow to the end of the block, turn around, and push back the other way, block by block. The front-end loader scoops up the snow while we're heading the opposite direction, dumps it into a truck, and then the truck heads out to the park to make those huge mountains of snow. System works great. The only problem is we ain't got enough equipment and drivers to get the snow moved fast. Caleb trained some new drivers over the summer, but we've only got so many trucks, but, then again, we only get this kind of a blizzard once every ten years or so."

After the last of the drivers left, Laurent closed her office door and made a cup of tea. All of them said the exact same thing. No one saw anything and anyone could have picked up the body and dumped it without their knowing. Especially early in the morning, when it was still dark. Interviewing the snowplow drivers added nothing to the investigation. Other than Theo was a bad driver and enjoyed getting petty revenge on Caleb. Great-grandfathers, grandfathers, fathers, and now sons. Theo jabbed at Caleb over and over again. Their own personal feud. Maybe Theo killed Dylan's girlfriend to get back at Caleb. Laurent frowned.

That's crazy. No one's going to risk a murder charge just to escalate a feud. Revenge isn't worth going to prison for.

* * *

"Dylan said he got to your office at four thirty. Is that correct?" Laurent was interviewing Caleb outside on a cement bench in between the sheriff's office and the township office.

It was early afternoon and the sky was darkening as snow clouds gathered. Tonight's forecast called for heavy snow as the winds were going to sweep down Lake Michigan and dump another twelve to fourteen inches on central Indiana.

Four years ago, Caleb had been elected road commissioner—the same election Laurent had won as sheriff. Throughout their first terms, Laurent's and Caleb's paths crossed frequently as they shared the same territory. Dead animals, especially deer, often had to be put down after colliding with a vehicle, and that sad task fell under the jurisdiction of the sheriff's department, but Caleb's department often reported the injured animals first.

"It was already dark, so, yeah. His headlights flashed in the front window."

"What was his demeanor?"

"Hungry and pissed."

"He said he went through the McDonald's drive-thru after school. How could he be hungry?"

"I wish I could eat like I was eighteen."

Laurent snorted. "What are you? Six-five? One eighty?"

Caleb grinned. "Six-six."

"Enough said." Laurent rolled her eyes. "Why was he angry?"

"It took a while for him to spit it out. I figured he and Dad argued before school or he was flunking physics. We argued about what channel to watch." Caleb shrugged.

"All of this sounds normal to me."

"It is. Then he told me about Stephanie being pregnant and how she didn't want to marry him and thought he was an asshole. I think she hurt his feelings."

"What did you say?" Laurent shifted from side to side on the concrete bench. Her butt was cold, but Caleb asked to talk outside. She assumed he didn't want anyone to overhear their conversation or see them talking. Her pen slid out of her gloved hand and landed next to her boot. Bending over, she picked it up and brushed the snow off.

"I wish I would've told him to grow up, but I didn't. I told him you don't have to do anything about it today, but this messes up college for both of you."

"Where's Dylan going to school in the fall?"

"Notre Dame."

"What was he most upset about?"

"I think he was afraid Dad wouldn't let him go. Make him stay home and work the farm. Begin earning his keep, as Dad would say."

"Do you think Dylan was upset enough to make this problem go away?"

Caleb pointed a gloved finger at her. "My brother did not kill his girlfriend so he could go to college. Period."

"Did you kill her?"

"What? No. Sheriff, you know me better than that."

"I had to ask." Laurent glanced at her notes. "When did Dylan leave your office?"

"He stayed overnight on Wednesday and all day Thursday and Friday. He was sitting in the TV room with a box of Cinnamon Toast Crunch and a gallon of milk when you dropped me off on Saturday morning."

"Could he have left and returned?"

"His Jeep was covered in snow. He didn't go nowhere."

Laurent squinted at Caleb. The township's secretary, Maggie, confirmed Dylan was still asleep on the couch when Caleb dropped her off at four thirty on Saturday morning. "Any issues with drivers?"

"Everybody hits a mailbox or two," Caleb said. "We repair them as quick as we can, but sometimes we can't do anything until the ground thaws."

"What about Theo?"

"I think he deliberately hits mailboxes knowing I have to fix them and pay for them. And I think he thinks no one knows it's him. Like giving me the finger. Asshole."

"Why don't you fire him?"

"I'm thinking about it. The problem is, I've only got so many people willing to drive a plow or a truck. All of the farmers are busy feeding their livestock and making sure the water troughs ain't frozen over with ice. There's not a lot of free hands available."

"What did you do on Saturday before I called you?"

"I picked up Maggie and then plowed out the village, township, your office, post office, and the courthouse and then I drove out to the park when dispatch called."

"After I dropped you off at your office, whad'ya do?"

"Dad asked if I'd plow him over to Uncle Vern's so he could check on him."

"What time was this?"

"Middle of the afternoon."

Laurent jotted a note. Emmit drove to Vern's cabin while she and her deputies were at Webster Park. By this time, everyone in the

Martin family knew Stephanie was dead and pregnant by Dylan. What did Vern and Emmit do? Did they tamper with evidence? Remove something from the deceased's truck? Make up a story about a fourth vehicle? If Vern lied about the fourth vehicle, she was chasing a nonexistent person. Was the Martin family trying to distract her from the truth?

"Those two phone calls from your uncle—what did you talk about?"

"He kept seeing headlights at the water tower," Caleb said. "I told him it was Stephanie and Dylan and then when Dylan got to my office, he told me about Theo clipping his mirror. So, when Uncle Vern called the second time, I told him about Theo's piece-of-shit car. Made him nervous, I guess."

"What's your impression of your uncle's mental health?"

"Uncle Vern's been through a lot." Caleb sighed. "People ask all the time. I was eighteen when Aunt Debbie drowned. It scared me. Everyone in the family drives over Turtle Lake bridge. Since Aunt Debbie couldn't have kids, I think her and Uncle Vern were more dependent on each other than most families. For a while, I wasn't sure he was gonna pull out of it. I was afraid Dad would drive over one day and find Uncle Vern had put a bullet through his head."

"I bet your father was afraid of the same thing," Laurent said. "And now?"

"He's better. For the first few years, he wouldn't leave the cabin or his property. Now, he goes to the library and checks out stacks of books. Stops in at Cook's and buys gas. Listens to John Cook yap. Dad says he's even talked about meeting everyone at the Skillet someday. I think he's on the mend."

"That's good to hear." Laurent thought Caleb's assessment of his uncle was accurate. Vern showed no signs of impaired mental ability and his dry sense of humor surprised her, despite the fact he had greeted her with a loaded shotgun. She glanced up. Even though it was only five, dusk was falling, and the overhead streetlights flickered on as she and Caleb sat outside on the concrete bench.

"Was your dad strict when you were growing up?"

"If he was, we usually had it coming. We weren't punished any more or less than any other kids around here. Everyone I know got their butt swatted at least once. Dad never took a belt to us, although we probably deserved it a time or two."

"Dylan was sitting in the middle of the kitchen surrounded by the rest of the family when I walked in. Was that normal?" she asked.

"As we got older, Dad wouldn't lay a hand on us. I think sitting on a chair all by yourself was more intimidating and worked better than screaming and yelling and swearing. Sometimes, he made us sit there for hours."

"Tell me about Dylan's temper."

Caleb's eyebrows shot up. "Dylan doesn't have a temper. He does dumb stuff."

"Like what?"

"A couple of years ago, he jumped out of the hayloft and broke his leg. Dad was pissed because he couldn't drive a tractor for spring planting."

"How many kids around here do that? He's not the first."

"One time he was racing on the ATV and he flipped it over and gave himself a concussion."

"Sounds like a typical teenager to me."

"He ran over the cat."

Laurent laughed. "Anything else you want to add?"

Caleb squirmed on the park bench. He dropped his head and hunched his shoulders over his knees. "Dylan got another girl pregnant last year. I helped him find a clinic for her."

"What'd your parents say?" *So, this was why Caleb wanted to meet outside in the freezing cold.*

"We didn't tell them. We claimed a sibling weekend, brothers only. Said we were going fishing up in Michigan on the Detroit River."

"And they never suspected?"

"Not one bit. Dylan asked me to get an appointment for Stephanie. Same deal, except we were going to have to come up with another excuse."

"Did you set up the appointment?"

"Didn't have time. You found her first."

"Lucky me."

CHAPTER TEN

LAURENT OPENED THE door to A Touch of Class Cigar Lounge and nodded to the owner. Choosing her usual seat next to the window, she adjusted the leather wingback chair to face the rest of the room and piled her personal mail on the end table. Normally, she smoked, but, with this cold, it'd be a waste. She couldn't taste anything, let alone breathe. And after sitting outside on the cold bench for the last hour interviewing Caleb Martin, she was glad for a nice warm chair. Her shift was over for the day, and she quickly walked the two blocks to the cigar lounge. It had been days since the blizzard dropped several feet of snow on Field's Crossing, and temperatures plummeted. The wind chill was forecasted to be below zero for the next week. Maybe two. The polar vortex was roaring down from Canada, crossing Lake Michigan, and freezing Indiana.

"May I join you?" Jim Cotter, the village attorney, was the king of the comb-over. A dozen black hairs covered the top of his head, glued down, right ear to left ear.

Laurent waved him over. Cotter pulled up another wingback chair, extracted a cigar and cutter, and lit up. She was glad he chose to sit and talk. With the election less than a month away, she'd have to start cultivating votes.

"What's the story on Stephanie Gattison?" Cotter asked.

"Not much to tell. I'm waiting for the body to thaw so Dr. Creighton can issue cause of death and a death certificate."

"The talk at the Skillet is she ran out of gas and tried to walk back to town during the blizzard and got turned around and finally fell down in exhaustion in the park. Went to sleep and never woke up."

"I've heard that, too."

"But you don't believe it."

"Do you know what else I've heard?" She didn't wait for his answer. "Her hand was cut off and she was shot by aliens."

Cotter laughed. "Don't you love the rumor mill in a small town? She wouldn't be the first to freeze to death in a winter storm. I've lived in the quad-county area for the last fifteen years, and this happens to the young and the old. It's always sadder when it's a young person." He blew out a stream of smoke.

"Did you know Stephanie?"

"She worked for the village, scanning in a bunch of old documents. I saw her around the office a few times."

"Why is the village scanning in old documents?"

"Saves space. All those old brown banker boxes sitting in the file room, and the fire two years ago in Alexander County scared the trustees."

"How long was this job going to last?"

"You'd have to ask Starr," he said. "She was her boss."

"I'll do that."

Jim Cotter wasn't on her list of people to interview, but another view of the deceased never hurt. Cotter confirmed everything Starr said.

"I hate to leave. This weather is a bitch, but I'm meeting a client in fifteen minutes. Nice talking with you, Sheriff."

"Stay warm." Laurent sorted her mail into piles. She slit open her internet bill and tucked it inside her *Midwest Gardener* magazine.

Glancing at the return address on the next envelope, her hand froze, hovering over the envelope. She read her address and the return address again before extracting a single piece of paper. Indiana Foster Care and Adoption. The paper fluttered to the floor. She squeezed her eyes closed, and concentrated on breathing. In and out. In and out.

"You okay, Sheriff?" The owner of the cigar lounge was emptying ashtrays.

She nodded. Bending over, she grabbed the paper off the floor and smoothed it on her lap.

The daughter she had given up for adoption thirty years ago wanted to meet her.

*   *   *

Laurent and David Lucroy had lived together during their senior year at Jacobs School of Music at Indiana University. After a shouting match in one of the practice rooms when Laurent informed him she was pregnant, he had gotten her dismissed from the university orchestra. Thirty years later, she still hated him and wished him ill will. She knew it was petty of her, but that wound never healed. And now the scab had been ripped off.

Clutching her mail to her chest, Laurent exited the cigar lounge and stepped into the frigid air. Darkness had fallen on Field's Crossing, and her breath shone in the overhead streetlights. She strode to the rear of the police station, where her little red truck was parked, fumbled with the UNLOCK button on the car fob, tossed the stack of mail on the passenger seat, and slammed the door. She needed to walk. Cold air and all.

She stalked down Field Street, hands in her pockets, shoulders hunched against the wind, her cheeks burning. Two months ago, the busy street had been filled with Christmas shoppers and window decorations. Every year, the department of public works built Santa's toyshop near the gazebo, and the Skillet passed out free hot chocolate, with and without marshmallows. Now the street was empty and lined with dirty snow.

Laurent passed the post office and Farmers Bank, recrossed Field Street, and slowed through the residential area. Why now? Why did this request arrive now? There was no room in her life for this. Forget that she had a murder to solve. Forget about the election next month. Forget about the feud escalating between the Martins and the Tillmans. She wondered if a request to meet had been sent to Lucroy. *What would that asshole do?*

Laurent kicked a pile of snow. Stopping at a four-way intersection, she glanced around before stomping across the street. Away from the downtown area, the front lawns of the cottage homes were filled with snowmen and snow forts, the sidewalks and driveways had been shoveled and salted, and cars were parked in garages. Light glowed from behind closed curtains as Laurent glimpsed the life she might have led. She had always believed her decision from thirty years ago had been the right one. But today's mail ripped open an unhealed wound. The night she gave up her daughter for adoption. The hospital stint. Losing her position in the orchestra. Her aunt dying of cancer. Her only sibling, Joelle, drinking her way through college. The weight of the burden she carried thirty years ago crashed over her, and she slipped on a chunk of ice in the sidewalk. She never expected this request.

CHAPTER ELEVEN

"The old guys at the Skillet have their finger in every pie," Glen said. "Literally. Dutch ate blueberry pie and ice cream for breakfast, and his mouth and fingers were purple. How does he stay so skinny eating like that?"

"I can't wait to get old. Are you sure you want to do this?" Laurent had asked her former boss to assist with the complete autopsy of Stephanie's thawed body. She smiled as Duke, the chocolate lab, circled the gray carpet in her office and stretched before flopping on his side in the sunshine and closing his eyes.

The blizzard had shot Laurent's budget to hell. Everyone in her department and public works was earning overtime pay. And even though there was an emergency fund, the trustees were reluctant to disburse those funds on overtime. She wasn't sure what they considered an emergency, but, in her mind, a blizzard fell into that category. If the money was used for overtime, so be it.

"It's not my first choice," Glen said. "But I understand the need to try and keep costs down. Getting those trustees to approve anything is a real bitch. You might want to give Cotter a heads-up about dipping into the emergency fund. Have you made any requests in the last year or so?"

"None."

"Then there should be buckets of money to pay for overtime," Glen said. "Come on, let's get this over with."

Laurent parked in back of the funeral home, and rang the doorbell. She opened it at the funeral director's shout. Henry Linville and Dr. Creighton were gowned and waiting. After her partial exam of Stephanie on Tuesday, and with the funeral director's assistance, the frozen body had been stripped of all clothing and left on the gurney at room temperature directly over a drain. A fine mesh sieve under the drain cover caught all debris. Henry emptied the sieve every four hours and bagged and labeled the contents.

The two sheriffs hung up their jackets and wriggled on masks, gloves, and gowns.

"Testing. Testing. One, two, three." Dr. John Creighton, local coroner for the quad-county area of north central Indiana, was a short man with stubby fingers. The green surgical suit was cuffed and taped around his ankles and bulged at the waist. His face was pale, his huge bulbous nose bright red from the wind, and his black goatee had been shaved close to his chin. He adjusted the height of the surgical tray and slid his half-moon glasses down on his nose.

"Today is Thursday, February seventh, two thousand nineteen. Time is nine a.m. I'm beginning a complete autopsy at Henry Linville's Funeral Home in Field's Crossing, Indiana. Present in the room are myself, Dr. John Creighton, funeral director Henry Linville, Sheriff Jhonni Laurent, and former sheriff Glen Atkins. The body before me has been identified as Stephanie Gattison, age eighteen, of seven W two forty-three Bees Creek Road, Field's Crossing, Indiana. Sheriff Laurent attests the body was initially identified by Caleb Martin, quad-county road commissioner, and confirmed by the deceased's father, Owen Gattison."

As Creighton droned on, Laurent wondered what he was feeling. In rural farm areas, a local doctor often performed the role of coroner as the nearest hospital or morgue might be hundreds of miles away. Creighton was completely professional, but she glimpsed angry eyes glaring out from behind his mask. Had he discovered something already? She was positive Henry pointed out the two dents in the head and the caved-in chest cavity. Was Creighton angry at her or Henry for stripping the body without him?

She really didn't want this to be murder and was hoping there was a simple explanation for the earlier discoveries, but the dread in her heart told her it was a false hope. Telling the Gattisons their daughter was *murdered* might be harder than telling them she was *deceased*. No parent wanted to hear that their child had been deliberately killed. The next question would be why or who did this. Who could kill an eighteen-year-old girl with her whole life in front of her? What could Stephanie have known or seen? A girlfriend's secret? Someone else's secret?

Stephanie lived at home, went to school, and held down two part-time jobs. Beaumon's and the village of Field's Crossing. Both Dylan and Claire told her Stephanie didn't have any other close friends. Laurent was pretty sure Claire hadn't killed her best friend. Dylan she wasn't so sure about. *If Creighton declares homicide, that's where I'm going to start.*

"Upon inspection of the skull, two circular indentations were noted, measuring one inch in width, with depression measuring one-quarter to one-half inch. The area around the indentations contains dried blood. A sample was procured. The external examination is complete." Creighton rolled his shoulders and flexed his fingers before picking up the scalpel.

"Question for you, Doc," Laurent said. "Is there any way the two dents are a birth defect or some other type of illness or disease? Any medical explanation?"

"No." He pointed his scalpel at her. "I brought this young woman into this world, cared for her over her short life, and now this. Someone killed her, and I'm counting on you to find the sonofabitch who did this."

As Dr. Creighton began the Y-incision and the internal exam, Laurent and Glen stepped back and watched as the local doctor and funeral director removed, marked, and weighed the internal organs. As far as Laurent could tell from the conversation, nothing was abnormal as far as the interior of the body. "Opinion, Time of Death: considering the body temperature, rigor, and livor mortis, and stomach contents, the approximate time of death was between six and ten p.m. on Wednesday, January thirtieth, two thousand nineteen. Cause of Death: Hypothermia secondary to accidental exposure. Manner of Death: Homicide. Remarks: Decedent originally presented to this office as an accidental freezing victim. Possible presence of suffocation and indentations of the skull and depression of the chest cavity suggest accidental freezing in this case is highly improbable. The sheriff's office was notified of this finding immediately upon conclusion of examination." Dr. Creighton shut off the tape recorder.

"She froze to death, but it wasn't an accident?" Laurent raised her eyebrows.

"Let me give you a brief overview of what happens to your body when you freeze to death." Dr. Creighton pulled off his gloves and mask and leaned against the stainless-steel counter, his arms resting on his round stomach. "First, your blood goes to the vital organs, which makes your fingers and toes feel cold, and your heart rate goes up, along with blood pressure and respirations. Then you start shivering. Shivering is the body's way to generate heat. After that, your skin turns white because there's no blood flow to the surface. Then you have to pee. The body produces more urine because of the increased blood flow to the vital organs. After that it becomes difficult to move. The cold seeps into the muscles very quickly. Then you become confused. When the core body temperature drops below a certain level, the brain becomes less efficient, which leads to a mental fog, confusion, and disorientation.

"After that happens, your extremities turn blue or black, but because you can't feel them, you won't know until you look at them. Your heart rate and breathing decrease, and you begin to hallucinate. The heart is pumping less blood and the brain is deprived of oxygen. Amnesia sets in. Finally, paradoxical undressing occurs. The blood vessels near the surface of the skin dilate because the muscles are exhausted from constriction. The victim is suddenly hot, and, in some cases, may rip off their clothing. Then, terminal burrowing happens as the victim tries to get into a small, enclosed space. In the end, the victim loses consciousness and the organs shut down.

"The initial pictures from when you recovered the body show the victim tried to burrow. Her body was curled into the fetal position and frozen in a chunk of ice," Creighton said. "That's why I declared hypothermia secondary to accidental exposure."

"What about the dents in the skull?" Glen asked.

"If the victim was unconscious, then the body would have taken over, which is why we see burrowing. The internal examination of the brain shows no blood clots or aneurysm, nothing abnormal in the brain, and even if there were abnormalities, the age of the victim would suggest the ability to overcome the condition or disease or situation. From a medical standpoint, the dents didn't kill her." Dr. Creighton shook his head. "I'm going to take a closer look at her lungs, and I may be able to declare suffocation as the cause of death. It will depend on the state of the lungs and if the weight of the snow caused her ribs to puncture the lungs. Essentially, the dents rendered her unconscious and the hypothermia killed her. But she may have suffered from a punctured lung."

"How long can a person survive with a punctured lung?" Laurent asked.

"Depends on the size of the puncture. If it's a small one, the lung may be able to heal on its own, but I'd like to view the lungs under a microscope. I might change the specific cause of death from hypothermia to suffocation, but the manner of death will remain as homicide."

"The bottom line is—someone hit her over the head on Wednesday. Whoever hit her and left her outside is guilty of murder, and she died either of hypothermia or suffocation, depending on the state of her lungs. Is that a correct interpretation of the autopsy results?" Laurent stripped off the gloves and gown and stuffed them into the stainless-steel wastebasket.

"You're correct," Creighton said.

*   *   *

"What's the autopsy going to say?" Ralph Howard of *The Crossing* stood on the bottom step in front of Henry Linville's Funeral Home and thrust a microphone in Laurent's direction. The tip of his beak-shaped nose was dull red, and a few white snowflakes rested on his angry, black unibrow.

"We should've gone out the back door," Laurent muttered under her breath to Glen. She didn't like talking to the annoying reporter. Normally, she wouldn't be rude to the media, but in the last twenty years, *The Crossing* had become known for sensationalism and biased and inaccurate reporting and was more of a gossip column than a newspaper.

"I bet Greene told him where you were," Glen whispered back.

"Whatever I say and however I say it, Ralph's going to blow it out of proportion." Laurent jogged down the stairs and strode past the reporter, heading for her SUV. "Dr. Creighton has declared the cause of death for Stephanie Gattison to be hypothermia and the manner of death to be homicide."

"Are you shittin' me? Homicide?" Ralph jogged next to Laurent—microphone aimed at her mouth.

"The victim presented with two dents in her head."

"Someone hit her over the head? With what? When?"

"I have no more information at this time," Laurent snapped.

"What are you going to do next? Do you know what to do next? Have you ever solved a murder?"

Laurent yanked open the SUV door, climbed in, and slammed it shut. *I'll find out who killed her and then, Ralph, you can eat crow.*

CHAPTER TWELVE

"SHE DIDN'T WALK two miles in the snow and ice," Glen said. "Her fingers were covered, but her nose, ears, and face should have shown signs of extreme frostbite, not mild. If she tried to walk in that weather, the uncovered extremities should have been black. Twenty minutes is all it takes."

After slamming the door in Ralph's face, Laurent and Glen sat in the front seat of the police SUV, heat cranked up.

"I don't think she walked anywhere," Laurent said. "I think someone picked her up at the water tower, drove her somewhere, hit her over the head, and tossed her into the snow or drove to the park and tossed her into the snow. Creighton says she died on Wednesday, which means she was hit over the head on Wednesday. I know he can't tell us if she was conscious or unconscious, but at least we have a window from when she was hit in the head to the time she died. According to Theo, she was alive at four thirty and Creighton says the time of death was between six and ten on Wednesday night. The last person to see her was Theo or the killer."

Laurent reached into the back seat, opened the small cooler containing her lunch, and pulled out two bottles of water. She twisted off both caps before handing one to Glen.

"That means there's a fourth vehicle, just like Vern said. But I don't think she was struck in her car. When I searched her vehicle, it looked to me as though she had settled in. She had water, candy bars, a pillow, a couple of blankets, and, God forbid, homework. Boredom and lack of cell phone coverage would have been her only problems. There was nothing in the cab that looked like it could cause those dents. At the time, I didn't check the back of the pickup because it was completely filled with snow. Jay Cook told me he had to shovel out most of it before he could tow it. The weight of the snow almost flattened the tires, and when Owen verified my inventory of the pickup, he said the only thing missing was the gas can."

"But we don't know what Vern did after his two calls to Caleb."

"There are gaps for Dylan, Caleb, and Vern," Laurent said. "The brothers alibi each other. I talked to all of the snowplow drivers, and Jay and John Cook were the first to arrive at the township offices on Wednesday night. They both said Dylan and Caleb were there."

"What time did the Cook brothers get there?"

"Seven." Laurent tapped her fingers on the steering wheel. "Whoever caused the victim to lose consciousness is guilty of murder. If we figure out how she got to Webster Park from the water tower, then we should have our murderer."

"That's a narrow way to look at the situation. Where's the crime scene? The murder weapon? We're assuming it's a hammer of some type. What if it isn't? What other items can make a dent like that? The only thing we know is that, from the angle of the dent, whoever hit her is taller than five feet four inches, she didn't see it coming, and it was someone she knew. That's it."

"That doesn't rule out many people. Her best friend said she knew everyone. But I get what you're saying. Figuring out how she got to the park may or may not lead to the murderer," Laurent said.

"Exactly. What I'm saying is—open your eyes. Look at everything. Don't make any assumptions."

"This could get ugly, especially when Ralph spins it, and you know he's going to. I can already see the headline." Laurent was tired of the constant bashing in the newspaper. Ever since the election four years ago, Ralph found something negative or nasty to say about her in *The Crossing*. During the budget process, he demanded an explanation of every single line item and that receipts, invoices, and payments be posted online, where citizens could see how much the sheriff's department spent on coffee and pens and air-conditioning. Fortunately, the trustees said no to itemized online billing and approved her budget without Ralph's requests. The reporter was a mean, spiteful little man, but she knew why he disliked her. What she really wanted to do was wipe the smirk off his face. She wasn't sure how to do that without causing more damage to herself and her reelection campaign. Keeping quiet was a bitch.

"Ralph's gonna do what Ralph's gonna do. Don't worry about that idiot. People around here got more sense than to believe anything he writes in that damn thing he calls a newspaper. Concentrate on the victim."

"What I'm worried about is Ralph will start pointing fingers, not only at me, but at who he thinks the murderer is. It's not going to be hard for him to find out Dylan was Stephanie's boyfriend and she accused Theo of stealing from Beaumon's. What if Ralph escalates the feud between the Martins and Tillmans?" Laurent put the SUV in gear and headed south on County Street.

"It might be in everyone's best interest if you had a chat with the two families. Separately. Take Dak with you when you talk to Neal and Theo. He'll scare the shit out of them. But we know Ralph's favorite topic is you, so be ready for him to ambush and bad-mouth you."

"I'm not sure how much support I have in the quad-county area. Reelection is going to be tough, especially with Ralph increasing his attacks on me every chance he gets."

"I think you have more support than you're giving yourself credit for," Glen said.

"If I can't arrest Stephanie's killer, I'll be viewed as incompetent and voted out of office. You know I love my job. I love my house. I don't want to move. But if Greene wins, he'll never keep me on as a deputy, and I'm not sure I'd want to stay."

"I'll admit the timing is bad, but you've got to remember, you've been sheriff for almost four years. Your actions in that time will determine the outcome of the election. People around here have long memories." He tugged on his seat belt. "Let's drive over to Beaumon's and measure the width and depth of a ball peen hammer. But let's stop at the drugstore first and fill that prescription Creighton wrote for you. Whatever you've got, I don't want."

Half an hour later, Laurent pulled into Beaumon's lot, and parked next to the handicapped spaces. To the left of the hardware store's entrance, Laurent recognized the store manager, Brent Kessel, shoveling snow. The man was well over three hundred pounds.

"What can I do for you, Sheriff?" Kessel stopped shoveling, leaned the shovel against his shoulder, and pulled a handkerchief out of his pocket and wiped his forehead. The big man was sweating in the frigid air, and his breath came in short bursts.

"I've got a few questions," Laurent said. "Want to go inside?"

"God, yes. I'll have the greeter throw down salt." Kessel headed for the front entrance.

Next to the rows of shopping carts sat a storage cabinet. The store manager propped the shovel inside the cabinet and pulled out a bucket of ice melt. Laurent watched as he steadied himself on the wall and pulled off both rubber boots and tossed them into the cabinet. He tugged off his gloves and shrugged out of his coat, stuffing his gloves into a jacket pocket before straightening his shirt and red apron.

"Do all employees use those big rubber boots?" Laurent asked.

"Those are mine. My wife got me new shoes and boots for Christmas this year. I've got big feet. She special orders 'em."

Laurent, Glen, and Kessel passed through the second set of doors.

"Walt, would you salt the front apron of the store for me? Sheriffs, let's go to my office."

Laurent liked the lumber and hardware store. The smell of sawdust, the bright red aprons, employees who could tell her how to fix her toilet. Since buying her farmhouse, she had become a regular shopper at Beaumon's. She nodded to several employees as they made their way through the forty-thousand-square-foot building to the store manager's office.

Kessel's office was tiny. A metal desk sat below an enormous flat-screen computer monitor hanging on the wall, cords dangling. A two-drawer filing cabinet occupied one corner. His chair was the only one in the room.

"What can you tell me about Stephanie?" Laurent leaned against the doorframe, notebook and pen in hand.

"Smart girl. Register was always perfect. Never late. Customers loved her. A bit chatty, but I'd like an entire store of Stephanies. I understand from customers her body was found under a pile of snow in Webster Park. What a shame." Kessel opened the bottom drawer of the file cabinet and propped one foot on it.

"When was the last time you saw her? How'd she seem to you?"

"The Saturday before the blizzard. I thought she was her usual cheerful self."

"Who were her friends here at the store?" Laurent asked.

"She was friendly with everyone. I never saw her leave with anyone, and I never heard any talk about going to the bars or stuff like that."

"What about Theo Tillman?"

"The longer he works here, the more entitled he thinks he is." The store manager grimaced. "He was a summer hire, and when two of our forklift operators moved, I kept him on. He walks around the store as though he owns it. Customers don't like him, and he's rarely helpful. He thinks he's going to make assistant manager, and I've told him in his reviews his attitude has to change before I'll promote him. With the incident between him and Stephanie, I've put him on probation. I'll probably fire him in thirty days."

"Why don't you fire him now?" Glen asked.

"If I don't follow through on the probation, he can go to the EEOC and make a complaint. I've got to dot all the i's and cross all the t's to fire someone who's been here over ninety days. Under ninety days, I can hire and fire at will. If his attitude doesn't change during this probationary period, I'll add more documentation to his file and fire him. He'll yell and argue and make a scene, but, in the end, he'll leave. It won't be pleasant."

"What kind of reference will you give him?" Laurent asked.

"I'm not going to offer an opinion. I'll only state his dates of employment. That's all I'm required to do by law. Word will get around Field's Crossing. He'll have a tough time getting another job here."

"He'll find one in Alexander County," Glen said. "They don't know him over there."

"I'd like to view the security camera footage of the incident between Stephanie and Theo."

"Follow me." Kessel led Laurent and Glen past the conference room into a tiny security room. Four video monitors sat side by side on a speckled black countertop, cords fed through pre-drilled holes and plugged into a tangled mess of surge protectors. "After I heard Stephanie died, I pulled this video and saved it to a flash drive. Let me get two more chairs."

"When was this recorded?" Laurent asked.

"Mid-January."

Laurent settled into a plastic chair in the security room as the store manager plugged a flash drive into the computer and clicked on the mouse. She watched as Theo extracted money from a cash register and placed it in the front pocket of his red apron. From off to the left, a female voice said, "Put it back." Stephanie came into view.

"Put it back."

"What are you talking about?" The pockets in Theo's red apron sagged below his enormous stomach, and his dirty blond hair was pulled into a ponytail wound tightly with a rubber band.

"The money you stole from the cash register. I saw you stick a wad of cash in your apron. Put it back or I'm telling Kessel." Stephanie grabbed Theo's arm, her purple fingernails digging in, blue eyes glaring at the overweight head cashier. "Now."

"What's going on?" From off-camera, Brent Kessel's voice was heard.

Stephanie pointed at Theo. "I saw him take money out of the register and put it in his apron."

"I was taking it back to the vault," Theo said.

"You can't carry cash through the store. Put it in a transfer bag and send it through the vacuum tube system. We've been through this. I'm not going to warn you again." Kessel walked into camera view—his hand held out.

Theo pulled a wad of cash out of the front pocket of his apron and handed the money to Kessel. As he walked away, Theo gave Stephanie the finger. "Bitch."

Laurent viewed the sequence three times before leaning back. "Thanks for the flash drive. I understand you're limited in what you can tell me, but do you think Theo is capable of injuring another employee?"

"I suspect Theo of a lot of things." Kessel leaned against the wall, arms crossed over his chest.

"Such as?"

"Stealing cash from the registers, damaging goods on purpose, and then either marking them down or throwing them away, which means he stuffs them into his truck. I think he smokes pot on his break and at lunch."

"What kind of goods?"

"Mostly food items, but I wouldn't be surprised if he stole other stuff."

"Hammers, drills, saws, tools, anything like that?"

Kessel shrugged. "Possibly. Pot smoking makes him hungry. He'll find a bag of chips and claim they were ripped open and the store can't sell them and can't return them. He's supposed to throw them away. I suspect he eats them."

"What about smoking on company premises?" Laurent asked.

"He parks in the last spot in the lot, and all I can see from the entrance is a haze in that beat-up old pickup. Cigarette smoking is allowed outside of the store, and I really don't want to deal with an angry Theo or a high Theo."

"Back to my original question. Do you think he's capable of harming another employee?"

"It's just my opinion, but I'm afraid so."

Laurent raised her eyebrows. "Can you elaborate?"

"I don't know if I should say anything."

"Just so you know, Dr. Creighton has declared Stephanie's death a homicide. You're cooperating with a murder investigation. Asking questions, interviewing coworkers is part of the process. You're not breaking any laws, but I don't know about Beaumon's store policy, whether or not you need an attorney present to speak to us."

"Stephanie was murdered? Really?" Kessel shoved his clenched fists into his red apron.

Laurent wondered if Kessel regretted showing her the video and giving her the flash drive voluntarily. Too late. She wasn't giving it back. "Why do you think Theo could hurt someone?"

"His size. He's intimidating. Add in the pot smoking, and you've got one crazy, big dude."

"Any particular incident you'd like to tell me about?"

Kessel shook his head. "He doesn't bother me, but I suspect that's because I sign his paychecks and I'm as big as he is."

"Does he bother other employees?" Laurent asked.

"No one has reported anything to me."

"Any friends?"

"Not that I know of."

* * *

Laurent slowed her pace as she and Glen climbed the front steps to Field's Crossing High School. The building was ten years old, white brick with black trim. Two sets of double doors opened into a small foyer, where the two sheriffs were assaulted with the scent of fried foods mixed with disinfectant. Trophy cases lined both sides of the foyer, and a custodian wheeled a gray garbage can down the hallway. The walls were painted gray and the classroom doors were red. The smell of the high school cafeteria lingered as Laurent and Glen followed the signs to the administrative offices, their footsteps echoing in the empty corridor.

"You still planning on building your greenhouse this summer?" Glen asked.

"Before I have the big barn demolished, I'm gonna have someone come out and take a look. It's over a hundred years old, and reclaimed wood seems to be the current decorating fad, aka modern farmhouse."

"You're kidding me. You think someone'll buy that old wood and make a couch out of it?" Glen raised his eyebrows.

"Not necessarily a couch, but end tables, side tables, a dining room table. Go look at 'Tiques and Things. That's all she stocks. Most people don't know the stuff's not a true antique."

"How big are you thinking of making your greenhouse? Won't the heating bill be huge?"

"I'm thinking of installing solar panels over part of it," Laurent said.

"Doesn't that block the natural sunlight? Sort of defeats the purpose of a greenhouse. How much does it cost to build a greenhouse?"

"Twenty-five grand."

"That's a lot of money to pour into a hobby."

"I might have an investment partner. Dak's grandma," Laurent said.

"Mrs. Aikens from the flower shop? I'll be damned. That's perfect for both of you."

"If I can sell the wood, there would be very little to demolish, and I should break even. The reclaimed wood should bring in enough to cover the cost of the demolition. If not, I may have to spread the greenhouse project over a couple of years."

"Another option would be to call the chief at the fire department and see if he'd burn it down and use the burn as a training exercise. They did that with the old Walmart a few years ago," Glen said. "Tax write-off."

"Yeah, but Walmart was in town. They trained in and out of that building for a month before they burned it down."

"Just sayin'. It's free."

"True." Laurent opened the door to the administrative offices.

"Sheriffs, come in. My secretary leaves at three thirty. I didn't know you were here," Principal Yoshida said.

The top of Principal Yoshida's head reached Laurent's nose. His suit coat was still buttoned and the striped tie centered perfectly. She glanced around his office. Neat and orderly. On the credenza behind his desk sat a Tiffany-style lamp, family photos, and a bonsai tree, and, on top of the bookcase, diplomas. Bachelor's degree, master's, and doctorate.

"You're here about Stephanie Gattison. Such a shame. After your secretary called, I pulled her file and had it copied, but I don't think it'll tell you much."

"Thanks for the copy. I'll read it over when I get back to the station." Laurent unzipped her jacket, and balanced her notebook on her knee. "What can you tell me about Stephanie? Her friends?"

"Nice kid, well liked. No problems whatsoever," Yoshida said. "I never saw her with anyone other than Claire or Dylan this past year, but she was on friendly terms with everyone. I understand you've already talked to Claire. She called me about doing something for Stephanie during the graduation ceremony. I'll make sure something happens."

"What kind of student was she?"

"Better than average, but not valedictorian caliber. I understand she was accepted to Indiana University and received a scholarship." Yoshida steepled his fingers.

"Did you see Stephanie on the Wednesday before the blizzard?"

"I didn't get out of my office that day. There's a lot of work that goes into calling off school. You'd think with the Weather Channel forecasting a blizzard closing school would be automatic, but I have to get permission from the school board and the superintendent. Then the bus company has to be notified, and emails must be sent to all the parents, and those parents without email have to be called. Then, after that we inform your office and public works that we're closing early, the crossing guards need to be in place, and, if needed, plowing the school grounds must happen. This is the first blizzard we've had since the school district installed system-wide email, so the lawyer for the district had to approve the announcement, written and oral." He shook his head. "I enjoy interacting with the students, but that Wednesday was an office day."

"I'd like to talk about Dylan Martin," Laurent said.

"We don't keep track of who is dating who, but this is a small town. Everyone knew Dylan and Stephanie were a couple."

"How well do you know him?"

"He's a good kid, despite instigating a few food fights and kicking in a locker or two."

"The food fights I get." She raised an eyebrow. "Kicking in lockers?"

"Dylan's impulsive and, at times, irresponsible," Yoshida said. "The locker incidents occurred during his freshman and sophomore years. I put it down to raging hormones. These farm kids are big and strong, but they don't dare release their anger or frustration at home. Too many things can go wrong and the consequences can be serious."

"Do you think it was just a phase?" Laurent asked.

"Absolutely. I've been an educator for thirty years. Any teacher will tell you, by the time the child leaves elementary school, we know who's going to be a problem in the upper grades. Dylan wasn't a problem."

"How has he been acting the last six months?"

"Senioritis sets in right after Christmas break," Yoshida said. "Happens every year. This year's been tougher because of the blizzard and heavy snow. So many of the kids have chores before school, and they're tired when they get here. Two years ago, we started offering breakfast between six thirty and seven thirty every morning, and the response has been huge. We receive food shipments on Monday, Wednesday, and Friday. Every Friday morning, we're sold out before breakfast is over, and lunch doesn't start until ten thirty. A lot of free peanut butter and jelly sandwiches are consumed in those three hours."

"It sounds like Dylan is a normal teenage boy. How long have you been principal at the high school?" Laurent knew Yoshida had been a teacher in the quad-county school district for a long time. One of her favorite days of the year was the first day of school. She parked and roamed the campus the entire day, talking with parents who were waiting to pick up their kids.

"Ten years at the high school, assistant principal for five years at the middle school, and a math teacher for ten years at the elementary school. Before that, I lived in Illinois."

"What can you tell me about Theo Tillman and Caleb Martin?"

Principal Yoshida leaned back. "Talk about a loaded cannon."

"Care to explain that comment?"

"I have moved through the Field's Crossing educational system with Caleb and Morgan and Theo. Caleb and Morgan are twins. In elementary school, Theo picked a fight with someone every week and frequently his target was Caleb. Caleb didn't back down. When they got to high school, Theo escalated to keying cars in the parking lot. And then he got caught."

"How?"

Glen cleared his throat. "I received an anonymous phone call and placed surveillance cameras in the high school parking lot. Took Theo two years to pay for the damage to all of the cars."

"Did Theo ever find out who placed that call?" Laurent tried to keep the smile off her face.

"Do you think Theo can put two and two together?"

Laurent snorted. And looked across the desk at the principal who was staring at the ceiling, a grin tugging at the corners of his mouth. "Small towns." She shook her head. "Even before Theo and Caleb reached high school, they didn't like each other. What does someone filled with long-term resentment do? What makes them snap?"

"I'm not a psychologist, so I have no idea what makes a person snap, but don't forget that while Theo and Caleb were in high school, Emmit and Neal had issues," Yoshida said. "Their fathers were in a bitter battle back then. Something happened at the co-op."

"Do you think Theo is or was capable of killing someone important to a member of the Martin family?"

"I'd like to say no, but I'm just not sure. He's a young man filled with resentment and anger, and I suspect financially he and his father struggle. I went into Beaumon's the other day and almost didn't recognize him. He's put on a lot of weight, apparently eating his anger." Yoshida leaned his elbows on his desk. "Do you think he had something to do with Stephanie's death? I heard it was an accident."

"The cause of death is hypothermia. The manner of death is homicide."

"Meaning?"

"Someone rendered her unconscious, tossed her in the snow right before the blizzard, and she froze to death."

CHAPTER THIRTEEN

"Do you wanna join your buddies and eat blueberry pie for lunch?" Laurent asked.

"Dutch and Art probably ate it all. I'll drive over."

Laurent walked Duke and Glen down the stairs and waved good-bye. The old dog limped almost as much as his owner. She went back to her office and settled behind her desk. Inserting the SD card into her computer, she loaded all of the autopsy pictures into a file and added the file to Stephanie's folder. Then she added the video from Beaumon's Hardware store and password protected both files. She flipped through the teenager's high school file. Nothing popped out at her.

Laurent hadn't known Stephanie before she was killed, but after seeing the video and hearing her talk, the girl came alive in her mind. And although she didn't care for colored streaks of hair, it looked good on Stephanie. Laurent hadn't had a haircut in the last two years. It was easier to braid it every morning and hide the increasing silver and white strands.

She closed her eyes and imagined Stephanie at school, at home, at work, with friends, and with family. In the short piece of video, she'd seen a determined, fearless, don't mess with me attitude. Where would that attitude have taken her? What would she have accomplished in her life? Stephanie knew she was pregnant. Laurent had been twenty-two with an unexpected pregnancy, Stephanie only eighteen. The end results were so different.

Laurent picked up her cell phone and then laid it back down on her desk. She needed to call the Gattisons and tell them about Dr. Creighton's findings and the fact their daughter had been pregnant and was murdered. It was already late afternoon, and she didn't want them to find out in *The Crossing* tomorrow. After she finished the paperwork, she'd drive out to the Gattison farm. Delivering bad news over the phone was the coward's way out.

Before dialing Indiana's Crime Scene Unit, Laurent accessed the DMV website. Emmit Martin owned eight registered and licensed vehicles, including a 2016 red Jeep. Vern, one. Neal Tillman owned four vehicles, his son, Theo, one. She touched the speakerphone and dialed.

"Crime Scene Unit, Whitmore speaking."

"Sheriff Laurent in Rogers County. I've got a homicide. I'd like to send some photos, a tissue sample, and a couple of DNA swabs."

"Is this about the body you recovered in the park?" Whitmore asked. "What'd you find?"

"The body was completely frozen when we dug her up on February second. It took five days to thaw," Laurent said. "Dr. Creighton performed the autopsy this morning and found two dents in her head and has declared the manner of death as homicide—cause of death is hypothermia, possibly suffocation. He wants to examine the lungs in more detail. He'll send in the tissue sample. I found boot prints in the snow next to the victim's vehicle, which was parked two miles away from where the body was found. They're too big to belong to the deceased. What I'm looking for is a match to the tread. That should lead me to the type of boot and size."

"Were you able to make a mold?"

"Negative. Obtaining footwear impressions in the snow is tough, and before we could even spray the print to insulate it, it snowed again. Lost it all."

"Send the photos," he said. "What else?"

"The voluntary DNA samples are from two individuals who saw her the afternoon before she died. I'd like a comparison between what Dr. Creighton's office sends and what I'm sending."

"I'll let the lab know and ask them to expedite," Whitmore said.

"I've also photographed the victim's boots."

"Why the boots?"

"First, to compare against the print I found in the snow. Second, the right shoelace is untied and the left is tied tight. I think she bent over to take off her boots and was hit in the head."

"Your persons of interest," Whitmore said. "Would the victim have been comfortable removing her boots in their presence?"

"Yes and no."

"Have you located the murder weapon?"

"We walked Beaumon's Hardware with the manager, and I wrote a list of items that fit the size of the dents in the victim's head. I think the murder weapon is either a ball peen hammer or a regular hammer. There are thousands of hammers in the quad-county area, so I'm not hopeful the murder weapon will lead me to the murderer." Laurent pushed her checklist to the side of her desk and leaned back.

"Send me a copy of the autopsy report and I'll run those specifications through our database. If any other items matching the dents pop up, I'll let you know. I'll handle all of this myself," Whitmore said. "We rarely hear from you out in farm country. I'd like to keep it that way. Give me a call if you need help or have questions."

Laurent said goodbye to the head of Indiana's Crime Scene Unit, and tossed her pen on the desk. She stared at her computer screen.

Thursday was her regularly scheduled day off. She usually started the day practicing in final preparation for her cello lesson on Thursday nights, but she'd canceled her lesson for tonight, citing her ongoing cold and murder investigation. It was the first time in the last ten years she'd canceled. Other than her job, her cello lessons were her top priority. And, every once in a while, the words out of her college-lover's mouth, David Lucroy, came back to haunt her. *You're not good enough.* With those four words, he smashed her confidence. Hours of practice evaporated. What she worked so hard for had been given to that asshole. Talent and ability oozed out of his fingers. Maybe that was why she never missed a lesson. She wasn't sure if she'd ever get her confidence back.

Tipping forward in her chair, she closed out of all of the tabs on her computer and put it into sleep mode. Darkness had fallen on Field's Crossing, and there was no snow in the forecast for tonight. A cold but clear night. After she spoke with the Gattisons, she'd go home, open a can of chicken noodle soup, and binge-watch something on Netflix. Clear her mind.

Almost a week had passed since she and her deputies uncovered Stephanie's body. As she and the former sheriff walked through Beaumon's earlier in the day, the glances from the employees told her one thing. Stephanie was well liked and her coworkers were saddened by her loss. Laurent wondered what the reaction would be if she walked through the hardware store tomorrow after *The Crossing* was published. Once everyone knew Stephanie had been murdered, the pressure to find and arrest the killer would be enormous. She knew the quicker the arrest, the more settled the community.

Unfortunately, she had very little hard evidence and even less experience. Even with offers of help from Glen and the head of Indiana's CSU, Laurent was worried. The weather had delayed the finding of the body and ascertaining the manner of death. Had the killer counted on this and was he still in Field's Crossing? She remembered thinking whoever committed this crime was local. Someone who knew all the excess snow was dumped in Webster Park. The problem was, everyone in town knew this.

CHAPTER FOURTEEN

OPINION/EDITORIAL PAGE
GATTISON GIRL MURDERED

February 8, 2019
Field's Crossing, Indiana
by Ralph Howard

In a rare moment of honesty, Sheriff Jhonni Laurent admitted the death of Stephanie Gattison was declared a homicide. At Linville's Funeral Home, the sheriff would only say she is beginning her investigation while awaiting lab results and would not comment. One wonders if she knows what to do.

In reviewing her history with the sheriff's department in Indiana, it's clear Laurent has never been involved in a murder case. Will she have to call upon her mentor and sole supporter, Glen Atkins, for assistance? The former sheriff was in attendance at the autopsy.

The autopsy report was made available to the public late Thursday afternoon and indicates the high school female was struck over the head, dragged into the snow, and left to die the afternoon before the blizzard.

Will the murder of an innocent young woman go unpunished?

A source close to the sheriff's office claims Laurent is floundering, interviewing the wrong people, and getting no closer to the truth.

CHAPTER FIFTEEN

"WHAT ARE YOU doing here?" Vern's blue eyes glared at Laurent from his cabin door.

"I've got some follow-up questions." Laurent half-expected him to slam the door in her face.

He blocked the doorway to the rest of his cabin, arms crossed, feet spread wide.

She squinted at Vern. "I'm searching for Stephanie's cell phone. Did you find it?"

"No."

"I'm going to call her number."

"Go ahead. I got nothing to hide."

Laurent listened for the corresponding ringtone. The cabin was quiet.

"Satisfied?"

She slid her cell phone into a pocket and sealed the Velcro flap on her pants. "Did Caleb tell you Stephanie was pregnant and Dylan was the father?"

"That little shit."

"Which one?"

"Both of them. Caleb for not telling me and Dylan for . . . Emmit told me. You're thinking Dylan had something to do with the Gattison girl's death, aren't you? What possible motive does Dylan have to kill his girlfriend?" Vern dropped his arms to his side, hands clenching and unclenching.

"You tell me."

"You're fishing."

"What do you think Emmit's reaction would have been?" Laurent asked.

"He'd be pissed."

"And then what?"

"He'd cool off. Jane would bring him around. Might not let Dylan go to college." Vern rubbed his unshaven chin. "I'll admit Dylan should have waited for Stephanie and that makes him partly responsible for her death, but he didn't leave her out in the cold knowingly. He's got the softest heart of all of us. Damn shame all around."

"Did you remove anything from her truck?" Laurent asked.

"You asked that question the other day."

"Remind me of your answer."

"No."

"Mind if I look in the barn?"

"Go ahead. Like I said, I got nothin' to hide."

"I'm going to walk around calling Stephanie's cell phone. Owen and Theresa don't know where it is, and phone records show no activity after four on Wednesday." Laurent tugged on her gloves.

"You think whoever's responsible for her death has her phone?"

"Strong possibility."

"I didn't kill Owen's girl." Vern slammed the door.

Laurent walked down the path to the barn, knowing if she glanced over her shoulder, she'd see Vern's silhouette in the mudroom window. Scowling. Might even be on the landline to Emmit.

The doors on the metal barn rattled in the wind. Grasping the barn door handle with both hands, she planted her feet and pulled. And tugged. And swore. Four feet of snow was piled at the base of the sliding door. Falling back on her butt as the door slid open, she landed in a drift and sat for a few seconds, catching her breath, before shoving to her feet. Her cheeks burned, but not from the wind. Vern probably saw the whole thing and was laughing his ass off. She pounded on the barn door before slipping inside.

Out of the wind.

The barn was pitch black; the faint musty odor of rotting hay lingered in the cold air, the sides shuddering back and forth in the wind. Laurent clicked on her Maglite and shone it over a tool bench. Hammers and saws were lined up neatly and extension cords and rope hung on pegs. Calling Stephanie's cell phone, she waited, but there was no answering ringtone. With her phone still calling, she walked deeper into the barn. Past shelves of propane tanks. At the rear of the barn, a vehicle sat covered with a tarp.

"Told you it wasn't here." Vern's voice cut through the semidarkness, his shadow blocking the faint light from the barn door.

"Goddammit, Vern. Are you trying to give me a heart attack?" Laurent snapped. She had been so focused on listening for a ringtone, she forgot he was a hundred feet away. And watching her. She shone the flashlight in his face and watched him stumble back out of the light. "You gave me permission to look around."

"I changed my mind. The phone's not here. You can leave now." Vern pointed to the partially open barn door.

Laurent trudged back to the water tower, stopping every fifty feet to call the missing phone. The battery was probably dead, and it might be spring before the phone was found. Reaching the police SUV, Laurent leaned against it and studied Vern's tiny cabin and barn. Was the occupant crazy? At lunch the other day, Starr thought Vern was off his rocker and so did Ralph, but John Cook and Caleb thought he was doing better. Much better. And Glen hadn't seen him in the last year. She had seen an angry Vern, a sad Vern, and a protective Vern. Part of her was glad she hadn't found the victim's phone on Vern's property and the other part, deflated. The leads she had to follow were growing fewer, and it was time to widen the search. For now, Caleb and Dylan alibied each other from four thirty to seven, but she was leaving that door open. She was going to focus on Vern. And Theo.

Laurent climbed into the SUV and called Dak. "Meet me in the parking lot in five minutes. I've got everything ready." She touched END on her cell phone and leaned against the front seat of the police SUV. The back of the vehicle was filled with items she had confiscated from Emmit's and Vern's farms. The only part of the warrant she hadn't executed was for the 2016 red Jeep, which was at Cook's Auto Body Shop for repair of the side mirror. The warrant was specific to location and vehicle to be searched, and with the Jeep not on the property, Laurent was hesitant to search it at the auto body shop. She was waiting for the judge to return her call.

Her deputy Dak Aikens had volunteered to drive the SUV south to the Indianapolis CSU lab so she could go home and curl up in misery. Her cold was at its peak, despite the antibiotic Creighton prescribed for her bronchitis. Fever, chills, stuffy nose. It was less painful to swallow, but she had no energy. Executing the warrant took most of the afternoon, and she'd left Vern's cabin for last. Her interview earlier in the morning hadn't gone well, and when she reappeared late in the day, he snarled at her. And stomped into his living room, rocking furiously in his chair.

Laurent turned into the police lot, parked in the empty spot next to Dak, and got out.

"How'd it go?" Dak took the pile of paperwork from Laurent and clipped it on a clipboard, adding a few more pages on the top. He signed and initialed the acknowledgment of transfer and tucked the clipboard under his arm. "You look like shit."

"Thanks. I feel like shit," she said. "Everything went fine. I'm waiting for Judge Jenkins to call me back about the Jeep at Cook's."

"Anybody give you flak?"

"Emmit stormed out to the barn, and I thought Vern was going to break his rocking chair, but other than that, no." She shrugged.

"Any of those treads look like the picture you snapped?"

"Hard to tell. One thing caught my eye," she said. "In Vern's mudroom there was a black backpack sitting on the floor next to his boot tray."

One of Dak's eyebrows raised.

"I moved it to get to a pair of boots."

Dak's other eyebrow raised.

"It was heavy and full of books."

"How do you know there were books in there? The warrant said nothing about backpacks."

Laurent raised a hand. "I didn't look inside. I picked it up by the side, not the strap or the handle. I felt a book. Books."

"Sheriff, you're walkin' a fine line there." Dak ran a hand over his bald head.

"The label on the back had the initials "DM.""

"What the fuck is Dylan's backpack doing in Vern's mudroom?"

* * *

Laurent shuffled to her front door, a blanket clutched in one hand under her chin, unlocked the door, and returned to the living room. She sank into the couch and pulled the blanket tightly around her. Starr had turned into the driveway, the headlights flashing in the windows. She was bringing soup from the Skillet. And Kleenex.

"You look awful. Are you running a fever?" Starr stood in the hallway, hands on her hips.

"Chills and shakes. I hate that. Started during work and, since I got home, I haven't been able to get off the couch." After interviewing Vern and walking around the musty old barn and then executing the warrants, Laurent had no energy left. None.

"Are you gonna get me sick?"

"I won't breathe on you, but the possibility exists."

"Give me a minute. I'll warm up the soup." Starr dropped her enormous purse on the carpet next to the couch and stomped back to the kitchen. "Where the fuck is a pot? Never mind."

Half an hour later, the fire in Laurent's throat eased and she could partially breathe through one nostril. "There's something I want to talk to you about."

"Okay, but I'm gonna sit on the other side of the room. Whatever you got, I don't want."

"You sound like Glen." Now that Starr was sitting across the living room from her, Laurent was nervous. She wasn't sure if the sweat dripping down her back was from the fever or nerves. Starr knew about Randi, the daughter she gave up for adoption. What she didn't know about was the letter asking for a meeting. The request was already a few days old.

"Read this." Laurent leaned forward and handed the envelope to Starr.

A puzzled Starr pulled out her reading glasses, perched them on the end of her nose, slid the letter out of the envelope, and smoothed it open.

"You've been sitting on this for a while. Are you going to contact her? She doesn't say why she wants to meet you, but invites you to her concert. Kinda weird. What are you thinking?"

"What do you think I should do? I've got so much going on right now. I feel like crap and, apparently, I look like crap. I've got a murder on my hands, and I'm running for reelection. I haven't got time for this."

"Sounds like excuses to me, other than the winter cold. Everyone's got a job. Yours is more public and complicated than most, but still, it's a job. If this request had arrived a month ago, before Stephanie was murdered and two months before the election, what would you have done? What would your excuse have been then? Too much snow?"

Laurent stared at Starr. She had been hoping for a reprieve. Understanding. Something like—now isn't the time to open this can of worms; you've got too much on your plate. As usual, Starr went in the opposite direction.

"That's what I like about you. You don't beat around the bush. Don't spare my feelings. You think I'm making excuses?"

"Aren't you? I'm not saying to meet her for lunch tomorrow. You'll get her sick and then she never will come back. But think about it. Wouldn't it be nice to make another friend?"

"Friend? Is that how I should think of her?"

"Maybe to start with." Starr's voice softened. "You have no way of knowing what she wants. That's why you have to meet her. She might be angry, but she's definitely curious or maybe she just found out. Maybe her adoptive parents didn't tell her until now."

"She's thirty. How could they have not said something?"

"Jhonni, you've never met Randi's adoptive parents. Who knows what motivated them? Who knows what their story is? You're always talking about the walking wounded. Well, you're one of them when it comes to this."

Laurent flopped her head back and stared at the ceiling. Starr's reaction wasn't what she'd been expecting. Certainly not what she wanted to hear. She thought Starr would have told her to leave the past where it belonged. In the past. Not set up a lunch date.

"Would you go with me?"

"To the concert or to lunch?"

"Concert."

"You buying?"

CHAPTER SIXTEEN

"SHERIFF'S OFFICE." LAURENT touched the ACCEPT button on the steering wheel of the police SUV.

"Jhonni, it's Bob Kane. I'm on the Five-and-Twenty heading home, and Neal Tillman's weaving all over the place behind me."

"How close are you to home?" she asked.

"A mile away."

"Are you buckled in?"

"Of course. My daughter would kill me if she found out I wasn't wearing my seat belt."

"Do you think he's following you?"

"I denied his loan request this week," Kane said. "You know how mean he is, but add in some booze, and he's liable to do anything."

"I'm five minutes away. Why don't you loop around and come back through town? Don't go home just yet."

"He's creeping up on me and he's got no headlights," Kane said.

"That ancient pickup has so many violations, it's a wonder the damn thing even starts."

"He's right on my fender."

"Slow down. Let him go by. Don't get out of the car."

"He's right next to me."

"Any oncoming vehicles?" The pitch of Bob Kane's voice rose and his words were short and choppy. *Don't panic.*

"No."

"Where are you?" Laurent said. "Be specific."

"Big left-hand curve by the drain culvert. Shit. Shit. Shit."

"Bob?"

"My cell phone's on the floor."

"I can hear you." Laurent leaned forward in the SUV and flicked on the red and blue lights and siren.

"Goddamn it."

"Bob. Stay still. Don't move. I'm on the Five-and-Twenty. Stay in your car. Do you understand?"

"I'm not going anywhere. I'm headfirst in the culvert and bleeding like a stuck pig. Bastard broke my nose."

"Breathe through your mouth. I'm two minutes away. Dak and Greene are coming in from the south end of the Five-and-Twenty. They'll pull Tillman over and stick him behind bars."

"I hear the siren."

"Stay with me, Bob. Concentrate on the siren." Laurent laid her cell phone across the dash and touched the radio on her shoulder. "Dispatch. Send Greene and Dak to the south end of the Five-and-Twenty. Tell them to set up a road block. Advise them Neal Tillman is drunk and weaving. Black pickup, no headlights."

"Ten-four."

"Send an ambulance to the left curve by the drain culvert on the Five-and-Twenty. Advise injured sixty-year-old man. Possible concussion, broken nose." Laurent released the talk button and then pressed it again. "Send a tow truck."

The siren wasn't necessary in the country, but Laurent wanted Bob Kane to know she was near and not to lose consciousness. Dak and

Greene would have the south end of the Five-and-Twenty blocked off in less than ten minutes. The only way for Tillman to get past the deputies was to drive into the ditch or into the police cars. Tillman might be crazy enough or drunk enough to do either.

Laurent killed the siren and parked diagonally across the road, her headlights shining on the Cadillac in the ditch. "I'm right behind you. Crack open your window."

"I see the headlights." She heard the sigh of relief in Kane's voice.

Laurent popped open the trunk of her SUV and grabbed a shovel. The night sky was pitch black as clouds covered the stars. The weather forecast called for tonight's air temperature to be below zero. It was a good thing Kane called her when he did or he might have died in his car headfirst in a snowdrift two miles from home.

"How long can you lock that asshole up for?" Kane yelled out the window.

"Cotter will probably spring him after forty-eight hours." She directed her voice at the driver's-side window. "How are you feeling? What hurts?" Laurent threw snow from side to side, stamping down a path to the Cadillac.

"There's blood on everything, but the bleeding has stopped," he said. "My head hurts like a sonofabitch, and I think I sprained my right wrist. Other than that, I'm fine."

"Count backward from ten for me."

Kane counted.

"What day is it?"

"Friday."

"Month? Year?"

"February of two thousand nineteen. The coldest and snowiest month in history so far," Kane said. "After I get out of here, I'm calling my daughter and thanking her for saving my life."

"I'm shoveling a path to your door. The temperature is dropping fast and the volunteer fire department won't arrive for another fifteen minutes. You don't sound concussed to me. Do you think you can crawl up the embankment into my SUV?"

"I'm sure as hell not gonna end up frozen under a pile of snow like the Gattison girl."

*   *   *

Neal Tillman turned left on Field Street and clipped the side mirror of the Buick parked next to the meter. He jerked back to his side of the street, an oncoming pickup blaring its horn. Spotting two empty parking spaces across from Farmers Bank, he made a U-turn in the middle of the street and shoved his pickup directly between the spaces. He spat out the window, tobacco juice mixing with black slush.

Five ten. Friday night.

Darkness had fallen and the overhead streetlights reflected off the snowdrifts. Tillman fiddled with the radio, settling on CTRY96, Indiana's best country radio station. Unscrewing the cap of his flask, he swigged a mouthful of cheap whiskey and watched as Bob Kane held the door open for his employees.

Right on time.

Tillman slouched in the driver's seat and pulled the brim of his camouflage baseball cap over his eyes. Three bank employees crossed in front of his truck, calling good night to each other. He snuck a peek to his left as Kane and the security guard locked the door and activated the alarm system. The two men walked in opposite directions.

Tillman straightened up as the bank president tossed his black briefcase on the passenger seat, and settled behind the wheel. Time to go.

Kane pulled onto Field Street.

Tillman followed. Headlights off.

The CEO turned onto the Five-and-Twenty. If Kane checked his rearview mirror, Tillman knew the banker wouldn't be able to see the dirty black pickup on the country road, where no overhead lighting existed.

Kane picked up speed. Tillman didn't bother to glance at his speedometer. It was broken.

Tillman pressed on the gas pedal. The Cadillac continued cruising.

Faster.

The country roads where Kane lived were plowed last. Both sides of the Five-and-Twenty were piled high with fifteen-foot drifts, common where the wind blew huge amounts of snow across the road, even with the orange lattice fencing. Drifting snow or black ice were often the cause of accidents, with cars and pickups ending in a ditch.

Tillman had driven the road earlier in the day, scouting out where the huge drifts were and where there were gaps. The perfect spot was coming up. It was a left-hand curve, almost ninety degrees, crossing a drain culvert. The snow was level with the road on the right, but on the left, the blizzard had blown the snow across the Five-and-Twenty into an enormous drift. A little nudge and Kane would be in a ditch, nose down, a mile from home. And he'd never know who hit him.

One-half mile.

Tillman inched closer. He figured Kane was going around fifty miles an hour on a road he knew well.

One-quarter mile.

In the distance, Kane's headlights illuminated the curve. Brake lights glowed red and reflected off Tillman's black pickup.

Almost there.

Tillman swung into the middle of the country road, sped up, and passed Kane's car. He yanked the wheel back, clipping the front end of the Cadillac.

The big car slowed. And slid. And turned. And disappeared into the soft snow of the drainage ditch.

Tillman fist-pumped and slapped his hand on the wheel. Big fat banker in a big fat car in a big deep ditch. Serves him right. *That'll be the last time he doesn't give me money.*

*   *   *

"What did the breathalyzer show?" Laurent asked. She had called Kane's wife, Shelby, and stayed with him until the ambulance arrived, insisting he go to Columbia Hospital to be checked for a concussion and to set his broken nose.

Neal Tillman was locked in a cell three stories below her desk. She pulled up the security settings on her computer, accessed the cell Tillman was sleeping in, and muted the sound. She didn't need to hear his snoring. "What happened on your end?"

She dipped her tea bag into the steaming hot water. The antibiotic Creighton prescribed for her had worked miracles. She could swallow without pain and breathe without using nasal spray, and some of her energy had returned. Deep sleep, however, eluded her.

"He refused to take it," Greene said. "Mean old bastard. What the hell was he doing all the way out on the Five-and-Twenty?"

"Trying to run Bob off the road because Farmers Bank refused his loan request. I think the Tillman family is having serious financial difficulties."

"Who gives a rat's ass?" Greene snapped. "We all go through tough money times. Why should he be any different?"

"Why do you think that?" Dak asked.

Dak's quiet voice calmed Laurent. The hackles on the back of her neck rose the minute Greene opened his mouth. Just being in his presence irritated her lately. "I chatted with Glen when he stopped by the other day. He mentioned a number of instances, usually before the snow melts and before the farmers can get out into the fields, where he tossed Tillman in jail and all Tillman groused about was money. Or the lack of it."

"He bitched about the Martins, too, I'll bet," Greene said.

"I'm sure he did."

"Should I call Jim Cotter now?" Dak leaned against the doorframe of her office, arms folded across his chest.

"Tillman's got to dry out before we can release him. Did he resist arrest?"

"Not enough," Greene said. "He was laughing and seemed very pleased with himself. What a dumb shit. I suppose you're gonna let him go tomorrow morning?"

"Probably."

"I'd lock him up and throw away the key. He's a menace on the roads and an asshole to boot." Greene shoved to his feet.

"If Bob wants to press charges, I'll keep Tillman until he posts bail. Otherwise, I'll let him sleep it off. And he's got to pay to fix Bob's Caddy."

"How's Mr. Kane?" Dak asked.

"Thank God for seat belts. Saved him from going through the windshield," she said.

"Did he see the front end of his Caddy?"

"He was in shock. Talked okay, but his eyes were glassy and he was shivering even with three heated blankets tucked around him. He's going to be very sore tomorrow." Laurent sipped her hot tea.

"Tillman was coming right at us," Dak said. "Greene flashed his headlights and turned on the spotlight, but the asshole kept coming.

I think when he saw both cruisers across the road is when he decided to run. No way that piece of shit pickup was going to do anything but dent a police cruiser."

"He tried to make a fast U-turn, but he slid off the Five-and-Twenty into a snowdrift. I was expecting blood and vomit when I opened his door," Greene said.

"Not a scratch on him."

"We dragged him up the embankment and laid him down in the snow. Dak cuffed him. That's when he started kicking and screaming and biting," Greene said.

"Did he break any skin?" she asked.

Both deputies shook their heads.

"We stuck him in the back of my cruiser. I waited until Dak turned off the engine, and locked and tagged that old piece of shit," Greene said.

"I confiscated his flask and added it to his personal items," Dak said.

"Book him on a DUI, resisting arrest, and causing a vehicular accident," Laurent said. "The paperwork should take the rest of your shift. Good job."

CHAPTER SEVENTEEN

LAURENT COCOONED HERSELF on the couch and pulled the coffee table close. She was feeling marginally better this morning and wondered if the stress from Stephanie's murder, combined with her daughter's request for a meeting had exacerbated her cold. After Starr left on Friday night, she'd taken her medicine and slept for nine hours. Yesterday's shift had been consumed by Bob Kane being run off the road by Neal Tillman. She was hoping if she spent Sunday on the couch and took a few more meds, who knows? *I might be back to my old self by tomorrow.*

She pulled her laptop on top of the blanket and started a file marked "possible suspects." At the top of the list was Dylan Martin. Boyfriend of the deceased. Angry. Left in a huff. Next seen at his brother's office by the public works secretary, Maggie, who left at four thirty. After that, Dylan's alibi was his older brother, Caleb.

Laurent was pretty sure Caleb didn't kill Stephanie. Maggie alibied Caleb from noon to four thirty. The two employees were preparing for the blizzard while Dylan and Stephanie were in school. But after Maggie left, what did the brothers do? The next people to see either one of the Martin brothers were John and Jay Cook, who showed up at seven that night. Dylan and Caleb had two and a half hours by themselves. What did they do? Where'd they go? No one in

Field's Crossing would find it odd if Caleb was out in his orange truck. That was his job.

Something to think about.

Now add in Vern. And Dylan's backpack in his mudroom.

Laurent paused, hands hovering over the keyboard. Dak was worried she had crossed a line by moving the backpack to confiscate the boots next to it. *I didn't cross a line. Might have stretched it a bit.* If it came up in court, would Vern remember where the backpack was in relation to his boots? Doubtful.

How did Vern fit in? Caleb thought his uncle was on the mend. Physically, Vern was fit as a fiddle. Mentally. What about his mind? What if Caleb or Dylan or both drove out to the water tower and then what? Killed Stephanie in cold blood? Hit her on the head then drove to Webster Park and dumped snow on her? There'd be no reason to involve Vern, but why was Dylan's backpack in the cabin? Why did Caleb and Dylan involve their uncle?

Because they were scared. *I'll buy that.*

Stephanie was killed in a moment of anger and then the cover-up began. Who did what and when?

Laurent sipped her tea and started on the next suspect. Theo Tillman. Theo admitted to seeing Stephanie at four thirty on Wednesday afternoon and said she was pissed and crying. He taunted her, throwing big-boobs Brittany in her face, suggesting Dylan was cheating on her. And he was. Stephanie's best friend, Claire, confirmed it. Did Stephanie suspect Dylan of cheating? Would Stephanie go anywhere with Theo? Laurent shook her head. *No way.* From the video at Beaumon's Hardware, Laurent saw a fearless, capable young woman. She wouldn't get into Theo's truck unless she was unconscious. Theo said she didn't, but what if he was lying? Laurent narrowed her eyes and stared at the darkened TV screen. Was it possible Theo didn't remember giving Stephanie a ride? Was it possible he didn't remember hitting her with a hammer? She snorted. Of course it was. *I'm getting a warrant for Theo's truck.*

Laurent sighed. It was going to take CSU at least two weeks to get the results of all of the items she had confiscated. *Let's hope it doesn't take that long. I'd like to solve this well before the election.*

What else? Laurent moved her laptop to the coffee table and picked up her mug of hot tea. Glen Atkins' narrative about the century-old feud between the Martins and the Tillmans echoed in her mind. Was there enough anger, hatred, or resentment for either Theo or his father, Neal, to kill someone important to the Martin family? Theo smoked weed. Neal was a drunk. Add in the threat of losing the farm. Neal seemed focused on hurting Bob, but what about Theo? Two weeks ago, Theo tried to steal from a cash register at the hardware store and was caught by the deceased. Was that enough to kill Stephanie, dump her body in the park, and cover it with snow?

She opened the file marked POSSIBLE MURDER WEAPONS. Conduit, copper piping, metal garden stakes, rebar. All of these items were straight, long, and short. Nothing with the curved head of a hammer. If something like that had been used, the wound would have looked more like a stab wound and, from the location on the victim's head, Stephanie would have had to have been lying down. The murder weapon was a hammer. No doubt about it.

Laurent picked up her cell phone and dialed Dak.

"You're supposed to take it easy," he said.

"I'm on my couch with hot tea and blankets, and I'm about to binge-watch something on Netflix, which means I'll fall asleep. Anything from CSU?"

"I would have called if something came in," Dak said. "Take a nap. You're gonna need your energy this week. More snow's coming."

CHAPTER EIGHTEEN

"I'M IN FRONT of your house right now, Mrs. Kane," Laurent said. "The driveway's been plowed, but I don't see your husband's pickup truck."

"Can you check the barn?" Shelby asked. "I'm in Tampa with my sister and Bob's not answering my phone calls. The Caddy should be at the auto body shop after Tillman's little escapade on Friday. Bob drives the pickup on the weekends."

"I'll call you back." Laurent parked the police SUV near the back door of the old farmhouse and jogged to the barn. She was hoping Bob's truck was gone. If the truck was there, she was afraid of what she might find.

Laurent pulled the door open.

No Cadillac. No pickup.

She exhaled a sigh of relief. She wasn't going to find Bob dead in his La-Z-Boy, TV blaring, remote gripped in his hand, food spilled on the floor. After calling Shelby back, she contacted her office and Caleb's office. Whoever found Bob needed to tell him to call his wife.

*　*　*

Laurent pulled the police SUV onto the shoulder of the road, behind Bob's pickup truck. One of the snowplow drivers had noticed Kane's vehicle earlier in the day and reported it to Maggie, Caleb's secretary. An inch of snow covered the pickup and faint sled tracks led to Turtle Lake.

She called in her location before exiting the SUV and walking to the driver's-side window. Laurent knocked and opened the door. The pickup was empty. She peeked over the front seat and found the usual emergency supplies. Slamming the door shut, she walked back to her vehicle and pulled on an orange vest. The outline of two sets of snow-covered footprints, along with rabbit, squirrel, and deer tracks, led down the slight incline to the lake. Laurent snapped a few pictures of the boot prints, slid her phone in her pants pocket, and started down the path, matching her footsteps to the ones in the snow.

Two minutes later, she perched on the edge of Turtle Lake. On her right stood the forest, to her left, the frozen lake. Ahead, a single ice-fishing tent billowed in the wind.

"Bob!" Laurent's shout echoed across Turtle Lake. The lake was an elongated oval, thirteen miles in perimeter and ninety feet at its deepest point. The Turtle River fed into the lake from the north. Bass, trout, perch, and crappie were plentiful. The lake was far enough away from Field's Crossing so high school kids didn't frequent it, but Laurent saw a few firepits filled with snow along the edge of the lake.

The trees were bent over, bare branches bending under the weight of the snow, a few limbs frozen to the icy lake. Wet snow clung to the trunks and the cold air was filled with the creaking and groaning of the old oaks, maples, and elms. Laurent skirted the tree roots choosing to travel into the forest a few feet rather than step on the edge of the lake's ice. She stopped opposite the ice shelter. "Bob!"

The ice shelter was zipped shut.

Laurent radioed her location before stepping gingerly onto the frozen lake. She wasn't an ice fisherman like Deputy Poulter. He had laughed at her description and called her "old-fashioned." She spent a lot of time outdoors and didn't need to encase herself in layers of clothing and sit on a plastic fold-up chair staring at a hole in the ice. According to Poulter, modern-day ice-fishing was much easier with gas-powered augers and sonar fish finders and portable heaters. And alcohol always helped.

"Bob!"

Again, no answer. To the left of the ice shelter, a sled used to drag ice-fishing gear onto the lake was anchored into the frozen lake. Laurent knelt on one knee and unzipped the tent.

Laurent sighed. She met Bob four years ago when she applied for the mortgage on her farmhouse and had spoken with him a few times at the weekly farmers market. She didn't know him well, but, from watching him interact with residents at the market, he was well liked, as was his wife. Shelby's banana bread had taken first place at the quad-county fair; Laurent's banana bread, second.

Laurent stepped over the lip of the tent and waddled, bent over to the body. She pulled off a glove and checked his pulse, knowing it was futile. Sitting back on her haunches, she touched her radio. "Dispatch. I've located Bob Kane. Send an ambulance and the fire department to the Turtle Lake bridge. They're going to need a body bag unless they want to roll a gurney on the lake for a quarter mile. Call Henry Linville and advise him we have another body to thaw."

"Ten-four."

"I'll inform next-of-kin after the body has been retrieved."

"Ten-four. Do you require any other assistance?"

"Negative."

The wind rattled the tent poles and polyester sides. Laurent crouched at the entrance, memorizing the scene in front of her before pulling out her cell phone and snapping pictures. Bob's right cheek was frozen to Turtle Lake, inches away from one of the three drilled ice-fishing holes and a rod holder holding two tip-ups. A thin layer of ice covered his entire head, the short white hair frozen straight up. A dribble of ice ran from his nose and down the side of his cheek, freezing his face to the floor of the shelter. He lay on his stomach, legs splayed wide, fingers frozen in a claw shape. Near one foot, a yellowish-brown patch of ice had formed, a broken beer bottle frozen on its side, label half-picked off. One ear warmer was missing; the other floated in the open hole.

A padded canvas chair perched in one corner and an open tackle box lay next to the chair. In the opposite corner sat a portable heater. Laurent reached over and turned the heater on. Nothing. She glanced at the gauge and saw the propane cylinders read empty. Scooting back to the entrance, she zipped it up, trying to keep what little heat the sun generated inside the shelter and the blowing snow and wind out.

The glare of the sun disappeared. Peering into the nearest ice hole, Laurent estimated Turtle Lake was frozen two to three feet down. The faint smell of beer hung in the ice shelter and broken brown glass lay next to the deceased's feet. She shuffled back to the body, leaned over, and sniffed the back of Kane's head. Beer. She parted a few strands of hair. Blood. Gashes. Did Neal Tillman come out here to finish the job?

A shadow fell across the tent.

Laurent froze. The zippered entrance to the ice shelter was four feet away. The ambulance at least ten minutes away. Did the shadow know she was inside the tent?

The shadow slid to the back of the tent.

Laurent pulled off her right glove. Her bare hand hovered over the gun at her side. She held her breath.

The shadow circled the tent, stopping at the zipped-up door.

The shadow knelt.

As the zipper crept up, Laurent unsnapped her holster. With her teeth, she pulled off the other glove. Two hands steadied the Glock. She exhaled silently.

The zipper moved up, the flap opened, and Vern's blue eyes met her gaze.

"Take ten steps back."

Vern raised his hands and stepped back.

"Turn around. Face the forest."

Hands raised, Vern turned.

Laurent duck-walked to the edge of the ice shelter, Glock shoulder height, eyes peeled on Vern Martin. "Take another ten steps." She waited until he was twenty yards away before stepping over the lip of the ice shelter. "Face me. What the fuck are you doing here?"

"Most fishermen take their shelters with them when they're done," Vern said, his gloved hands raised. "This one's been standing here for the last two days. I thought I'd take a look."

"You walked all the way from your cabin to look inside an ice shelter?" The wind tugged at the hood on her parka and whipped her pants. It was hard to read a person's expression when they were talking through a scarf, but Laurent thought she saw a flicker.

"Ice-fishing equipment is expensive. Whoever left it is an idiot."

"How'd you get here?"

"Cross-country skis." Vern jerked his head toward the edge of the lake. Standing in a crook of a tree were two skis and two poles, the wrist loops swaying in the wind. "I cut through Perry's cornfield."

"Did Caleb call you?"

"Yep. And since I had nothing else to do, I skied over."

Laurent holstered her Glock. Her heart rate slowed. Off to her right, she saw the red-and-white ambulance park next to her SUV. Both doors popped open and a hand waved in the air.

"What do you need the ambulance for?" Vern asked.

"Do you know Bob Kane?"

"Everybody knows Bob. Is he hurt or dead?"

"Deceased," Laurent said.

"That's the only reason he left his stuff here. Bob's a banker and a cheapskate." He lowered his hands. "How'd he die?"

"That's for Dr. Creighton to determine."

"How do you think he died?"

"What I think is irrelevant," she said.

"You're a smart lady, Sheriff. What's your opinion?"

"It looks like he fell, hit his head, and never woke up."

"Not a bad way to go."

"Who does he usually fish with? Have you seen him out here before?" Laurent asked.

"Ask Shelby."

"She's the one who called me to track him down."

"Why doesn't she know where her husband is?"

"She's visiting her sister in Tampa for the next month. When Bob didn't call her back, she called my office. Someone from Caleb's office called in the pickup," Laurent said.

"Field's Crossing hasn't had a blizzard-related death in ten years," Vern said. "Now there've been two in two weeks."

"And somehow, you've been at both scenes."

"So have you."

"I'm supposed to be," she snapped. "You inspected Stephanie's truck before I got there. Were you trying to do the same thing here?"

"Strictly coincidence. I'm going home now. You've got enough to do. You know where to find me." Vern walked backward until he reached his skis.

"Who else did you see ice fishing this week?"

"There were a couple of other tents out here. You'll have to ask them."

"Them who?" she asked.

"The old guys at the Skillet."

Laurent narrowed her eyes as Vern reattached his ski boots to the skis, looped the straps around his wrists, and shoved off without sparing her a glance. Everyone knows there are no coincidences in a murder case. What was Vern's motive for killing Bob? What was the connection between the two frozen bodies? If any. Why would Vern or anyone in the Martin family want the banker dead? Laurent exhaled. *Slow down.* Just because Vern scared the crap out of her was no reason to assume he had anything to do with Bob's death. She was having trouble getting a read on him. Asking questions but not answering hers. Tight-lipped. Was that how he normally behaved? She didn't remember ever having a conversation with him. Emmit always did the talking.

She crouched in front of the tent again and waited as the paramedics and volunteer firemen struggled through the snow, their equipment slowing them down. There was nothing that said Kane was murdered, but how did he get that gash on the back of his head? There was no way he hit himself over the head, even though his hair smelled of beer.

Kane's eyes were closed, the bruising from Friday night covering the eyelids and the entire eye socket. Laurent stepped into the tent. Six feet wide by eight feet long. One fisherman or two? Three holes and two rods. That seemed odd to her. She'd have to ask Poulter. Bending at the waist, she half-stood over Bob's body. The faint outline of a boot tread was imprinted on the back of the banker's jacket. Laurent snapped a few pictures. This wasn't an accident. Who wanted Bob dead? Only one person came to mind.

CHAPTER NINETEEN

"So why won't the sheriff release any more information?" Ralph Howard perched on a stool at the counter sopping up egg yolk with the last bite of toast.

"I can't comment on an ongoing investigation." Laurent closed the inner door to the Skillet and tucked her gloves under one arm. She strolled to the middle of the diner and dropped her headband on the checkered plastic tablecloth. The décor in the Skillet reflected the 1950s, complete with black-and-white checkered linoleum, a soda fountain with red plastic stools, and antique road signs. Laurent thought the signs might have been scavenged from local farm sales and auctions. "Just hot tea this morning."

"I read the autopsy report," Ralph said. "Stephanie Gattison froze to death, but why was she out in the snow? Where'd the dents in her head come from? Have you found the murder weapon? What are you doing about that?"

"I'm investigating." Laurent had hoped to find Art and Dutch alone. The old guys at the Skillet were always the last to leave. *Bad luck finding Ralph here.*

"What's that supposed to mean?"

Laurent squeezed a lemon wedge in her hot tea and considered her options. Thanks to the local newspaper, everyone in the quad-county area knew Stephanie's death had become a murder investigation. Keeping quiet would look like she was trying to hide something and in today's era of transparency, any hint of hiding information from the public would be seen as dishonest. "The manner of death is homicide. It appears the victim was struck in the head twice with a hammer and left in the snow."

"A hammer? Whose hammer? What have you done since Creighton issued the death certificate?"

"Other than find Bob Kane's body?" She sipped her tea and added another lemon wedge. "I've been investigating. Talking to people."

"Who have you interviewed? Who are your prime suspects?"

"You know I can't comment on that." Laurent's dislike of Ralph increased every day. The irritating reporter always found a way to make her look incompetent while, at the same time, riling up the community. If he knew the last two people to admit to seeing Stephanie alive were Theo and Dylan, he'd dredge up the old feud.

"Is that why you need Glen Atkins' help? Can't do this on your own?"

Laurent raised her eyebrows. Did Ralph have spies perched on every corner in Field's Crossing? She blew on her tea, hoping the biased reporter didn't know the former sheriff accompanied her to Beaumon's Hardware and the high school. "Glen frequently stops by. Duke, too. I believe he drove to the Skillet to chat with friends."

"We had a good long chat with him," Dutch said. "He's got too much time on his hands."

"Who doesn't?" Art snorted.

"What evidence have you been able to collect?" Ralph asked.

"No comment."

Ralph slid off his stool and pointed his finger at Laurent. "I'm not done with this story. If you don't find Stephanie's murderer before the election, I guarantee you won't get reelected. The residents of the quad-counties deserve a competent sheriff, and that's not you." He slapped a ten-dollar bill on the counter and stalked out.

A blast of cold air shot through the diner as Ralph opened the outer door before the inner door closed. It was midmorning and the Skillet had emptied out, leaving Laurent with the two old farmers.

She dipped the tea bag again, and squeezed in another lemon wedge. After laying the tea bag and spoon on the red-and-white checkered tablecloth, she looked up to find two pairs of eyes trained on her.

"You know he's going to call his buddy Mike Greene," Art said. "What a snark."

"Everyone knows Ralph's 'unnamed source' is Greene. The question is how far over the line will Greene go? I won't bash a fellow officer, even if I'm running against him. I won't engage in negative campaigning. I'll leave the bad-mouthing to Ralph. He's got enough for everyone." Laurent blew on her tea. "The election is three weeks away. What are the voters going to think if I don't find out who killed Stephanie? Do you think they'll vote me out? Is Ralph right about that?"

"Finding the murderer isn't going to change the outcome of the election," Art said. "The real question is—does the Howard family and *The Crossing* have enough influence in the quad-county area to elect Mike Greene? The paper's been here since paper was invented."

"I think their influence is long gone," Dutch said. "And papyrus has been around since before Christ. Thank God, Ralph's family hasn't been around that long. Sheriff, you're worrying over nothin'. No one in the quad-counties has any respect for Ralph and that rag he calls a newspaper. My wife uses it to wash windows. Vinegar and newspaper. You're a better sheriff than Greene could ever be. Me and Art are in your camp, and we'll tell everybody."

"Thank you, both. Greene would never keep me on as a deputy, and I couldn't stomach him as a boss. You know I love Field's Crossing and my home. I accused Glen of being attached at the heart, but I'm exactly the same. I'll fight to stay here."

Laurent cupped the mug of hot tea in both hands as the two old farmers sipped their coffee in comfortable silence. Dutch's and Art's bodies might be letting them down, but their minds were sharp. She enjoyed talking with them.

"Who wanted that girl to die?" Dutch asked.

"I can't say anything other than I'm perplexed."

"Was Bob's death an accident?" Art asked. "Folks are real upset about that. Everyone trusted Bob. He never talked shop. No one ever knew how much money the other guy had. Good banker."

"I've got to check a few things, but it looks like he hit his head hard enough to knock himself out and then hypothermia set in and he froze to death. It's also possible he had a stroke. Dr. Creighton will be able to determine cause of death after the body thaws."

"He fell asleep and never woke up," Art said. "I'd like to go out that way."

"We all would," Dutch said. "Two deaths this winter. You know the saying, 'death comes in threes.'"

"That's superstition." Art snorted.

"I'd rather not have another dead body. Two is enough."

"Just sayin'."

"How well did you know Bob?" Laurent sipped her tea and squeezed in another lemon wedge. Sometimes she wondered why she bothered with a tea bag. The hot water with lemon soothed her throat and warmed her.

"Known him for years," Dutch said. "He started at the bank as a young fella and never left. I remember him complaining about all the computer stuff he had to learn over the years. Said he was getting tired of keeping up with technology. He'll be sorely missed."

"He's been at Farmers Bank for decades," Art said. "Think of what he knows about people's money. Who has it; who doesn't."

"He didn't strike me as the talkative type," Laurent said. "I never heard him talking about clients or personnel at the bank."

"He would've kept that all to himself," Dutch said. "Only Shelby would've heard, and she's just as close-mouthed as he is. I never kept anything from my wife. If I had, she'd have found out. Couldn't even keep her fiftieth birthday party a secret."

Art slapped the table and laughed. "She was so mad at you for throwing that party. She didn't want anyone to know how old she was."

"Everyone in town knew how old she was," Dutch retorted. "She still throws it in my face when she's pissed at me."

"Who did Bob go ice fishing with?" Laurent knew the two old guys wandered from topic to topic. Where the conversation started wasn't where it would end.

"Bob and Jim Cotter have been fishing or hunting every weekend for as long as I can remember. No comment from the peanut gallery." Dutch glared at his best friend.

"Who else ice fishes around here?"

"We'll write you a list," Art said.

"Appreciate it." Laurent cleared her throat. She was nearing the end of her cold, and her throat was no longer on fire, but she still had a few more days left on the antibiotic Creighton had prescribed for her bronchitis. She thought about how to phrase this question without giving away her concerns. "What's your opinion of Vern Martin's mental health?"

"He's coming around," Art said. "He stopped in right before Christmas and stayed for almost two hours. Didn't say much. Just listened to me and Dutch argue."

"Healthy as a horse," Dutch said. "Spends all his time choppin' wood, walkin', or skiin' around Turtle Lake. Last time my daughter was at the library, he was checking out a pile of books and said hello. For a while after his wife died, he wouldn't speak to anyone. Just Emmit. Why are you asking about Vern?"

"I had to speak with him recently," she said. "He struck me as angry."

"That's gonna come up," Art said. "Especially if you were asking about a family member. He's always been protective of the family, and since his wife drowned, maybe even more."

"You're a crafty old badger, aren't you?" *Not only are you sharp, but you're quick-thinking.* Laurent drained the last of her hot tea.

"As much as the whole town thinks we spread rumors, we don't," Dutch said. "We just know things, but we'll spread the truth as far as we can. If you want the rumor mill, talk to Ralph. *The Crossing's* responsible for more hurt feelings than me and Art."

"Gentlemen, breakfast is on me." Laurent rose and tugged on her gloves. As she closed the outer door to the Skillet, she breathed a sigh of relief. The two old guys calmed her fears about her reelection bid and Vern's mental health. Her only question—was Vern so protective of the Martin family he'd cover up a murder? How far did family loyalty go? And how was he connected to Bob? She settled her sunglasses on her face. It was time to check a few things.

* * *

Laurent closed all the tabs on her computer and pushed away from her desk. "I'm walking to Dr. Creighton's office to get his final autopsy report on Stephanie and a prelim on Kane. I shouldn't be too long. Hold down the fort." She snugged her headband over her ears and pulled on her gloves.

"You know one of them Martins killed that girl," Greene said. "You don't want to admit it because you like the family and they gave money to your campaign four years ago. You'll believe Caleb's alibi for Dylan, but not Neal and Theo alibiing each other. What do you think that says?"

"Which Martin? Pick one and show me the evidence."

"One of those hammers you confiscated is gonna have hair from the girl and prints from one of the Martins. I don't know which one yet, but, mark my words, that snotty family killed her 'cause they didn't want an unwed mother laying claim to their land." Greene leaned back, laced his fingers behind his head, and smirked.

"My feelings about potential suspects are irrelevant, and Emmit and Jane get to decide who their inheritance goes to, not you, not the victim, not even their own children, so your motive is weak. Nonexistent, actually. And second, you're living in the past. Whatever they donated last time doesn't mean they'll do it again."

"How much have they contributed this time?"

"Not one red cent. When we get the lab results back, that's when we'll act and not before." Laurent stomped to the squad room door and yanked it open.

"So, you're gonna stall the investigation until after the election. How much are you asking for?" Greene sneered.

"Are you insinuating I'm accepting bribe money?"

"Maybe not yet, but you've thought about it."

"I have not, but you've obviously considered it. Has someone offered you a bribe?"

"Don't try and turn the tables on me. My record is impeccable." Greene shot to his feet, his chair slamming against the back wall.

"Oh, really. Never fixed a DUI for your buddy Ralph Howard? How about the time you wrote a ticket for a traffic violation when the vehicle wasn't even there? You were pissed at the kid because his dog shit on your lawn so you made something up. You're lucky they didn't sue us."

"That little SOB is a reckless driver. He deserves everything he gets." Greene's fists were clenched at his side and his face was red. If they had been outside, Laurent was certain steam would have been coming out of his ears and off the top of his head.

"Finished with your unfounded accusations of me and the Martin family? Get back to work and keep your mouth shut until we have proof." Laurent stormed down the stairs and exited through the back door of the sheriff's office. Turning the corner, she inhaled the cold air. And exhaled. The argument with Greene had caught her by surprise, and she reacted without thinking. Somewhere in something she said, Greene was going to misconstrue it and call Ralph. She could almost read the next day's headlines. SHERIFF ON THE VERGE OF ACCEPTING BRIBE. She hoped Greene wouldn't be that stupid because she'd slap a defamation of character lawsuit on *The Crossing* the next day. She really didn't like her deputy. He was mediocre at best and an outright liar at worst. After she got back from Creighton's office, she'd make a record of their conversation. Greene's words echoed in her head. The insinuation. Bribe money. *That asshole.*

Laurent marched down Field Street. The merchants had shoveled and salted their sidewalks, and a few people were out. The kids were back in school and everyday life had resumed, but a shadow of sadness enveloped the community. Spirits were low, hers included. Everyone was tired of the snow and cold but knew there were another six weeks to endure along with a few more heavy snowfalls. And with two deaths in the community, spring never looked so good.

"Jhonni, you come to order flowers for the Gattison girl?" Behind the counter of the floral shop stood Dak Aikens' grandmother. Mrs. Aikens, the owner of Roses & More, was in her late sixties and was determined to live up to the name of her shop. The four-foot, ten-inch grandmother wore a flowered turtleneck and flannel jeans, and her rose-painted fingernails flashed as she clipped the ends off the long-stemmed yellow roses. Red rose earrings hung from both ears and the strong smell of vanilla and jasmine permeated the shop. "Somethin' upset you."

"Trouble at the office." Laurent smiled ruefully and pulled off her headband. "You're not wearing gloves?"

"Thornless roses, and I got hands like leather," Mrs. Aikens said. "I'm sorry for your troubles. Let's talk about good things. When you gonna build that greenhouse?"

"As soon as the big barn is demolished and it's warm enough to pour concrete. End of April." Laurent liked Dak's grandmother. Not only had she raised her grandson, she saved him from a gang in Detroit. Laurent never got the entire story about how her deputy and his grandmother had come to live in Field's Crossing, but she was glad they had. No one knew more about flowers than Mrs. Aikens. When Laurent had begun laying out her perennial gardens at her farmstead, Dak had driven his grandmother out to Laurent's house. Mrs. Aikens' approval and pleasure, while strolling in her gardens, still warmed Laurent. And she had implemented a few of the grandmother's suggestions. An oak tree here, hydrangeas there, and maybe a wrought iron chair or two with flagstone stepping-stones.

"I'm looking forward to seeing it," Mrs. Aikens said. "What message are you trying to send with the arrangement for Stephanie?"

"None of us knew her, but . . ." Laurent hesitated. How did you say I'll find your killer with flowers? She looked at Mrs. Aikens and realized the older woman knew what Laurent wanted to say.

"I ain't an expert in floriography for nothin'. How about black-eyed Susans for justice and pink carnations and forget-me-nots for never forgetting. Looks good in an arrangement, too."

"Those are all spring and summer flowers. Where are you going to get them?"

"You leave that to me. I ain't Roses & More for nothing."

Laurent pulled out her wallet.

"Put that away." Mrs. Aikens' sharp words startled her. "Here's my price." She pointed her scissors at Laurent. "You catch that sonofa-bitch and you win reelection. Get a move on, Jhonni. I want your campaign poster in my window by the end of the day. You hear me?"

"Yes, ma'am." No one messed with Dak's grandma.

Laurent crossed Field Street and opened the door to Dr. Creighton's medical practice, wincing at the weird smell of clean. Creighton shared the building with a dentist and an orthodontist, and the entire building smelled of disinfectant and alcohol prep.

"This way, Sheriff." Laurent followed a nurse into Creighton's office. "He's finishing up with this morning's schedule. He'll be with you shortly."

Laurent dropped her gloves and scarf on the chair in front of the large desk and bent over to peer at a red-and-white truck. Creighton collected Tonka trucks. The old metal ones, not the new plastic pieces of junk. A few trucks in his collection had spots of rust, which Laurent thought gave the vehicles character. Some had dings and scrapes; others were in pristine condition, as though they had never been played with.

The door opened behind her.

"You've added a few things since I was last here."

"I love eBay. I picked that one up a month ago. A Coca-Cola semitruck. Cost me five hundred bucks. Worth every penny." Creighton dropped a stack of manila folders on his desk and shrugged out of his white lab coat. He hung the coat and his stethoscope on the hooks behind the door before plopping into his worn leather chair.

"How much money have you spent on toy trucks?"

"Probably the same as you spend on cello lessons, music, recordings, concerts." He shrugged. "Obsessions cost money. Passions cost money."

"Touché." Laurent settled into the chair opposite the chubby doctor. "What do you have for me?"

"You're not going to like it."

CHAPTER TWENTY

"I CAN'T BELIEVE he's dead." Bob Kane's secretary, Donna, was in her midsixties with dyed black hair pulled into a knot on the top of her head; a pencil stuck through as a barrette. The secretary perched on the edge of a chair in front of the CEO's desk, a tissue tucked in her sleeve at her wrist.

"What can you tell me about Bob's last few days at the bank?" Laurent leaned back in the banker's brown leather chair and waited for the printer to finish. She'd forwarded a week's worth of emails to Dak and Greene and a list of recent bank transactions. Everything looked normal, but another set of eyes never hurt. She was personally going to review the larger transactions and accounts.

"Everything was slow," Donna said. "Blizzards in February tend to do that."

"What do you mean by everything?"

"No customers in the bank, very few phone calls for customer service, only one loan application, even online banking activity was down due to losing power from the storm. I think online banking is changing the way people handle their money, and it's going to put small brick-and-mortar banks out of business. When you add in E-DocuSign, no one needs a signature card on file anymore and apps like Venmo let you move thousands of dollars at a time. I think Mr. Kane was glad he was close to retirement. Keeping up with technology and new rules and regulations was getting hard for him."

"How was he feeling?" Laurent asked.

"I think he was a little lonely. Shelby left for Tampa, and he seemed to hang around the break room a little more often. Part of me is glad Mr. Cotter made him go ice fishing and part of me is sad."

"How often did they fish together?"

"A couple of times a month, all year long. Mr. Cotter must be devastated."

"The one loan application—was it approved?" Laurent asked.

"Mr. Kane denied the application."

"Isn't that how banks make money? Loan it out and collect interest and charge late fees." The printer had finally finished. Picking up the stack, Laurent straightened and tamped down the pile.

"The applicant hasn't been able to pay off his loans for the last several years. It appears he has a gambling problem and is about to lose his farm. My cousin works at First Federal and the applicant applied and was turned down there, too."

"Name of applicant?" Laurent said.

"Neal Tillman."

The application and Kane's denial lay on top of Laurent's pile. "Other than Neal, was there anyone else mad at Bob for any reason?"

"No one at the bank. He was easy to work for and was always asking after our families. He'd been here for years, knew all of his customers, and they liked him." The secretary pulled out a tissue and blew her nose. "Is there anything else I can help you with?"

"That should do it."

Another bank employee knocked. "Old man Dawson is here. He wants to talk to Mr. Kane."

"Send him in. I'll tell him about Bob. After that, I'll have him talk to the vice president." Laurent shrugged into her parka. "Mr. Dawson, I'm sorry to tell you, but Bob Kane passed away this weekend."

"What happened? His heart give out?" The elbows in the old farmer's coat were worn through, and his blue flannel shirt was peeking out.

"I found him in his ice-fishing shelter on Turtle Lake."

"I'm sorry to hear that. I'll drive over and sit with Shelby for a while." He cleared his throat. "Bob was a good man, a fair man. He'd bend over backward to help. I'm mighty sorry he's gone."

"Me, too. He was extremely helpful when I was renovating my farmhouse. Knew which contractors did the best job at a good price."

"He loved the farmers market," Dawson said. "Sometimes I think he bought food and took it straight back to the bank for the employees for lunch, and when the bank held their annual summer picnic, he bought everything from the vendors at the market. Don't know what he did at Christmastime. He'll be missed."

"What did you want to see him about?" Laurent asked.

"I wanted to see if Jim Cotter has the cash for our agreement."

"What agreement?"

"Cotter's been after me to sell him the eighty acres between our properties. We agreed he'd pay me two grand a month for the next ten years and then the property would be his and, in return, I'm letting him hunt and fish all he wants."

"You'll have to talk to the vice president about that," she said. "When did this start?"

"We shook hands on it last fall. October, maybe." He twisted the green and yellow John Deere baseball hat between his hands. "Sheriff, I gotta ask ya somethin'."

"What can I do for you, Mr. Dawson?"

"You runnin' for reelection?"

She nodded.

"Don't you pay no never mind to that snake Ralph Howard. People 'round here got more sense than that."

CHAPTER TWENTY-ONE

"How much money am I gonna make?" Neal Tillman was meeting Noel Smith, the windmill representative from Renewable Farm Energy, at Nick's Pizza Palace for lunch.

The old brick building was divided into an order/pickup counter and a dining room. The brown sepia carpet was stained and flecks of pizza sauce dotted the red pepper shakers. The two men picked up their beers and slid into a booth near the rear of the building. The thin crust pizzas would be ready in twelve minutes.

"Windmills are another source of income for you. You can be paid via fixed payments, royalties, or both, and you can continue farming, grazing, and hunting." The windmill rep tore a paper towel off the roll, and placed it on his lap.

"Got that." Tillman swigged half of his beer, and tossed his camouflage baseball hat on the torn red seat next to him.

"A windmill needs sixty acres, but only three acres are used for the turbines, substations, and access roads. The other fifty-seven acres are a buffer zone. You have to preserve the wind flow, which means you can't build any structures restricting the flow of air. No barns, grain bins, cell towers, houses, anything that obstructs the wind flow. There will be height restrictions placed in the lease."

"I ain't planning on puttin' up any new buildings."

"The windmill lease will affect your property rights now and into the future. Leases are usually twenty-five to fifty years, so any decisions you make now, you should discuss with your heirs."

"I don't have no heirs. Theo don't wanna farm." Neal picked at the label on the sweaty beer bottle.

"Are you planning to sell your land when you retire?"

"Of course I'm gonna sell, but not to Emmit."

"Renewable Energy isn't interested in who you sell to, but if you have a mortgage, the bank will have to sign off on the lease. That's usually not a problem because it's steady income for you, and banks like money coming in."

"Bastards, all of them." Neal slid out of the booth, and sauntered to the pickup counter. He returned with two pizzas and two more beers. "If I sell before the lease ends, what happens?"

"Renewable Energy will insist on a clause stating that if you sell, the lease agreement goes with the land. The new owner will have to abide by all of the stipulations you do, but they won't have to renew for an additional twenty-five years."

"How do I get paid?"

"We'll pay you an initial sum of money in good faith and choose what acreage we plan to build on. After that, Renewable pays a mixture of fixed payments and royalties. Royalties are based on gross revenue."

"How is gross revenue defined?" Tillman pointed his drooping slice of pizza at the windmill rep. "You may think I'm a simple country farmer, but my daddy instilled the math in me."

"Gross revenue is negotiable. For example, gross revenue can be based on each individual turbine or the entire windmill farm. The revenue may or may not include sales credits or renewable energy credits from the government. The contract will clearly spell out how your payment is calculated. Expect three to five percent of gross earnings.

"We'll also pay a minimum rent, whether or not the turbines are generating power, and we'll raise the royalty percentage at specified intervals. In the beginning, the royalty percentage will be lower because Renewable's costs are much higher. Later on, both you and Renewable will be on a much more even keel."

"I'm gonna want to look at your books. Make sure you ain't cheating me." Neal folded another piece of pizza in half and bit. Red marinara sauce oozed down his face. He swiped at his chin.

"We'll include an audit clause for you to verify the revenues produced. I need to inform you that a windmill farm may affect your neighbors. If we have to alter your drainage patterns, it may increase or decrease water retention on land not owned by you. Snowplowing may be affected as will aerial crop spraying. The crops directly under the arms of the turbines cannot be sprayed. That area is better used for grazing or hunting. We don't want a lawsuit where a crop duster got hit by the arm of a turbine and crashed into one of your fields."

"I sold all of my cattle a few years back. The only trees on the property are from the tree line to limit the amount of blowing snow. Ain't no hunting there."

"You might face a lot of opposition."

"I got nothin' to lose. What are they gonna do to me?" Neal slammed the beer bottle on the table.

"Not to you, but they can try to change the zoning laws after we submit the permit. We'll beat that in court. Restraint of free trade. The new laws were changed to keep us out. Look at the timing."

"Legal costs are all on you. What else do you think they'll try?"

"Your farm is in unincorporated Rogers County. The village of Field's Crossing can't do anything. The quad-county area currently has zoning laws in effect for windmill farms, and our legal department will have to research that. We may need to apply for a few variances."

The windmill representative leaned back. "I understand you know Emmit Martin. How about Owen Gattison?"

"Leave Owen alone. His daughter froze to death in Webster Park. Foolish girl ran out of gas and tried to walk into town before the blizzard last week." Neal grabbed the last piece of pizza. "Emmit's dead set against windmill farms."

"His farm is adjacent to yours."

"My farm is directly between Emmit's and his brother's. Emmit bought out his brother ten years ago when Vern lost his marbles. There's nothing Emmit would like better than to buy me out, and that ain't ever gonna happen."

The windmill rep didn't speak. Neal wondered if he overplayed his hand. Renewable didn't need to know about his ongoing feud with the Martin family. And he needed that check. The manager at Gray Fox Casino had called this morning. He'd pay off everyone except Farmers Bank with the money. Let Bob stew in that. *Money-grubbing asshole shouldn't have turned me down. Hope it costs him a fortune to fix his Caddy.*

"Emmit's going to raise the most objections and be the hardest to fight so, before you retire or think about selling, we'll help you find a buyer who believes in wind energy." Smith laid his briefcase on the greasy table. "It certainly sounds to me as though we can do business, Mr. Tillman. I have a one-page letter of intent for you to sign, and then I can write you a check."

Neal Tillman reached for the pen.

CHAPTER TWENTY-TWO

"WHAT DID YOU do after we released you?" Laurent glared at the slovenly man.

Neal slouched in the folding chair, legs splayed out in front of Laurent's desk, his gray hair smashed to one side, several black eyebrow hairs plastered on his forehead.

"Nothin'."

"Be more specific. You threatened Bob in his office on Wednesday. You sideswiped him on Friday night and on Monday I find him dead. There's a bunch of time you need to account for. Let's start with your conversation at the bank on Wednesday." Laurent picked up her pen.

"I didn't kill Bob."

"But you wanted to."

"Hell, yes." Tillman pointed his baseball hat at her. "Asshole wouldn't loan me any money. He'll loan money to Emmit all day long, but he won't lift a finger to help me."

"What was the loan for?"

"Farming."

"Anything else?"

"Maybe."

"I talked to the manager at Gray Fox Casino," Laurent said. "How much do you owe?"

"Shit." Neal propped his elbows on his knees and twisted his baseball hat in his hands. "Don't matter. I paid it off. You know the rest. I went and got drunk and shoved Bob and his big old Caddy into a ditch and then you locked me up."

"I want to know what you did after we let you go."

"Theo posted bail for me. I went home and slept and then we watched TV."

"You never left?" Laurent raised an eyebrow.

"You ever heard of binge-watching. Stupid. No sense of anticipation anymore." Neal snorted.

Laurent tipped her head. Not a point worth arguing about. No one watched the news on TV anymore. *If anything happened anywhere in the world, your cell phone alerted you. Not a fan.*

"Did you and Theo go out for breakfast on Saturday morning?"

"We got food at home."

"You went directly from jail to your house?"

"We got my truck out of the pound and I got gas."

"Then what?" Laurent jotted a note.

"This is chickenshit."

"Are you sure? Because now I've got two different stories."

"Brown bottle flu."

"Still hungover. Great. What'd you watch on TV?" Laurent asked.

"I don't know. Ask Theo. I fell asleep on the couch."

"What livestock do you own?"

"Sold everything a few years ago to pay the mortgage. Fat lot of good that did me. Still owe the goddamn bank."

Laurent stared into watery brown eyes. A lifetime of sadness and resignation lived there. It took alcohol to bring out the chip on Neal's shoulder. She believed him when he said he went home and slept it off. The man refused a breathalyzer, but the smell of alcohol when he opened his mouth had been overwhelming. Dak told her that when he went downstairs to release Neal from his cell, the entire floor stank. The vomit next to Neal's cot didn't help. "I've got paperwork from five different banks in the quad-county area all denying your loan applications."

"Tough shit."

"Planning on putting anyone else in a ditch?"

Neal shook his head.

"Why Bob?"

"Easy target. Drives that big ol' Caddy. Look, Sheriff. I got drunk and shoved him into the ditch. That's it. I was nowhere near Turtle Lake, and I sure as hell don't ice fish. Stupid waste of time."

"Cross-country ski?"

"You think I got time for all that foolishness?"

"I'm obtaining a search warrant for your property," she said.

"Go ahead. You won't find nothin'."

"So, you're saying after Theo picked you up on Saturday morning, all you did was eat, sleep, and watch TV?"

"Yep."

"What did you do on Sunday?" she asked.

"Nothin'."

"You never left the house?"

"Nope."

"Do I need to check the video at the casino? The liquor store?" Laurent leaned back. Why was Neal so relaxed? Like he didn't have a care in the world? What had changed?

"Go ahead." Neal folded his hands across his stomach and smirked.

"For someone who's having financial difficulties, you seem extremely nonchalant."

"I solved all my financial problems."

"How?" she asked.

"Met a guy. Noel Smith."

"Who is Noel Smith and how was he able to solve your money problems?"

"We made a deal. I'm leasing out the northwest corner of my land for a windmill farm."

Laurent dropped her pen. "Right next to Emmit."

*　*　*

"Is Creighton positive on the manner of death?" Dak asked.

Laurent had called Dak and Greene into her office to discuss Dr. Creighton's latest findings. "Kane's lungs were filled with water. His steel-toed boots chipped holes in the ice. His fingernails bled. The ice around the edges of the holes had blood on them. His face was scratched. Creighton is listing the initial cause of death as drowning. He wants the body to thaw more before he lists the manner of death, but he's leaning toward homicide. The back of Bob's head had several gashes and smelled like beer. Someone hit him over the head, knocked him unconscious, and held his face underwater until he drowned."

"Is that why you hauled Neal in? But you have no proof. Why don't you take your own advice? Keep your mouth shut about unfounded accusations." Greene smirked.

Laurent mentally kicked herself. She had walked right into that one. "I don't know who killed Bob, but things are going to get ugly."

"Why do you say that?" Dak asked. "Drunks and gamblers aren't killers. They're guilty of poor judgment, but not murder."

"Neal signed an agreement to lease the northwest corner of his property to a windmill energy company."

"That man is hated enough, and now he's going to piss off all of the farmers, especially Emmit," Greene said. "Everybody in town knows how Emmit and Vern feel about windmills. What an idiot."

"When did he sign the agreement?" Dak asked.

"Last day or two. With the money from Renewable, he paid off his gambling debt to Gray Fox Casino and had some left over in the bank."

"With the agreement, he's out of debt and still owns his farm. He's got no motive to kill Bob," Dak said. "And he gets back at the Martin family."

"He starts up that goddamned feud again," Greene said. "How many fights are we gonna have to break up because of those two?"

"When Bob was killed, Neal was deep in debt and pissed," Laurent said. "I'm going to have a chat with Noel Smith from Renewable and see when he first talked to Neal. Just because Neal signed a contract today doesn't mean he didn't kill Bob last weekend. He claims all he did from the time we released him until the time I found Bob's body was eat, sleep, and watch TV with Theo, and I don't consider Theo to be a reliable alibi."

"There's no way we're going to be able to track either one of them. Too much time has passed," Greene said.

"Neal could have killed Bob out of sheer meanness," Dak said.

"I'm obtaining a new search warrant for the Tillmans and their property."

"Why? Whad'ya think you're gonna find? I'd wait until the doc declares manner of death. If it's not homicide, a search warrant is extra work that's not necessary," Greene said.

"Theo was the last person to see Stephanie alive. Neal runs Bob off the road and two days later, I find Bob dead in an ice shelter on Turtle Lake. Something's not right and the Tillmans are part of it. I snapped a picture of a boot tread on the back of Bob's coat. I'm looking for a match," she said.

"So, you're going to waste more valuable time. You'll never find the Gattison girl's killer and the people of Field's Crossing are going to hold you responsible, one way or another. And you're guessing about

Bob. The old man drowned." The belligerent deputy shoved to his feet and stalked to his desk.

Laurent sighed and looked at Dak. "The first warrant was for the Martin family and property. I'm trying to match a print there, too."

Dak raised both eyebrows at her. "You think they're connected. Same boot print puts the same person at both scenes. That's why you want molds of all the boot prints at the Tillman farm. The son kills the girl, the father kills the banker. Both out of meanness and revenge. Let's hope we get a match." He tilted his head toward Greene. "What in the hell's wrong with him?"

"You know I can't comment."

"Well, I sure can."

*   *   *

Laurent closed her office door and smoothed *The Crossing's* latest op-ed on her desk. She massaged her knees under her desk. She knew who the unnamed source was—Greene. Would he keep his mouth shut? How was she going to fight the lies and innuendos printed by the local newspaper while trying to find a killer? Her first obligation was to the victim and the victim's family. Everyone in the quad-counties was watching and judging her, including the victim's family and friends. Maybe she should give Owen and Theresa a call or go visit them with an update. She had given them three of the greatest shocks of their lives in the last month. First, their daughter was pregnant, second, that she was dead, and third, she had been killed. The problem was, she had nothing to tell them. Her entire investigation was based on a partial boot print by the driver's door. The results of the DNA swabs wouldn't be back until the end of next week. Same with the hammers.

Dr. Creighton told her yesterday the gashes on the back of Bob's head appeared to match the broken beer bottle pieces, but he wanted confirmation before declaring homicide. He sent the broken pieces to the CSU lab. What was going on in Field's Crossing? Two people hit over the head and left to die out in the elements. At first glance, the two victims appeared to have nothing in common. Where did their paths cross? Were the two deaths even related? Maybe she should be looking for two killers. When Bob's death was declared a homicide, how was Field's Crossing going to react? Vote her out of office? If she couldn't solve these two homicides, maybe she didn't deserve to be reelected.

Laurent picked up her cup of tea and wandered to the window. Greene was totally useless. Maybe after the election she should fire him. Or strongly encourage him to retire. It seemed to her that all he wanted was to sit behind a desk and tell people what to do. She had never seen him walk down Field Street to chat with business owners and residents, and his favorite pastime was to park at the high school exit and issue tickets to students. He certainly wasn't a good, conscientious deputy like Dak. She'd like a few more deputies like Dak on her staff.

Laurent gathered all of her cups and mugs and jogged down the stairs to the break room. It was late afternoon and the squad room had emptied out. She was the only officer working tonight. As she washed out her mugs, she wondered how Emmit would react when he heard the news about Neal's agreement. The rumor mill worked quickly in small communities, and Laurent was positive Greene had ignored her directive and called his best friend, Ralph, with the news. She'd never be sure. Neal could have spilled the beans to a dozen people.

Murder, feud, reelection. In her almost four years as sheriff and the previous fifteen as a deputy, Laurent's professional life had never held more conflict or more uncertainty. She thought about pulling in all parties to the feud and decided against it. There were four people in the Martin family and two in the Tillman family directly involved in

the feud. When she envisioned the scene in the conference room . . .
Laurent shook her head. Bad idea. Yelling. Finger-pointing. Threats.
And that was Emmit and Neal. Vern wouldn't say a word. He didn't
have to. Toss in Theo, Caleb, and Dylan, and she'd have a fight in the
parking lot before they even entered the building.

Laurent stacked the clean mugs in the rack and dried her hands.
Flicking off the light, she climbed the stairs to her office. She loved her
job. Cold winters and all. If she lost her job, the chances of being re-
hired anywhere in the state were slim. Age discrimination did exist.
So did sexism. After being sheriff, could she even go back to being a
deputy?

Old man Dawson's words reassured her. Somewhat. She was positive he had a TV with rabbit ears, and only read the newspaper. His
contact with the outside world was the radio. The crop report. An
all-news radio station. And whoever he talked to. She was glad for his
support but thought his influence in the quad-counties was minimal.
Mrs. Aikens liked her. She could talk for hours about flowers with the
tiny grandmother. Laurent suspected the shop owner was a bit lonely,
even though the last few days would have been hectic.

Murder, feud, reelection. Her priorities. In that order. Her personal
life didn't exist right now. Sinking into her office chair, she thought
about the request for a meeting with her daughter.

She had abandoned her daughter once. How many chances would
she get to make amends? Say she was sorry. Explain her decision, her
situation at the time. What would her daughter think if she said no?
That she was ashamed? Embarrassed? What did she, Jhonni Laurent,
want out of a relationship with her daughter? The request included an
invitation to a concert this Saturday night in Indianapolis. Starr said
she'd go with. *Stop being a chicken and procrastinating. Go online and
buy the tickets.* There was nothing that said she had to introduce herself. She'd wait until that night.

CHAPTER TWENTY-THREE

"WE DROVE SEPARATELY because I had an appointment. Bob dropped Shelby off at the airport earlier in the morning, and I was piling the gear on the sled when he got to the bridge pull-off sometime around nine." Jim Cotter picked up his whiskey glass and sipped.

Laurent was perched on a counter stool, her notebook on the marble kitchen island. It was after dinner on Wednesday night, and she'd agreed to meet Cotter at his house. They both lived on Turtle Lake Road, two miles apart. The stinging smell of disinfectant in Cotter's house tickled her nose. She pulled a Kleenex out of her pocket.

"That area where you were fishing, is that your land?"

"Not yet. Old man Dawson and I have a deal. He's selling me eighty acres over the next ten years, and we agreed I can hunt and fish during the buyout."

"What time did you leave Bob?" Laurent asked.

"Eleven thirty."

"Who was your appointment with?"

"Rogers County Currency Exchange."

She knew not to ask about what was discussed. Attorney-client privilege. "How many fish did you catch?"

"I don't know. Bob was taking home the catch. My freezer's full."

"How long have you and Bob been fishing together?"

"Forever. I can't remember a time when we didn't fish or hunt on the weekends."

"What was he doing when you left?" Laurent watched as Cotter gulped his whiskey and wondered if drinking was a regular habit for the attorney. She had never seen him drunk. Was talking about his best friend that difficult? How would she react if Starr died? A drink or two might not be a bad idea.

"Sitting in his chair, staring at the hole, drinking a beer." Cotter stood on the other side of the island, one hand curved tightly around the leaded crystal tumbler, the other hand shoved in his pocket.

"How warm was it in the tent?"

"It's February and we were sitting on a frozen lake. I doubt the air temperature in the tent was above forty."

"I thought these new heaters kept you warmer."

"Don't want to melt the ice."

"It would take a lot to melt two to three feet of ice with a space heater." She wiped her nose again. Cotter's cleaning lady must be thorough. "How was Bob feeling?"

"He was pissed at Neal."

"What'd he say?"

"The man's driver's license should be revoked. Asshole probably didn't have insurance to cover the repairs on Bob's Caddy."

"You know that's not going to stop him from driving. Theo bailed his father out. Are you going to represent him in court?" Laurent asked.

Why was Jim Cotter so tense? He looked like he wanted to pace but, instead, leaned against the counter, arms crossed over his chest, one hand holding his whiskey and water. Knuckles white. Laurent jotted in her notebook. *Check timing at currency exchange.*

Cotter shook his head. "I'm done with traffic tickets and DUIs. They're nothing but headaches, and no one wants to pay for a good defense. Even if I get them probation, they all think they deserved it and I did nothing to help their case."

"What are your areas of law?"

"It's a small town. I handle a lot of stuff, but real estate and wills and probate, which includes farming and inheritance laws, are my main areas."

"People buying and selling houses, drafting and signing wills and trusts, and waiting for people to die," she said.

"Farming law is more complicated than that. You have to know inheritance laws going back fifty years and disinheriting relatives and how to set up your farming business so the government doesn't get it all in taxes when you die. Old man Palmer's been farming his whole life and never paid a dime of taxes in his entire life to either the state or the federal government, and when he dies, his land will be sold and the money divided between the two agencies to be used for back taxes. His kids get nothing."

"Do they know this?" Laurent raised both eyebrows.

"It's not up to me to inform them, but yes, I think they do. That's why they all left town. There's no inheritance waiting for them."

"What did you and Bob talk about?"

"Local gossip. You'd think we were a couple of old men. As bad as Art and Dutch."

"Who were Bob's enemies?" Laurent tugged at the collar of her turtleneck.

Jim's kitchen was warm and, even though it was cold outside, she was looking forward to finishing up the interview. Between wiping her nose and the sweat trickling down her back, she was uncomfortable.

"The only one I can think of is Neal. Bob denied his loan application and, two days later, Tillman ran him off the road. Tillman's lucky he didn't kill Bob then, but maybe that was his intent and he botched the job. Maybe Bob's injuries from landing in a ditch were greater than he knew. Maybe he had a heart attack or a stroke after I left. If Creighton concludes the injuries Bob sustained from being forced into a ditch contributed to his death, I'm going after Neal. Have you questioned him? I bet he followed us and waited until I left to finish the job. You might want to look at that son of his. Maybe Theo killed Stephanie."

"Theo kills Stephanie and Neal kills Bob," Laurent said. "I see the father's motive far more than the son's motive. Why would Theo want to kill Stephanie?" *Cotter had the same thought she had.*

"How would I know? What's that saying? Once you eliminate the impossible, whatever remains, no matter how improbable, must be the truth."

"Arthur Conan Doyle," she said. "What was your relationship with Stephanie?"

"There was no relationship. Starr was her boss."

"Never chatted with her?"

"I have nothing in common with snotty high school seniors." Cotter held his glass under the automatic ice maker before splashing more whiskey into his tumbler. "But as long as you brought it up, how's the investigation?"

"We've got some leads, a few theories."

"Evidence?"

"Not much," she admitted. "Owen thinks she tried to walk into town because her car was out of gas and she got turned around and froze to death in Webster Park."

"Autopsy?"

"The autopsy says differently."

"In what way?"

"I'm sure you read *The Crossing*. Dr. Creighton has amended the manner of death to homicide. The victim was hit in the head and tossed into the snow and froze to death while unconscious."

"Because of the weather, there's no evidence. You're going to have a tough time getting a conviction." Cotter sipped his drink.

Laurent flipped back a few pages in her notebook, reviewing her notes. "You were the last person to see Bob alive. What was his state of mind?"

"He was missing Shelby, but that happened every winter since she's been visiting her sister. He was calm, relaxed. Said he was retiring in two years, when he turned sixty-five, but turning the bank over to someone else was going to be hard for him."

"The browser on Bob's office computer showed he had been looking at several of your personal and professional accounts. Any reason why?" Laurent asked.

"Every year we conducted a review. See where I needed to move my money, what vehicle was earning the most interest, how much longer I needed to work before I could retire. Financial planning stuff." Cotter shrugged.

"Did Bob ever talk to you about customers at the bank?"

"Never. He considered that information as sacred as the attorney-client privilege."

"What did you do after you left the currency exchange?" she asked.

"I ran a few errands in town, came home, did some work, and went to bed around ten thirty."

"Anything else you'd like to add?"

"When will you release the autopsy report on Bob?"

"We have the same issue with Bob as we did with Stephanie. The body needs to thaw. It'll be another few days before a full autopsy can be conducted." Laurent slid off the barstool and lifted her parka off the back of the chair. She'd put it on in the SUV. "Just so you know, I'm submitting a request to release some emergency funding to pay for overtime due to the blizzard. Any help you can give me with the trustees will be appreciated."

"Consider it done." Cotter led the way to the mudroom and hit the button for the garage door opener.

"That's a big freezer for one person." She sneezed into her elbow.

"Have some perch. Wrap it in foil with butter, salt and pepper, and bake it at three fifty for ten minutes. Poor man's lobster."

*   *   *

Why did Jim lie?

Laurent exited off Turtle Lake Road into her driveway, the four pole lights cutting through the black night. Dropping her keys into the ceramic bowl in the mudroom, she paused in the doorway to the kitchen and flicked on the overhead light. The faint smell of bacon lingered. Crossing the kitchen to the stove, she picked up the tea kettle, filled it, and turned on the gas flame. A little chamomile tea before bed.

Jim had been wound tight, gulping two whiskey and waters in the forty-five minutes she had been in his house. Was he a heavy drinker? Most of their encounters had been at the cigar lounge or village hall, and she had never seen him drink. In fact, she had never been inside his home before tonight. It had been obvious to her he was missing his best friend. His white knuckles on the whiskey glass. Snapping at her about the intricacies of inheritance law. But he had been nonchalant about his money problems.

All of the documentation she accessed from Bob's computer browser indicated Jim was deep in debt. Her brief perusal of the bank's records showed Jim was six months past due on his mortgage and owed over fifty thousand on his credit cards, and he had a shiny new pickup in his garage. What else was he hiding? She assumed his meeting at the currency exchange was a business matter, but perhaps it was something else.

Laurent unlocked the French doors to her music room, and walked to the bay window. She stared at her reflection. Dark smudges under her eyes and wind-burned cheeks. She pulled her long braid over her shoulder, removed the rubber band, and began unwinding her hair, the familiar motion soothing.

Earlier in the week, Dr. Creighton had discussed his preliminary findings and thoughts with her. If the broken glass found in Bob's ice shelter matched the gashes in the back of the banker's head, Creighton was going to label the death a homicide. Even though she had been expecting this result ever since she sniffed the back of Bob's head in the ice shelter, she was worried. Two homicides in one month in small-town Indiana.

The tea kettle whistled. Wandering back to the kitchen, Laurent finger-combed her long hair before settling it over her shoulders. She filled a coffee mug with hot water, and dropped the tea ball in. Picking up the heavy mug, she turned toward the living room and bumped the counter, the cup of hot water slipping out of her hand and shattering on the ceramic tile floor. Hot water splashed onto her pants and soaked her socks. *Damn it. Wet socks and broken glass don't mix.* She twisted to the right and reached back, opening a drawer and pulling out several dish cloths without moving her feet.

Fifteen minutes later, she trotted down the stairs dressed in her comfy clothes and warm slippers and started her tea ritual all over again. Tearing off a paper towel, she carried a new cup of tea into the living room and relaxed into her recliner. She clicked on the TV and muted the sounds of the hockey game.

Pulling a yellow legal pad and pen out of the end table's drawer, she began with Bob's timeline. Neal's loan application had been denied on Wednesday, and on Friday night, Neal's little stunt sent Bob to the hospital. On Sunday morning, Bob dropped his wife, Shelby, off at the airport and then went ice fishing with his best friend, Jim. On Monday, Laurent discovered Bob's body frozen to the ice on Turtle Lake. While the paramedics retrieved the body, Laurent had walked back to the bridge on the ice, following the sled tracks. The tracks stopped in front of Bob's pickup, exactly where Jim said he parked.

What happened in the ice tent? Did Jim kill his best friend? Bob was a banker. If anyone knew how to get out of debt, it would be him. Did Bob threaten Jim? She was assuming the banker knew about Jim's financial situation, but she couldn't see Bob threatening anyone. It wasn't in his nature. Every bone in Bob's body was filled with kindness. Same for his wife. His loss to the community would be immense. Trust in bankers was hard for everyone, and maybe farmers more than others. Who was going to fill that gap?

Laurent read through Bob's schedule for the next month and noticed a board of directors meeting set for February 28. She hadn't read the agenda, but did banks regularly review clients' accounts or those that were overdue? What did Bob know about other people's money? Did someone kill him because of that knowledge?

Her two suspects in Bob's death were Neal and Jim, but the motives were weak. She'd have to track their alibis for the entire weekend. Today was Wednesday. Bob's autopsy was scheduled for Monday. Five days. How long could she keep her inquiries to herself?

This might be one of the few times she was grateful for *The Crossing's* inflammatory stories. Neal signing with Renewable Energy was going to ignite the community and move the recent deaths off the front page.

CHAPTER TWENTY-FOUR

"GLEN GAVE ME the historical background on the feud between Granddad Martin and Granddad Tillman, but what's going on with Emmit and Neal? It has to be more interesting than your discussion about shoe polish." Laurent settled into the corner booth at the Skillet restaurant and ordered a tuna on rye, french fries with barbeque sauce, and a large Diet Coke. It was late Thursday morning and breakfast had been several hours ago.

"It started right after Sheriff Atkins hired you," Art said. "Tillman was president of the co-op, and he either ordered the wrong seed or the seed that was delivered wasn't stored properly or we got shipped bad seed. The seed company fixed it and made a special delivery to Rogers County, but Emmit, along with a few others, lost about three days of good planting time. No one said anything, but this had never happened before."

"I understand how important the weather is to farmers, but is the seed problem possible?"

"You bet and the next year tweren't no problems with spring plantin'." Dutch picked up the story where his best friend left off. "But when it came time to audit the books at the end of Neal's term, the numbers were off. Not by a lot, but enough for everyone to raise an eyebrow or two. And the year before was the bad seed year."

"The president's term for the co-op is two years, with an option for another two if reelected," Art said. "Everyone puts in their time and then passes the baton."

"No one likes the job?" she asked.

"It's considered a necessary evil," Art said. "Co-ops were founded so groups of farmers could buy at bulk prices. The actual building is nothing more than a big metal barn with shelving. Farmers place their orders with the co-op and the co-op bands them together and places one big order with the seed company or the fertilizer company or whatever company."

"Does the co-op employ anyone?"

"Usually, one or two people. Farmers' kids. Someone's got to sign when the order is picked up and someone's got to sort and shelve the orders and unload the semi. The co-op's not open all the time and now, with the internet, all you gotta do is drive over and pick up your stuff."

"The feud started because of some bad seed and poor accounting?" Laurent tilted her head and raised an eyebrow.

"Neal was planning on using the bylaws for a second term."

"I thought the president was a volunteer position and no one liked it."

"It mostly is, but Neal had Theo workin' at the co-op, and we pay those kids," Dutch said. "They bust their balls when those semis arrive. Except Theo. He got caught smokin' pot durin' workin' hours while drivin' the fork. What a dumbass."

"Vern and Emmit and Caleb were there when it happened," Art said. "Plus a few other guys, and Emmit told Theo he was fired."

"Was Emmit president then?"

"Nope. Pissed Neal off royally. Emmit didn't have the authority to fire Theo. The two of them got into a shouting match and then Theo pushed Caleb, and the two of them started throwing punches," Art said.

"Caleb broke Theo's nose and that's when the sheriff pulled up," Dutch said.

"Did Glen arrest anyone?"

"Nah. He knew we'd sort it out ourselves," Art said. "Tillman wasn't reelected. Guess who was?"

Laurent snorted. Of course, Emmit had been elected. Payback was a bitch. She was certain those who remembered the reason for the feud felt justice had been served and that was that. Time to forget it. With the exception of the Tillman family. How far would the Tillmans go to get back at the Martins? "Then what happened?"

"First thing Emmit did was fire Theo and hire Caleb," Dutch said. "Then he asked Vern to review the books."

"What did Vern find?"

"Five thousand dollars was missing."

"Everyone assumed Vern was telling the truth?" she asked. "Did it cross anyone's mind that Vern and Emmit were setting Neal up?"

Both of the retired farmers shook their heads.

"The Martins got a helluva lot more money than Neal. They don't need five thousand dollars for nothing," Art said.

"What'd Emmit do?"

The two old guys winked at each other.

"He let the results be known and then he let it hang there," Art said.

"That had to be worse than a direct accusation."

In one stroke, Emmit had shattered Neal's reputation.

"The whole thing was forgotten when Vern's wife drowned that spring," Art said.

"I vaguely remember this," she said. "The bridge washed out?"

"It was rainin' to beat all hell. Middle of the day. Pitch black. Wind blowin' everythin' sideways. The trees and bushes on both sides of the bridge were huge and overgrown. Halfway across, Debbie hit a downed limb layin' on the bridge. Twisted it just enough to snap the railin', and she slid into the river. Got a call off to Vern before the car snagged on an underwater root and got stuck. She drowned before Vern got there. That didn't stop him from pullin' her out through the window he broke." Dutch curled his hands around his coffee cup.

"We had to hold the funeral at the high school. So many people. Came from all over the state, not just the quad-counties. Vern quit farming right after that. Holed up in that little cabin way out on the edge of town. Let his crops rot. Emmit had to plow them under. Land laid fallow for two years," Art said. "Emmit bought Vern's farm, which put Neal's farm directly between the two farms Emmit now owned."

"Then what happened?"

"Emmit adjusted the drainage and row configurations on Vern's farm to hook up with his, which ended up flooding a corner of Neal's farm," Art said.

"Is that legal?"

"Not illegal and he told everybody what he was doing. Didn't hide it or sneak around," Art said.

"I heard he sent a letter to Tillman and asked if he wanted to hook into the new drainage system," Dutch said.

"What did Neal say?" Laurent asked.

"No way in hell," Dutch said.

"And then what?"

"Neal tried to sue Emmit, but that went nowhere," Art said. "Emmit did everything by the book and then some. He tried to be fair, and Neal spit in his face."

"Neal got what he deserved," Dutch said. "But he lost the trust and respect of everybody with the fiasco at the co-op. He's never been able to dig out from that."

"Having a pothead son doesn't help," Art said. "Lazy sloth."

"Isn't that redundant?" she asked.

"Sloths move slow, but it doesn't mean they're lazy, so it's not redundant," Art said.

"Is there anything else to the feud?"

"Caleb beat the pants off Theo in the election for road commissioner four years ago," Art said.

Art and Dutch raised their coffee mugs and clanked them together. Both old farmers had grins and, as Laurent looked at them, she was glad they were on her side. She had a feeling anyone who crossed with their sense of justice wouldn't fare well in Field's Crossing or anywhere in the quad-county area.

"Last question. Did anyone in the Martin family accuse anyone in the Tillman family of foul play in Debbie's death?" Laurent asked.

Both men shook their heads.

"That was a godawful accident," Art said.

Laurent nodded and dipped a french fry before changing topics. "You'll read about this in *The Crossing* soon. Neal has signed an agreement to build a windmill farm on his property. With all of the talk about emissions, climate change, and global warming, why is an alternative source of energy such a hot topic with the farming community?"

"How long you got?" Dutch asked. "In a nutshell, windmill farms in Iowa have shown decreased milk production in cows."

"But no one has been able to definitively prove it," Art said. "Cows are animals, just like humans. Other environmental factors might upset the livestock. There's just no way of knowing or proving it with absolute certainty."

"Another main factor is you can't grow crops under a windmill," Dutch said. "No crop dusting allowed there. Grazing and hunting only."

"I would think the land at the base of a windmill would be ideal for growing crops. Almost like getting twice the value for the land," she said.

"If you can't spray for pests and animals, the crop will be eaten before it comes to harvest, so it's wasted land," Art said.

"With all of the roads that have to be built to maintain and repair the windmills, who pays for road maintenance?" Dutch asked. "We live in the Midwest, where you got concrete freezin' in the winter and then boilin' in the summer. Road maintenance is a bitch."

"And those in favor of wind energy? What's their argument?" Laurent asked.

"Steady income," Dutch said.

"Better for the environment," Art said. "Right now, about three percent of people employed provide one hundred percent of the world's food supply. That three percent is shrinking, while the population is increasing. Farmers have to become more efficient, but I'm not sure wind energy is the answer."

"What's the answer?" Laurent looked at the two retired farmers.

"Vertical farming," Art said.

"What?"

"Look it up," Art said.

The two old farmers bundled up and shuffled out of the Skillet.

Laurent never knew the root of the feud, but once respect and trust were lost, it was very difficult to earn it back. Did Neal's slide into gambling and alcoholism stem from the loss of respect? Even if Neal had stolen the five thousand dollars from the co-op, he'd never admit to being guilty. Paying back the money now would be an admission of guilt, ten years after the fact.

The bell above the Skillet's door rattled and a gust of cold wind rushed through the restaurant as Ralph strolled through the diner and plopped on the counter stool across from Laurent's booth. "How much is Emmit paying you?"

"What are you insinuating?" She played with her earring. Just the sight of the reporter put her in a defensive mood.

"I'm not insinuating anything," Ralph snapped. "Dylan, son of Emmit and Jane, supporters of your campaign for sheriff four years ago, has been questioned in the death of his girlfriend, Stephanie. My question is simple. How much money has Emmit contributed to your spring campaign fund to keep his son out of jail?"

"All of my campaign donors and their contributions are listed on-line at the secretary of state's office through the election board. As far as I know, no one has contributed to my campaign this year." Laurent switched to hot tea before going out into the cold again. She debated whether to accidentally squirt a lemon wedge into the sneering report-er's eyes.

"You better be damn sure. But, on to your other problems. How are you going to solve this murder? I looked into your history. You've never been involved in a murder case. How are you going to find the girl's killer? What took you so long to get started?"

"First, the medical examiner changed the manner of death to homi-cide. The investigation began the minute I was informed. Second, the body was frozen. Thawing took a week. Dr. Creighton obtained fluid samples a few days ago and sent them to the lab. And third, this is all standard procedure, and you know it. I suggest you look for a headline out in the snow. There's plenty of it."

The clock on the wall of the Skillet ticked over to one o'clock. Laurent glanced around the restaurant. The only other person in the dining area was the waitress, Karen, who was clearing and wiping down tables.

"I'm checking with the Indiana State Election Board. Anything within a hair of election law will be front-page news."

"Will the fact I'm in total compliance make front-page news? I think not. If my opponent, your best friend, isn't in compliance, will that make front-page news?" She shrugged into her parka, strolled to the cash register, and laid down a ten-dollar bill. "You better give me my change, Karen, otherwise Ralph will think the tip I leave is a bribe."

"You barely got elected four years ago, and it was only because there were more female voters in the quad-county area than male voters," he hissed. "That's not the case this time. Farmers are traditional and old-fashioned. They don't want you and they don't like you. The only reason they voted for you was because Sheriff Atkins endorsed you. His influence is gone and soon you will be too."

"You tracked me down to accuse me of improper campaign contributions and potential voter fraud? What happened to unbiased reporting?" Laurent slid her wallet into a pocket.

"I'm stating facts. As of today, there are more registered male voters than female voters and, by extrapolation, you're going to lose in two-and-a-half weeks."

"How about we let the voters decide?"

CHAPTER TWENTY-FIVE

"I HATE THAT woman." Ralph slammed his car door shut and cranked the heat on high. February in Indiana sucked. There was no news except it was cold outside. No shit. At least it was an election year. Two school board appointees. One village trustee. And the sheriff's office.

Sheriff Jhonni Laurent. He wanted her gone. He cringed behind the steering wheel, memories flooding through him. Three DUIs. A ticket for passing a stopped school bus while children were getting off. A ticket for going around the gates as a train approached. But the worst one was when Laurent knocked on his door at two in the morning, his son in cuffs, higher than a kite and accused of dealing. In the dim light on the porch, he thought he had seen the amusement on her face, and heard the insincerity of her voice. Embarrassment. Anger. He hated her ever since and vowed to repay the humiliation.

Four years ago, he and Greene hadn't taken her candidacy seriously, and she had been elected. This time around, she wasn't going to have Glen's backing. The old guy was retired. No one listened to him anymore.

Ralph jerked his car into gear. He needed dirt on Laurent. Her cigar smoking was well known, as was her cello playing. She gave a free performance every summer at the band shell in Webster Park. Last summer, she had given two performances and packed the lawn both times.

The question was, were any election laws violated when she gave a concert? Did she use any campaign funds for the off-duty officers directing traffic? Fliers in the stores? Buttons, stickers, pencils, anything handed out before, during, or after the concert?

He never attended these events but knew a lot of people who had gone. He only needed one person vaguely remembering something. Whether or not it was true was irrelevant. The newspaper could issue an apology or redaction or revision, but the damage would be done.

* * *

"I talked to dozens of people and no one would say Laurent used her concert to promote herself as sheriff," Ralph said. "What the hell's wrong with these people? Standing up for her. Idiots. Can't they see she's incompetent? I may have to go back further in her career or personal life. Was she ever married?"

"I have no idea. If she was, she never talks about it," Greene said. "You should have heard the pile of bullshit she tried to lay on me the other day. She claimed she wasn't covering up for someone in the Martin family and that no one's given her a penny for reelection. What a crock."

Ralph and Greene were eating dinner at Buffalo Wild Wings in Columbia. The two friends were planning Greene's campaign attacks against Laurent. For the next two weeks, Ralph wanted a negative article about Laurent on the front page of every edition of *The Crossing*. "I checked her campaign contributions online at the secretary of state's office, and no one has donated, so there's no story there. Not yet. What's the connection between the Martin boy and the victim?"

"Gattison was pregnant," Greene said.

"How do you know this?"

"I read the report. The kid told the sheriff they had an argument on Wednesday afternoon at the water tower, hours before the blizzard."

"Pregnant teenager tells dickhead boyfriend. Nothing illegal there," Ralph said.

"She was out of gas."

"He left her at the water tower with no gas?" Ralph stared at his best friend. *What if he insinuated the Martin kid was responsible for his girlfriend's death and Laurent was looking the other way until after the election?*

"In the report, he claims he didn't know she was out of gas, and there's no way to prove it."

"Lie detector test."

"I doubt the sheriff'll take it that far. According to the autopsy report, Gattison had two dents in her head, but they didn't kill her. Whoever hit her in the head and tossed her in the snow killed her," Greene said.

"The murderer could be Dylan, especially if he was trying to get rid of a pregnancy problem," Ralph said. "Did you find a hammer or a murder weapon in the boyfriend's car?"

"Everything's been sent to the lab, but it'll be two weeks before we have any results. Finding Bob has put the investigation on a temporary hold. And it's fucking February. I don't want to go out in the goddamn cold and search vehicles and property."

"How'd you get access to the autopsy report?"

"Laurent always leaves her computer open. The screen might be blank, but she's got windows open at the bottom. She went to stretch her legs. I sat down at her desk, and clicked on the windows. Took me less than five minutes."

"Anybody see you in her office?"

Greene shook his head, his mouth full of chicken wings, barbeque sauce on his chin. He wiped his mouth. "I've got another tidbit for you. Neal leased his land for a windmill farm to pay off a gambling debt. You can confirm this with Gray Fox Casino and Renewable Energy. Neal was overheard bitching about Bob and banks in general. Next thing you know, Neal sideswipes Bob out on the Five-and-Twenty. Three days later, Bob's found dead in his ice shelter on Turtle Lake."

"Was it murder? Is Neal a suspect?"

"Laurent's waiting for Creighton. She thinks he's gonna declare Bob's death a homicide because of a broken beer bottle and a gash in Bob's head. I think the old man had a stroke or a heart attack and the bottle broke when he fell face-first into a hole and drowned. It's as simple as that."

"There's no story unless Columbia Hospital was negligent and shouldn't have let him go home. The hospital will have milked the ER visit for all they could. Chest X-ray, brain scan. The goal is to get rid of Laurent. None of this will do that. The windmill farm will escalate the feud and the bad feelings in this town, but that's down the road. We need something now. I can only go so far in what I say without being accused of slander. Innuendos and insinuations are all we have. We have to discredit her." Ralph slammed his beer bottle on the table. "Everyone has a secret."

CHAPTER TWENTY-SIX

LAURENT UNCLIPPED HER bow from the cello case, and picked up the cake of rosin. Tapping the "A" key on the piano, she tuned her cello and began a series of warm-up exercises. Major scales, minor scales, arpeggios, diminished scales, forte, pianissimo. After half an hour, her fingers were moving freely, the bow singing. She glanced at the clock in her converted music room, opened her laptop, and clicked into the videoconference with her cello teacher. Laurent had been taking on-line lessons for the last ten years. *This kind of technology is awesome.*

Night had fallen and the bay window in her music room overlooking the southern edge of her five acres reflected the trees in Turtle Lake Forest. She was working on Shostakovich's Cello Concerto No. 2 and, after setting the tempo on the metronome, the deep tones of the cello filled the soundproof room.

Two hours later, she wiped down her cello, loosened the strings on the bow, and checked her phone. No calls.

Laurent wandered into her kitchen, and filled the tea kettle. She had spent most of the day trying to track Neal's movements on Sunday. Creighton told her Bob died on Sunday, sometime between nine in the morning and three in the afternoon. She wasn't sure if Neal was an accessory to murder or a contributing factor in Bob's death or had killed the banker outright. He had motive, but then that motive disappeared. When and where did Neal meet with a representative from Renewable? Before or after Bob's death?

The autopsy of Bob's brain might reveal a stroke or an aneurysm, either of which could have led to his death, but could one of those medical situations explain the claw marks or boot chips in the ice? Laurent had only seen one stroke victim in her life. She received a call from the consignment store owner who said one of her customers was walking around talking crazy and half of his face drooped. His right eye was down by his mouth. Laurent arrived before the paramedics and led the customer to a quiet area of the store and made him sit down. He was talking, but no words were recognizable. The paramedics instantly diagnosed a stroke, and drove lights and siren to the hospital. The man recovered only to have another stroke three weeks later and died in his home.

If Bob had a stroke while ice fishing, could he have fallen face-first into the hole and drowned, kicking and clawing, not knowing to lift his head out of the water? But what explained the boot tread on his back?

The tea kettle whistled. Laurent poured the hot water into the teapot, added two tea bags, and carried the cup, pot, and ramekin filled with sliced lemons to the living room. The side table next to her favorite chair was stacked with *Guns and Ammo*; *Midwest Gardening*; the latest Dan Brown novel, *Origin*; and a yellow legal pad.

Two minutes later, she laid the gardening magazine on the end table. She couldn't focus.

Renewable Farm Energy explained the large sum of money in Neal's bank account, but did he take matters a step further and kill Bob out of revenge? She would have expected Neal to gloat, not kill. Did he show up at the ice shelter after Jim left? With the payout from the windmill company, Neal's need for money disappeared, but revenge remained. How would Neal have known where to find Bob? She shook her head. Small towns. Finding Bob on the weekend was easy.

Laurent squeezed several lemon wedges into her hot tea, and thought about her interview with Jim. He hadn't seemed upset his longtime friend was dead. Why was that? Was the whiskey covering up his shock? Possibly. But why lie? Jim's former landlord had told her he kicked him out for nonpayment of rent. Starr told her Jim wasn't paying rent to the village, but maybe he had an arrangement with the trustees. Other trustees frequently used office space at the township building, but Starr didn't think any of them conducted personal or professional business there, and she had never seen any of Jim's clients.

There was no review scheduled for Jim with Bob. Laurent had checked both the physical calendar on Bob's desk and the one his secretary kept online for him. Jim's name didn't appear anywhere in the first half of the year. How was he going to get out of his money pit? He certainly didn't have the option of a windmill farm like Neal. And Neal, in solving his financial problem, unleashed a storm of a different kind. Was that his intent or was he grasping at straws? Bob's secretary told her no bank would lend Neal money. Was signing with a windmill company his last resort? Was it possible to renege on the contract with Renewable? Maybe Neal just bought himself time. She needed to talk to the Renewable rep.

Jim's motive was even weaker. The two men were best friends and whatever financial hole Jim dug for himself, Bob would have been able to help him get out of it.

She sipped her hot tea and leaned her head back against the worn leather chair. Her head hurt. Thanks to Creighton's prescription, she had finally gotten rid of her winter cold and bronchitis, but there were so many things to think about. Her hand hovered over the yellow paper. She dropped the pen and pulled out the request from the adoption agency. She didn't know what to do. The initial shock had worn off and her subconscious had begun to process possibilities. What would be the worst thing to happen if she met her daughter? Anger? Accusations? Maybe she deserved it.

Then what?

What if her daughter wanted answers and nothing else? *Tell me my background so I can know and bring closure to myself, and then I'll disappear. I don't need you in my life.*

Did she want her daughter in her life?

Did she dare hope? Forgiveness. Was that possible? Acceptance. Understanding. Future friends.

If she did nothing, she would never know. Life would go on as usual. Maybe that was all she needed for now. The usual. No upsetting the apple cart. Besides, finding a killer and winning reelection were two monumental tasks. Her potential relationship with her daughter would have to be put on hold. After that, maybe she'd change her mind.

CHAPTER TWENTY-SEVEN

OPINION/EDITORIAL PAGE
TILLMAN SIGNS AGREEMENT FOR WINDMILL FARM

February 15, 2019
Field's Crossing, Indiana
by Ralph Howard

Renewable Farm Energy has announced a new windmill farm will begin construction in the fall of 2019 on the outskirts of Field's Crossing, Indiana. Permits with Rogers County and the state of Indiana have been applied for, and approval is expected midsummer. The agreement between Renewable Farm Energy and Neal Tillman is the first in the quad-county area.

The Tillman farm is located due east of Turtle Lake and sandwiched between Emmit Martin's farm and Vern Martin's old farm. Emmit bought Vern's farm after Debbie Martin died and Vern was no longer able to farm due to health issues. Field's Crossing can expect a vicious fight from the Martin family and other farming families along the Five-and-Twenty, East Road, and Bees Creek Road. The quad-county area has regulations already in place to deal with windmill farms. Will the trustees of the quad-county area grant variances to Renewable, if needed? How will each trustee vote? Norm Johnson, one of the current trustees, is stepping down due to personal health issues and his son, Junior Johnson, is running unopposed for that spot. How will he vote? Is it too late for another candidate to enter the race?

Will the village be given access to reduced electrical costs, or will Renewable sell the energy elsewhere? In order for Field's Crossing to receive this benefit, Tillman will need a stipulation in the contract or can the trustees require free or reduced electrical costs for everyone in the quad-counties before granting a variance? This requirement would be a huge financial savings for many families in the area, which makes the election of a new trustee suddenly important. This reporter intends to canvass the trustees and ask how they will vote on any and all proposed variances for windmill farms.

CHAPTER TWENTY-EIGHT

"JAY, HOW'S MY car coming along? I've got a lot to do today." Jim Cotter closed the back door to the auto body shop, the sleeve of his coat catching on the dead bolt. The sun was rising, and the auto repair shop's heating system was on high, noisily rattling overhead, the down drafts shooting streams of heat into the cavernous building. A few strands of hair lifted off Jim's almost-bald head.

"BMW is awfully slow in shipping the parts," Jay Cook said. "I keep getting flak about not being one of their authorized dealers."

"Have you explained to them the vehicle isn't drivable due to the damage?" Jim was annoyed. As much as he loved driving his new Ford F-450, everyone in Field's Crossing owned a pickup truck. His Beemer was recognized.

"Twice. And twice they offered to tow it to an authorized dealer."

"At my expense, no doubt."

"You got it. Any way to make a buck. When I slid underneath, there's more damage than what you can see from here. I ordered all the parts, and they're supposed to ship this afternoon. Cross your fingers." Jay dropped a screwdriver onto his tool cart and wiped his oil-stained hands. "Can I ask you a question? Do you have any idea what Shelby wants to do with Bob's Caddy? I'm not calling and asking, and I hate to move it outside in the cold and snow."

"I have no idea, but I'll ask. What's the red Jeep in for?"

"Depends on who you talk to." Jay stuck his hands in his pockets and rocked back on his heels. "If you ask Emmit, Theo hit Dylan and knocked off the side mirror. If you talk to Neal, Dylan hit Theo. It's a three-hundred-dollar fix, so I'm guessing Emmit's going to pay for it, but he may make Dylan chip in."

"Irresponsible brats. When did this happen?"

"Wednesday afternoon before the blizzard. Idiots shouldn't have even been on the damn road."

"Snot-nosed kids think they're immortal." Jim strolled to the rear of his BMW, hand in his pocket. He had pre-programmed the auto body's phone number in his cell. He hit SEND. "I need to get something out of the trunk."

Overhead, a phone rang. "Let me get your key before I answer that."

"I've got my spare. Go ahead. Answer the phone." Jim pressed the trunk release, grabbed everything in it, and slammed it shut. Walking quickly across the stained concrete floor, he slipped through the back door and hurried to his Ford F-450. Pulling his cell phone out of his pocket, he tapped END, cutting off Jay's "hello, hello."

*   *   *

Jim ordered a Western omelet with extra cheese, hot sauce, wheat toast, and coffee. He was the first customer at the Skillet this morning, and the sizzle of bacon permeated the diner. He cocooned himself in a corner table, visible and approachable, but alone. Stirring cream into his coffee, he scooped up a mouthful of eggs as Dutch and Art stormed in, the heated debate of the day already in progress.

"Do the two of you start the day with an argument?" Karen, the Skillet's oldest waitress, asked.

"Only when he's talking like an idiot," Art said.

"You're afraid of losin' this argument like all the others you lost." Dutch touched his friend on the elbow and nodded toward the back of the restaurant. "Jim, we were sorry to hear about Bob. I went to kindergarten with this old geezer and, even though we argue a lot, I'd miss him somethin' terrible if he died."

The two old farmers hung their baseball caps and coats on the hooks on the end of the booth and settled in the table across the aisle from Jim.

"We've been fishing or hunting almost every weekend for the last ten years. I don't know what I'm going to do with myself," Jim said.

"Where'd you go last weekend?" Art asked.

"Ice fishing at Turtle Lake."

"I did that once. Damn near froze my ears off," Dutch said.

"I heard Neal put Bob in a ditch on Friday night and the sheriff found Bob dead on Monday morning. What's the connection?" Art asked.

"When Neal sideswiped Bob into the ditch, he broke Bob's nose and sprained his wrist. I think the accident might have triggered a stroke or a heart attack or a blood clot formed, an aneurysm maybe. The autopsy will tell us more." Jim wiped his mouth on a napkin and picked up his mug of coffee.

"Haven't you gotten Neal out of jail before?"

"I have, but no more. Theo posted bail for his old man, and I told Neal I wouldn't represent him in court on this matter. Besides, he didn't have the money to pay me. Bob told me when we were out fishing, Neal's going to lose his farm. Soon."

"How far in debt is he?" Art asked.

"Bob didn't give me a number. He said Farmers Bank denied his most recent loan application, and that's why Neal ran him off the road."

"Emmit's going to gobble up Neal's farm," Art said.

"Neal will file for bankruptcy before he sells to anyone in the Martin family," Dutch said.

"He'll get more money than if he sells outright to Emmit."

"Neal's too stubborn and there's too much bad blood between them."

Jim didn't want to listen to the two old farmers and didn't want to get drawn into their petty arguments. He drained his cup of coffee, stood, and pulled on his long wool coat. "And, gentlemen, on that note, I take my leave."

*　*　*

"Starr, what are you doing here so early in the morning?" Jim stopped at the bottom of the stairs and brushed the light dusting of snow off his coat. After leaving Art and Dutch, their latest argument raging, he'd driven to the township office, assuming the building would be empty.

"Jhonni asked me to send over a copy of the stuff Stephanie did on the last day she worked. I was just getting to it."

"Why does the sheriff need this information?"

"I didn't ask. That poor girl. Theresa and Owen. How do you bury your child?" She crumpled another Kleenex and shoved it into the overflowing wastebasket under her desk. Plucking another Kleenex, she wiped her eyes and clicked on the mouse.

Jim peered over the office manager's shoulder. "What was the last thing she worked on?"

"The 2009 Field's Crossing Capital Development Fund, but it seems to be a duplicate," Starr said. "Wait a minute. *Capital* is spelled differently on this account. You're the finance manager for the village. What's the difference between the two accounts?"

About a million dollars.

"I'll take a look and forward the appropriate file to the sheriff's office. My guess is she made a typo. Capital with 'al' versus Capitol ending in 'ol.' Why don't you close out of the scanned files and I'll finish up?" He smoothed his few strands of hair from left to right. "Is there anything else the sheriff asked for?"

"I already sent her my last text with Stephanie."

"What did that say?"

"I told Stephanie not to come in on Wednesday."

Jim climbed the stairs to his second-floor office and laid the laptop on his desk. Erasing the secret file posed no problem for him, especially since this PC wasn't tied into the village's computer system.

He flipped up the top and frowned at the black screen. Starr knew there were two capital fund account files. What if she checked the actual file boxes? He had become careless. Ten years of embezzling from Field's Crossing had made him lazy. He needed to lug both boxes up to his office and compare them with the laptop before he took the box with his false invoices and bank statements. Those he'd shred at home.

Jim trotted down the back stairs and opened the storeroom door. The room was half-empty. In five months, Stephanie had scanned in forty years of paperwork. He grimaced.

"Can I help you with something?" Starr poked her head out from behind the gray metal shelving.

He grabbed his chest. "Give me a heart attack, why don't you?"

"Sorry about that. You look lost."

"I want to make sure I don't delete the wrong file. Where's the 2009 box?"

"Sitting on the floor next to my desk. Whenever Stephanie finished scanning a box, she left it for me so I could spot-check it. She was thorough. I never found anything missing."

"Two thousand ten?"

"I don't think she started on that box. It should still be in here."

"I'll take the 2009 box up to my office and do the spot-check for you," Jim said. "My schedule is pretty light today."

"That would be one less item on my to-do list. Thanks for your help. After you're done, stick it back at my desk, and I'll shred it."

Trying to hide his shortness of breath, Jim carried the brown bankers box into his office. Tossing the lid on the floor, he picked up a stack of papers, signed onto the laptop, and searched.

An hour later, he had two piles. One he returned to the 2009 box, the other he shoved into his briefcase. How was he going to retrieve the remaining years? Starr would be suspicious if he offered to look at the other boxes. He needed to get her out of the office for a few hours. Maybe longer.

A sharp stab shot through his shoulder blade. Pressing his fist against his chest, he opened the middle desk drawer, popped a little yellow pill, and plopped back in his leather chair, sweat breaking out on his forehead. The angina would disappear in a few minutes.

CHAPTER TWENTY-NINE

A LIGHT BULB lay shattered beneath her boots, the back door un-locked, the window next to it smashed in. Laurent clicked on her Maglite, the beam catching the auto body shop's sign in its glare. Her boots crunched on the ice-covered snow as she trained the light along the outside rear wall of the darkened shop. With her shoulder, she pushed the back door open until it struck the side of the cinder block wall. Her gloved hand fumbled along the wall. Where was the light switch? As she shone her flashlight on the walls searching for a switch, she touched the radio on her shoulder and whispered, "Dispatch. Send backup to Cook's Auto Body on Woodruff. Advise possible break-in."

"Ten-four."

Inside the shop, four vehicles faced Woodruff Street, bay doors down and locked. Laurent angled the flashlight down, not wanting to fall into of one the bay holes that sat below street level. She always had the oil changed in her Chevy Colorado pickup at Cook's and knew the mechanics positioned the vehicles directly over the gaping hole to drain the old oil. When the mechanic was finished underneath the vehicle, he climbed the stairs and new oil was pumped in from an overhead hose. Same with the windshield washer fluid. And the vac-uum. But where were the stairs? She didn't remember seeing them.

Spotting a row of switches outside the office door, Laurent crept along the west wall, her boots squeaking on the concrete floor, the greasy smell of oil assaulting her nose. She paused at the corner, searching for the stairwell. There it was. In the middle of the north wall. She'd have to veer around it to get to the light switches. As her eyes adjusted to the dark shop, she stared across the cavernous building at the office. Was that a shadow?

On the other side of the stairs, the office door creaked. Keeping her back to the wall, Laurent slid into a squat. Was the intruder a thief? The auto body shop held a lot of tools. Expensive tools.

Laurent duck-walked along the north wall. *Scrape.* What was that noise? She squatted again and shone her flashlight under the four vehicles. Three tool carts were lined up to the left of the office door. To the right of the office door, a pair of legs. The driver's door to the red Jeep was open, the shadow distorted on the cinder block wall.

"Stop! Police!"

"Motherfucker." The shadowy figure picked up a wrench and heaved it at her.

"That's assault, asshole." Laurent ducked and touched the radio on her shoulder. "Where's my backup?"

"ETA. Two minutes." Dak's calm voice spoke in her ear.

What was the intruder doing? With a screech, the dead bolt on the front door slid open and the shadowy figure darted through, the heavy metal slamming against the outside wall. Sprinting around the stairwell, Laurent caught the door as it swung back. Propping the door open with her shoulder, she peered outside. The snow was packed tightly on the ground and there were no cars in the front parking lot. The only light came from the illuminated shop sign.

Crunch. To her right.

"Dak. I'm outside. Intruder exited on Woodruff. I'm guessing he's heading over to County Street. Meet me at Oak and County."

"Ten-four. I'm five blocks south of you on County. Description?"

"Dark clothes. Heavyset. Hooded." Laurent held the heavy front door until it rested, slightly ajar, and ran outside, past the bay doors. Peering around the corner, she saw no one, her breath shooting out white streams of air. The rear parking lot held two pickup trucks, but no dark figure. She stalked between the vehicles and glanced left and right on Oak Street. The only vehicle was her SUV. She jogged over to County Street and flagged down Dak.

"Follow County all the way to the Five-and-Twenty then cut over to Field and follow it south. There can't be that many people on the street this time of night, even on a Friday. The bars closed an hour ago."

"Don't stay in this cold for too long, Sheriff. You don't need frostbite."

Laurent pulled her scarf over her nose and half-jogged, half-walked, looking into every doorway and scanning every storefront. Nothing. The overhead street lighting cast a yellowish glow on the dirty mounds of snow. Six blocks later, she cut over to Field Street. *Lost him. Damn.* She paused to catch her breath and scan Field Street. No shadowy figure. He probably parked here. *There's Dak.* "Anything?"

Dak shook his head.

"Keep cruising this area and some of the residential area next to the shop. Jot down any license plates of parked vehicles. It's probably a long shot, but maybe he parked on a side street and circled back. We'll check them tomorrow. I'll call Jay Cook and get him down here. He's got a broken window and an unlocked front door."

"Did the intruder steal anything?" Dak asked.

"I couldn't tell. Jay's gonna have to do an inventory."

"Hell. He knows every single tool he owns. It won't take him but a minute to know if anything's missing."

Half an hour later, Laurent watched as Jay Cook scoured his shop.

"He threw this at you? Good thing he missed. This wrench would have knocked you out and left a nasty bruise. You don't want it for prints?"

"He was wearing gloves. Anything missing from your office? I know he was in there." Laurent's SUV was warmer than the auto body shop at night, and she stamped her feet on the cold concrete floor.

"Nope."

"So, the only thing out of place was the open door on the red Jeep and the wrench on the floor? What's wrong with the Jeep?"

"Broken driver's-side mirror."

"Does this vehicle belong to the Martin family?" she asked.

"How'd you know that?"

"Lucky guess." Laurent touched the radio on her shoulder. "Dak, swing by the office and grab that new warrant we got for the Martin farm and vehicles. Dylan's Jeep is here at Cook's with the driver's door open, and Jay's positive all the doors were closed and locked."

"Give me ten minutes."

"Thanks, Dak." Laurent turned to Jay Cook. "How much longer are you going to have the Jeep?"

"Just waiting for the replacement part. Should be here tomorrow." Jay took off his baseball hat and scratched his head before settling the cap back on. "Sheriff, I don't know if you know this or not, but I make a quick inventory of what's inside every car before I work on it. I know it's crazy, but a few years ago ol' lady Parks accused me of stealing her purse out of her Lincoln Town Car, which, of course, I didn't, and she threatened to sue me and close my shop and have me thrown in jail like a common thief. After that nasty incident, I now make a list of what I see in the vehicle. I don't open the glove box, but if you've left an umbrella on the back seat, I write that down. Same with the trunk. I ain't ever going through that again."

"Jay, I'm going to obtain a new warrant from Judge Jenkins for all your notes, paperwork, invoices, and anything related to the work you're doing on this vehicle, and I'd like you to do another quick inventory tonight." Laurent sank into a plastic chair outside Jay's office. "What happened with Mrs. Parks?"

"Crazy old lady left her purse at the grocery store and one of the clerks stole all the money out of it."

*　*　*

"You're going to compare what Jay inventoried against what we find," Dak said.

"That's the plan." After watching Jay lock up his auto body shop, Laurent met Dak in her office. "I'm going to file a report and, first thing tomorrow morning, I'm getting a warrant. Jay said he'll stall until the end of the day on Monday if I need it."

"I sure as hell ain't waking up the judge at two in the morning. He'll be pissed enough you're calling him on a Saturday."

"I've got another task for you," she said. "On Monday and Tuesday, I want you to visit all of the auto body shops in the quad-county area and get me the make and model of any vehicles with front-end damage in the last two weeks, and if the owner is willing to tell you who owns the vehicle, even better. Vern said the fourth vehicle was a car, not a pickup. It's possible that whoever killed Stephanie did some damage to the vehicle."

Dak raised his eyebrows. "No warrant?"

Laurent shook her head. "I haven't got a leg to stand on. Just a hunch. If there really was a fourth vehicle, maybe the driver scraped the front end climbing out of a ditch or veered off the road. You know how hard it is to drive when you've got blinding, blowing snow. Can't see for shit. Vern said the last car was a low-slung vehicle. I hope who-ever it was broke an axle."

"That's still no proof that the driver of the fourth vehicle killed Stephanie."

"I know, but a list with names will be another avenue to trace. I've got very little to go on until CSU gets back to me with the results of the boot treads. Knowing that a hammer is the murder weapon is of no help."

CHAPTER THIRTY

LAURENT SCOWLED IN the bathroom mirror. She unleashed her long dark hair out of its customary braid she used for work, letting it lay in waves around her face and down her back. Dammit. Where did that silver streak come from? She narrowed her eyes. Was that a gray hair in her eyebrow? *Not fair.* Rummaging in the bathroom drawer, she found her tweezers and plucked the lone gray hair from her eyebrow.

She took a deep breath. In the letter from her daughter there'd been an invitation to a concert tonight in Indianapolis, and she wasn't sure she could meet her daughter by herself. Thank God Starr was going with. Still, she was nervous as hell. She'd already sweated through one blouse.

Laurent applied lipstick, blotted, and dropped the tube in her jacket pocket. Starr would expect a full face of makeup, but Laurent's slightly darker skin tone was smooth and unblemished. Nothing more than moisturizer with tint, mascara, and lipstick were necessary. She wasn't going to win her daughter over with her appearance.

Laurent let out a sigh. She tugged the collar of her black turtleneck and wiped her palms on the black dress pants. Time to stop being a coward.

* * *

Jalapenos was not well-lit. Two walls of the Mexican restaurant were painted bright orange and two walls were teal. Sombreros and ponchos were tacked to the walls, and shelves overflowed with colorful glass bottles, succulents, and trinkets. Jalapenos had been open for a few years and was doing well. Farmers got tired of meat and potatoes. Or maybe it was the tequila. The Mexican restaurant was filled every night during the winter months.

Starr ordered a half-pitcher of margaritas. Salt, on the rocks. Two glasses. And chorizo dip with andouille sausage.

"How's the village of Field's Crossing holding up?" Laurent wasn't ready to talk about the upcoming evening. Not yet.

"We got a lot of complaints when you closed Webster Park and the new hands-free driving law is ticking people off, but other than that, all's well. You look fabulous. You should wear your hair down more. A little makeup goes a long way." Starr poured two margaritas and the women clinked glasses. "I've been thinking about Stephanie."

"Who hasn't?"

"Stephanie made a comment about Jim Cotter. She thought he was having money issues. She said she overheard him on the phone with the bank, and he told them he'd pay off his loan on Tuesday."

Laurent relaxed back in the booth and glanced around the restaurant.

Starr outshone every other patron. Tonight's ensemble for the concert was black and white, solids mixed with polka dots, an armful of bangles, and enormous hoop earrings, white with black crystals.

"That's what I said. I don't know how lawyers can even guess how much they're going to make or when they're going to get paid. He was extremely helpful the other day, which was rather odd for him. He's not usually like that, but I guess with Bob dying, he was feeling his mortality. Stephanie made a mistake and named two files the same, except for the spelling of 'capital.' He cleaned up that mess for me. Would have taken me hours." Starr sipped her margarita. "Have you set up your campaign fund?"

"I never closed the old one."

"Is that legal?"

"I talked to the election board. As long as I report income and donations every month, the election board says I can keep it for as long as I want," Laurent said.

"That makes reelection easier. We shouldn't have a hard time defeating Greene. Again."

"According to Ralph, there are more male voters in the quad-county area than the last time I ran. He thinks I'm done for."

"That snake is the most biased reporter in Indiana. I'd love to beat the crap out of his best buddy."

"He tracked me down at the Skillet and vowed to watch me like a hawk." Laurent sipped her margarita.

"I heard he's trying to dig up dirt on you." Starr's bracelets jangled as she dipped a chip into the chorizo appetizer. "Your concerts in the park. He's trying to find someone to say you distributed campaign materials without a permit at a free event on public grounds."

"I did not."

"The truth doesn't matter to him. Ruining someone's reputation is more important, especially yours."

"I know why he dislikes me, but I did everything by the book. I even recommended community service for his son. He could have gone to prison and, with Ralph's DUIs and moving violations, he could lose his license. Doesn't he get that?"

"The problem is Greene looks the other way on his DUIs, but you, Dak, and Poulter don't put up with his bullshit." Starr finished her margarita. "Another round? Why aren't you eating?"

"Not very hungry today. I'm done drinking, but you can have another one."

"Today? You weren't hungry last week when we went to lunch."

"I'm worried about the election. It's a little over two weeks away. What if I don't arrest Stephanie's killer? Will I be voted out for incompetence? Ralph's been making that suggestion over and over again. At some point, it's going to stick." Laurent stared across the brightly flowered tablecloth at Starr. "I love my job. I don't want to lose."

"Ralph spooked you. You've got nothing to worry about. People in Field's Crossing like you."

"It's a quad-county election. Field's Crossing isn't the only town with a vote." Laurent's voice was sharper than she wanted.

One of Starr's heavily penciled-in eyebrows rose. "Little nervous, tonight?"

"My palms are sweaty and my heart's racing a mile a minute."

"How are you going to introduce yourself?"

"I'm not sure I'm going to."

"What the fuck? I thought that was the purpose of going to this concert. To meet your daughter."

"I'm having second thoughts. What if she doesn't like me?" Laurent asked.

"She doesn't know you and she really shouldn't make up her mind over a five-minute, sure-to-be-awkward conversation."

"That's just it. What if she wants me to tell her the whole story? Right there in the lobby? I can't do that." Laurent's hand shook slightly as she lifted the margarita and set it back down without drinking.

"Why not?"

"It's not a story that should be told like that. It's a private conversation. I want to explain my decision without sounding defensive or like I'm making excuses for myself. I want her to understand how depressed I was, how my world crashed down on me, how I saw no way out. And I can't talk about that in the middle of a lobby with tons of people milling around chatting about the concert." Laurent stared at Starr as her throat closed shut and tears threatened to spill down her face.

"How about this? We introduce ourselves and make awkward small talk, and then I'll mention we need to get going because you have the morning shift and suggest that the two of you exchange phone numbers. Do you think you can do that?"

"I can do that."

* * *

Ralph checked his gas gauge before following Laurent and Starr out of the Mexican restaurant parking lot. The tank was less than half-full. Enough to go 200 miles. Maybe less. As he pulled onto Route 31 South, he stepped on the accelerator. Where were they going in such a hurry? He switched on the CTRY96 country music radio station and settled into the driver's seat. This was the main highway south to Indianapolis.

An hour and a half later, he eased into a spot in the free parking garage and walked three blocks to the front entrance of the concert hall. He bought the cheapest ticket available, and climbed the stairs to the top tier. After relaxing into a red plush seat, he scanned the crowd for the two women. Main floor, center aisle, halfway up. Not the cheap seats.

Ralph debated whether or not to go home. He hated classical music. It didn't surprise him that Laurent attended these concerts and dragged Starr along. The house lights flashed three times. The audience sat down. The musicians tuned their instruments and perched on the edge of their chairs.

A stifled cough.

From his vantage point, he saw the stage manager nod to the conductor.

The tuxedoed man strode onstage, bowed to the audience, and stepped onto the podium. Picking up his baton, he opened the score on the black music stand. He raised his arms.

Ralph fell asleep.

*　*　*

"Why didn't you talk to her? Wasn't that why we went?" Starr whispered in the dark.

The two women waited until all of the musicians had exited the side door before walking to Laurent's car and starting the drive north to Field's Crossing.

"I'm such a chicken. Why didn't I at least say hi? I'm sure she's disappointed."

"She doesn't know you were there. She might be disappointed, but you don't know that."

Laurent's knuckles were white on the steering wheel, and her eyes blurred. She snatched a tissue out of the side pocket of her car and blotted her eyes.

"You missed the ramp to the highway," Starr said. "You want me to drive?"

"Shit." Laurent moved to the left lane and did a U-turn in the middle of the block. "What'll she think of me? I've got nothing to offer her as a mother."

"You must be upset. I've never seen you break a traffic law before. Sure you don't want me to drive?"

Laurent shook her head. "I'll get it together. I won't kill us."

"Thanks. Appreciate it." Starr settled back in her seat. "She's got a mother. What she's looking for are answers, and you're the only one who can give them to her."

"But what if she wants to know about her father?"

"She can contact him separately. You don't have anything to do with that relationship."

The two women were quiet as the miles passed. It was a clear, cold night, the pavement dry, the highway empty. Farmhouses, barns, and silos dotted the miles of barren cornfields on both sides of the interstate. After finding the correct entrance ramp and leaving Indianapolis in her rearview mirror, Laurent finally relaxed. Veering into a ditch along a deserted section of the highway was dangerous.

"Do you want to talk about the father?"

Laurent sighed. "I was so stupid. We were musicians at Indiana University thirty years ago. He didn't deny paternity. He just refused to pay support. And now, he's famous. Me, not so much."

"You know the old saying—men are assholes, and if you forget, they'll remind you. Do you think he'll bad-mouth you? Call you a slut or worse?"

Laurent nodded.

"Are you embarrassed about the life you've chosen?"

"Not one bit. I love being a sheriff. I'm afraid she'll find me lacking because I didn't keep up my musical career, that I settled for less, that I compromised to save myself and took the easy way out. Most musicians don't make enough money to put food on the table and end up teaching to survive. I did that for a few years and then I gave up, especially after my aunt died."

"You think your daughter is going to condemn you because you survived? You did what you had to do at enormous emotional cost. I think you should be proud of your life and your accomplishments. Do you know that less than one percent of the three thousand twelve sheriff's offices nationwide have a female as top cop? And you haven't given up on your musical career. So, maybe you're not some famous cellist. You practice every day, you take lessons, you give concerts, and you go to all of the local concerts, even the elementary school ones where it's all out of tune and squeaky. You give back, and that's what's important. When you were younger, you couldn't. Alcoholic sister, aunt dying from cancer, giving a child up for adoption. That's a lot for anybody. And now that you can give back, you do. That's more than most people."

"Yeah, but Randi's making a career out of it. She's making it work."

"You don't know that. You have no idea how much her adopted parents are supporting her, financially and in every other way. That's something you never had."

Laurent was quiet. She had never considered herself a survivor. She simply did what she thought was best at the time. And she was proud to be a sheriff. The thought of losing to Greene made her sick to her stomach. But she hadn't told her best friend the entire story. About the night she gave her daughter up for adoption.

"I'm being a baby."

"Kinda."

Laurent snorted. "Don't hold back. Tell me what you really think."

Both women chuckled.

"Talk to her, Jhonni. She may surprise you. You may surprise yourself."

CHAPTER THIRTY-ONE

OPINION/EDITORIAL PAGE
ESCALATION OF FEUD

February 16, 2019
Field's Crossing, Indiana
by Ralph Howard

> *With the signing of a contract between Neal Tillman and Renewable Energy, can Field's Crossing expect an escalation in the century-old feud between the Martins and the Tillmans? To what lengths will each family go in order to secure the necessary votes to grant or not grant variances to Renewable? How will each trustee vote?*

> *At the time of this printing, none of the current trustees or those up for reelection would comment, saying only that they would have to see what Renewable was asking before making any decisions. Small-town politics at its best.*

> *The contract signing comes at a tense moment in Field's Crossing as this reporter has learned both Dylan Martin and Theo Tillman are suspects in Stephanie Gattison's murder. The Martin*

boy was the father of the deceased's unborn child, but the deceased also had a fight with the Tillman boy at Beaumon's Hardware, which was captured on security cameras.

What about the trustee position being vacated by Norm Johnson? Will his son vote the way Norm would have? Is a proponent of wind energy going to pop up on the ballot as a write-in candidate? What if Emmit Martin or Neal Tillman ran for the vacant trustee spot? Despite the obvious conflict of interest, this would put both men in a position to influence the vote. Would either one abstain? Would the other trustees ask them to abstain?

With two weeks before the election, the positions of sheriff and trustee of the quad-counties have become quite contentious.

CHAPTER THIRTY-TWO

LAURENT BURST THROUGH the rear entrance of Beaumon's Hardware store, Dak on her heels. "I'll take Tillman."

"I'm on the Martin kid."

"You fucker!" Dylan screamed, grabbing one of Theo's blond locks and punching the employee.

"Let go of my hair, you little shit!" Theo kicked Dylan's leg and fell on his butt as Dylan's grip loosened.

Laurent grabbed Theo's wrist and twisted his arm up behind him. Wrenching his other arm up, she cuffed him and waited as Dak cuffed Dylan. It was closing time on Sunday night at Beaumon's Hardware store and five employees lingered near the rear exit.

"Dylan, sit your ass down. On the floor," Laurent said.

"He left her. He left her crying at the water tower." Tears streamed down Dylan's face, and he rolled to his knees before Dak shoved him back.

"I might have left her, but you got her pregnant," Theo said.

"Murderer!" Dylan said.

"Sit. Down." Laurent towered over the two slightly bruised young men. No blood. No broken bones. *But another Martin-Tillman fight and this one in public.*

The cavernous receiving area had two bays for semis to back into and unload, and a battery area to charge the forklifts. The entire back wall was filled with shelving for overstock.

"He started it," Theo said.

"You hit me with a cart," Dylan said.

"Just like a Martin. Can't control your temper," Theo sneered. "Everyone knows all about you. How you got another girl pregnant last year. You're such a screwup."

"I am not!" Dylan shrieked.

"You left your pregnant girlfriend with no gas in her pickup in the middle of nowhere," Theo said.

"So did you."

"Shut up, both of you." Laurent glared at the handcuffed fighters. She was disgusted with both young men. She turned toward the employees lingering near the exit. "Go home. All of you. This is none of your business."

"Dylan! What the hell?" Caleb ran across the concrete floor.

"He left her," Dylan said.

"What?" Caleb asked.

"Theo left Stephanie at the water tower. He said she was crying. He was there after me," Dylan said.

Caleb stalked to Theo.

"Stand back, Caleb, or I'll arrest you, too." Laurent grabbed Caleb by the wrist and thrust her shoulder into his bicep. She wasn't going to let this incident get out of control. It was bad enough Beaumon's employees had witnessed the initial fight between Dylan and Theo.

"Getting fired today wasn't enough for you? You had to pick a fight with my little brother. You piece of shit." Caleb kicked the floor.

"You fired him?" Dylan gawked at his brother.

"He hit all of the mailboxes on the Five-and-Twenty. On purpose," Caleb said.

"You don't know that," Theo said.

"I got reports all the way up and down the road. More than one person spotted you veering out of your way to hit their mailbox. My inbox is full of complaints, and they're all about you." Caleb spat on the floor.

"Have fun fixing them," Theo said.

"Let's go." Laurent released Caleb's arm and grabbed Theo's, hauling the sneering kid to his feet. "One question—why didn't you give Stephanie a ride into town?"

"She told me to fuck off. Dylan's the one who shouldn't have left her," Theo said.

"I didn't know she was out of gas." Dylan sat, crumpled on the cement floor, all of the fight drained away.

"Both of you are morally responsible for Stephanie's death. Whether or not one of you hit her over the head with a hammer and threw her under a pile of snow is another story," Laurent said.

"Why don't you check his Jeep? It's over at Cook's Auto Body getting a new side mirror. I bet he's got a hammer in there." Theo pointed his chin at Dylan.

"Go ahead, Sheriff. I've got nothing to hide. You fat fuck." Dylan glared at Theo.

"I'm gonna beat the shit out of you." Theo lunged at Dylan.

Dak stepped in front of the teenager, one large hand pushing Dylan back to the floor, the other planted firmly on Theo's chest. "Back off."

Laurent yanked on Theo's arm, spinning him around, and clamped her other hand on the back of his neck, forcing his eyes to the floor. "March."

* * *

After locking both young men into separate jail cells, Laurent and Dak climbed the stairs to her office. She opened her mini-fridge and handed a Diet Coke to Dak. "What'd you think?"

"I'd wait to call Neal. You know Caleb's already called Emmit, and you don't want Emmit and Neal here at the same time. We've only got three cells." Dak popped the tab on the can and gulped. "Are you going to charge them? Disturbing the peace."

"Dylan's angry and upset. Theo capitalized on it, knowing it wouldn't take much to provoke him. I don't want this feud to escalate. It's bad enough the two of them were the last ones to see Stephanie alive, other than the supposed fourth vehicle. They clipped mirrors on Field Street and are pointing fingers at each other. And now a fight in the hardware store, to say nothing of the fact Neal signed a windmill farm agreement guaranteed to piss off Emmit. These little incidents get out of hand fast." She sipped her bottle of water.

"What happened with the new warrant?" Dak asked.

"When I compared Jay's inventory with what I found in the Jeep, there's an extra hammer. Brand new. I'm going to ask Kessel to conduct an inventory of hammers and review the security tapes for the last few days." Laurent looked at her deputy. "I think Theo broke in and planted the hammer in Dylan's Jeep in the hopes we'll arrest Dylan."

"Silhouette look familiar?"

She nodded. "Theo's a big dude. I'm betting he threw that big-ass wrench at me."

"You think he's trying to stir up more trouble to get Dylan put behind bars for murder, or is he trying to throw us off his trail? Maybe something did snap in his little pea brain and now he's panicking."

Laurent sank into her desk chair. "But what makes a person snap? I asked Principal Yoshida that question, but he had no answer for me other than Theo's put on a lot of weight."

"When did Caleb fire Theo? Before or after the break-in?"

"After, I think, but I'll double-check."

"So, Neal signs with Renewable. Theo gets fired by Caleb. Who's got the upper hand? Are we just going to seesaw back and forth putting out these little fires? We gotta find Stephanie's killer before someone else dies." Dak shot his empty can toward Laurent's wastebasket, just missing.

"I chatted with the librarian and, according to her, Vern comes in about every two weeks, a beat-up black backpack slung over one shoulder. He slides all the books he's returning through the slot and then spends an hour roaming the library and checking out another five or six books."

"You think that's the same backpack in Vern's mudroom you moved so you could take his boots?" Dak asked.

"Yeah."

"Don't look so glum. You never believed Vern was the killer."

Laurent eyed her deputy. "Neither did you."

Dak grinned at her. "Now that we all agree Vern didn't do it, who does that leave?"

"Theo and Dylan."

"Two hotheaded young men, both with motive and both capable of losing it," Dak said.

The two cops were quiet for a minute.

"Here's some bad news. Dr. Creighton is going to declare Bob's death a homicide." Laurent picked up Dak's empty can and tossed it back to him.

"What the fuck?"

"The gashes in the back of Bob's head match up with the broken beer bottle and, from the angle, there's no way Bob hit himself in the head. I also found a boot print on the back of Bob's jacket and sent it to CSU."

"Same as by Stephanie's truck?"

"I can't tell." Laurent leaned forward. "When you start canvassing auto body shops, also check the dry cleaners. I'm looking for a winter coat with beer spilled down the sleeve."

"What if the bottle was empty or the coat doesn't need dry cleaning?" Dak shot the empty Diet Coke can again. "Nailed it."

"Then I'm sending you on a wild goose chase."

"Do you think they're related?"

"I think we've got two killers."

CHAPTER THIRTY-THREE

"Did Neal kill my husband?" Shelby added another sprinkle of flour and rolled and kneaded the dough with the heels of her hands. Picking up the dough, the widow slapped it down on the countertop. Again and again. Slap. Knead. Slap. Knead. There seemed to be something deeply satisfying about beating the dough, and Laurent resolved to try it the next time she found herself stressed or anxious. It didn't matter if the bread tasted good or was even bakeable; the act of kneading looked like it released a lot of tension.

Shelby had dark circles under her eyes and deep crow's-feet at the corners. Her tightly wound permed curls were gray with white streaks, and flour dusted her right cheek. A blue-and-white apron hung from her neck and was tied around her ample waist. Glasses perched on the top of her head.

The renovated farmhouse kitchen smelled of freshly baked bread. Four loaves covered with dishcloths sat on the countertop in loaf pans and it looked to Laurent as if Shelby had been up before dawn baking bread.

"Your husband's autopsy will be this week," Laurent said. "It seems to me he fell and landed on his face, knocked himself out, and drowned. Whether or not the injuries he suffered from Neal running him off the road contributed to his death remains unclear. Dr. Creighton will examine the brain in minute detail."

"What's he looking for?"

"Evidence of a stroke or aneurysm. He's also going to examine the heart and surrounding areas. Was Bob on any medication?" Laurent counted the loaf pans on the countertops, the ones in the oven, and the one Shelby was starting. "Do you always bake this many loaves?"

"It's how I deal with stress. And grief. If my hands are busy, my mind is busy. My daughter buys the store-bought stuff with all those preservatives, so I'm sending her home with a few loaves. But to answer your question, Bob was diabetic and taking metformin. He was very conscious of his sugar intake. He also took a multivitamin and PreserVision." Shelby dusted her hands, rolled the dough up, tucking the ends under, and plopped the next loaf into another pan and covered it with a dish towel.

"What's PreserVision?"

"It's used to slow down macular degeneration. Bob was losing his sight. We caught it early and the doctor thought, with treatment, he'd be fine for a long time."

"Will his toxicology report come back with alcohol?"

"How in the world men can sit on a frozen lake in the middle of winter in a flimsy plastic tent staring into a hole and drink whiskey is beyond me." Shelby shook her head. "Damn fools."

"Ice fishing befuddles me, too. Must be a male bonding thing."

"I'm sure Bob drank a beer or two while ice fishing," Shelby said. "So, if Neal is responsible or partly responsible for my husband's death, then what?"

"Columbia Hospital took X-rays on Friday night when Bob went to the ER. A radiologist will compare the one on Friday with the one from the autopsy and send me the results. I'll confer with the state's attorney on how to proceed," Laurent said. "Can you tell me what Bob said about Neal?"

"Not in polite company." Shelby pulled on oven mitts, removed a loaf pan, and tapped the top of the loaf. "If it sounds hollow, it's ready. Want a slice?"

"I thought you'd never ask." Laurent slathered butter on the warm slice and bit. Melted butter ran down her chin, and she grabbed a napkin and wiped. "Did Bob ever talk about stuff at the bank?"

"Bob started at Farmers Bank forty years ago, when all transactions were done by hand or phone. He loved talking to people, but, as technology increased, he got tired of keeping up. All of us older folks are. You learn to do something one way and then they go and change it and nothing's the same. The screen's different, the headings, the colors. Why can't they leave well enough alone?"

"Those of us who learned how to use a computer later in life are going to struggle. Forever. Anything else at the bank bothering him?" Laurent asked.

"We discussed employees from time to time. He thought of them as his family, and if someone was struggling, Bob would come up with a way to give him or her a few extra days off without deducting anything from their paycheck."

"Every employee I talked to at the bank had nothing but great things to say about Bob and you. A lot of them cried the whole time." Laurent crumpled her napkin into a ball. "What can you tell me about Bob and Jim's relationship?"

"Jim moved here about fifteen years ago. He said he was tired of big-city politics and big law firms. Busting your butt so you might make partner someday. He was sick of it. He grew up in a small town, Greensburg, and decided to return to the small-town feeling."

"Why didn't he go back to Greensburg?"

"I never asked. Bob was so glad to have an attorney in town, one who knew his stuff about inheritance law, and the stubbornness of farmers. Add in the fact that Jim bought on Turtle Lake Road with access to the lake. It was a match made in heaven. Bob did mention he thought Jim overextended himself, but he was sure something would turn up. It always did." Shelby opened the oven and slid in two more loaves.

"I don't understand."

"Money went through Jim's hands like water, but he always managed to catch up if he got behind on his mortgage or credit cards."

"I imagine as a lawyer it would be hard to predict income." Laurent shrugged into her jacket. "Thanks for everything. I'll call you after I talk to the state's attorney."

"One loaf or two?"

Laurent held up two fingers.

CHAPTER THIRTY-FOUR

OPINION/EDITORIAL PAGE
SHERIFF'S OFFICE HIDING SUSPECT

February 18, 2019
Field's Crossing
by Ralph Howard

Is Sheriff Laurent stalling the murder investigation of Stephanie Gattison until after the election? Is justice being delayed by an incompetent sheriff or a sheriff who wants to win at all costs, even to the point of letting a murderer roam free while she campaigns for office? Laurent has been a regular at the Skillet and A Touch of Class cigar shop.

If Laurent is protecting Dylan Martin, how much money is the Martin family contributing to her spring campaign in the hope she will delay the inevitable, or worse, not seek the truth? What will she do? Where will her loyalties lie if Dylan killed his girlfriend? A list of Laurent's campaign donors is available online at the election board website through the secretary of state's office. The link is posted below. At the top of the list are Emmit and Jane

Martin, who contributed a great deal of money to Laurent's election bid four years ago.

With the election two weeks away and with Laurent bungling the murder investigation, her chances of being reelected are growing dimmer. The quad-counties need a change in leadership for justice to be done.

*   *   *

GATTISON FUNERAL SCHEDULED

The body of Stephanie Gattison has been released to her parents for burial. Funeral arrangements have been made for Saturday, March 2, 2019. Wake and viewing will be held at Henry Linville's Funeral Home on First Street on Friday, March 1 from 3 p.m. to 7 p.m. Funeral service will be held at Field's Methodist Church located on the corner of Jacob Street and Fifth Avenue at 10 a.m., Saturday morning, with burial procession ending at Field's Crossing Cemetery. A funeral luncheon will be served at the church at noon in the basement.

In lieu of flowers, the family asks for donations to the 4-H Club of the Quad-Counties in Stephanie Gattison's name.

CHAPTER THIRTY-FIVE

"DID YOU HEAR about Bob Kane?" John Cook said. "Sheriff found him dead in his ice shelter on Sunday. That'll be forty-two dollars."

Vern Martin pulled out his wallet and dropped two twenties and two singles on the counter. The gas station/mini-mart was the closest place to fill up his old pickup. He wasn't going to tell chatty John Cook the sheriff had pulled a gun on him at the ice shelter. He rubbed his chest. Just mentioning the incident quickened his heartbeat.

"Is your brother, the quiet one, still doing auto body repair?"

"Yep. Do you want me to ring him up for you? What work do you need done?"

Vern held up a hand. "Just want to see how much a new front bumper would cost."

"You really ought to scrap that old thing and buy a new used one."

"Bit of an oxymoron." Vern slid his wallet into his back pocket.

The cowbell above the gas station/mini-mart door jangled, and he left John to drive his next customer crazy.

Vern didn't need a new bumper. Or a new used truck. His 2001 Ford pickup was comfortable, the seat conformed to his back and butt, and the smell of the old truck was familiar. He was looking for a fourth vehicle. The sheriff seemed to think his nephew Dylan was responsible for Stephanie's death. Dylan's attack on Theo at

Beaumon's didn't help. And even though he didn't believe anything written by Ralph Howard in *The Crossing*, he didn't like being the object of slander and innuendos. There was nothing wrong with his mental health.

Vern pulled out of the gas station/mini-mart, and drove through downtown Field's Crossing, gaze darting back and forth. The downtown area was familiar. The bank, the post office, the Skillet, the schools. Nothing much had changed in fifty years. The high school he and Emmit attended had been torn down and a new one built. Same for the elementary and middle schools.

He turned right on Woodruff into Cook's Auto Body Shop and parked in the rear, out of sight of prying eyes. The back door was unlocked, plywood covering the window. He blinked in the bright lights of the auto body shop. The smell of oil and grease and burnt coffee filled his nostrils.

"Come in where I can see you," Jay Cook said. "John tells me you need a new bumper. What year is that truck of yours? You look great. Are you keeping busy out at the cabin?"

"All of you Cooks talk a mile a minute. I thought you were the quiet one."

"I'm the least talkative Cook. That means I still talk more than everyone else. You ought to be at one of our family reunions. Enough food to feed the entire town and enough gossip to last a decade. What year is your truck? Anything older than ten years I'll have to search for."

"Two thousand one."

"This is going to take a minute."

"Mind if I wander around?"

Cook waved a hand, phone pressed to one ear. "I'm starting with Pete in Alexander County. He's usually got the best supply of old stuff. You really should think about getting a new used truck."

"Same oxymoron." Vern closed the heavy office door and looked at the four vehicles sitting in the bays. Dylan's red Jeep, a Cadillac, a BMW Roadster, and a Camry. He crouched next to the left front tire of the Caddy and brushed his hand over the scraped paint. A slight dent creased the wheel rim and a four-inch swath of paint was missing. The dent was easy to fix. The number of coats of paint to repair the scrape was time consuming.

He strolled to the BMW and looked at the front end. He glanced at Jay in the office before squatting next to the car. The damage to the front end was extensive. The underbelly of the bumper was scraped and the front grille was dented. The paint was scratched. He pried a piece of gravel out of one of the scratches. A paint chip broke off. He pocketed both.

Next. The Camry. A huge dent creased the center grille, and the hood was crumpled back to the windshield. It looked like the driver had run into a telephone pole. The Camry wasn't the vehicle he was looking for. Only the BMW fit the picture in his head, but the number of low-slung vehicles with front-end damage in the quad-county area would be high, and he had four more shops to visit. He was going to have a lot of quotes for the bumper of his truck.

CHAPTER THIRTY-SIX

"Do you know what that asshole Neal did? Every farmer on the Five-and-Twenty and East Road will hate him and his family forever." Emmit Martin had arrived at his brother's cabin to check on him after the second round of heavy snow and subzero windchill temperatures.

"There's only one topic that pisses you off this much. He leased his land for a windmill farm," Vern said.

Emmit's dislike of wind energy had increased over the last decade as other counties in Indiana allowed wind farms to be built, many along the I-65 corridor. Vern and Emmit had driven over one afternoon to a new windmill farm construction site to watch an arm being hoisted and attached. The closest they could get to the site was half a mile away. The blade hung six feet off the back end of a flatbed semi, and the crane used to pick up the arm sat on sheets of plywood that had been laid to ease soil compaction. From where the two men sat and watched, they had been able to observe the entire, time-consuming process and see the half-acre divot the huge machinery left in the land.

"What a dumb shit." Emmit stalked to the window and then back to the fireplace. Repeating. Window. Fireplace. "Does he realize how those windmills are going to affect the quad-county area?"

"Wind farm regulations vary from county to county in Indiana. Fortunately, the quad-counties have all adopted the same set."

"Perry owns land all over the state, but we both own land next to Neal and both of us are a no."

"Renewable isn't going to ask your opinion. You're both so far out in the country you can't make the claim your home values will drop, even though no one wants to build or live next to a wind farm," Vern said.

"I'm claiming anything I can. And I'm going after increased set-backs—increase the minimum distance from a neighboring property, not the house, the property line. Make it half a mile." Emmit stalked to the tiny kitchen and spat a stream of tobacco juice into the sink.

"That'll piss him off."

"He should have thought of that before he signed with Renewable. I swear to God, I'll build a barn so tall it blocks the wind. Does he realize Renewable can sell the energy to anyone they want? Neal's not going to require them to provide energy for Field's Crossing either free or at a reduced rate. Even he won't get it for free unless he puts it in the contract."

"Do you know how long he leased his land for?" Vern asked.

"At least twenty-five years. With an option to renew for another twenty-five."

"His decision will affect Caleb, Morgan, and Dylan. You and I aren't gonna live another fifty years."

Emmit grunted. "Don't remind me."

"You might want to talk to Jim about your rights," Vern said. "What are your options if milk or crop production decreases and how can you prove the windmills are the cause?"

"You know we went through this ten years ago. I was able to talk Perry out of signing a lease."

"You're not going to be able to talk Neal out of it. He hates your guts. Got any idea why he decided to do this now?" Vern asked.

"The rumor at the Skillet is he's been a regular at Gray Fox Casino. Started up again right after Christmas."

"How much is he in for this time?"

"I have no idea."

"Does Tillman realize this is just a quick fix? No amount of revenue from the windmills is going to continually make up for gambling losses at the casino," Vern said.

"I'm gonna talk to all of the farmers along the Five-and-Twenty and East Road in the quad-county area. Their farms are going to be affected, too. I'll see if one of them will talk to Neal. I think I'll also check with the supervisor at the county office and see if there's anything I can do to stop it. And I'll give Jim a call."

"Good thing it's the middle of winter. You've got time on your hands." Vern rolled up a magazine and tapped it against his knee. "What are you going to do about Dylan?"

"He didn't kill Stephanie."

"We both know that," Vern said. "The boy's a big mush puddle. But *The Crossing* is making a bunch of noise and some people listen to that noise. Any truth to the rumor about another girl getting pregnant last year?"

"Dylan says another girl did wind up pregnant last year, but he never dated her."

"Think Theo killed her?" Vern asked.

"Kid's a bottleful of resentment."

The two men were quiet.

"The kid didn't stand a chance after his mother left and with Neal as his father," Vern said.

"Still no excuse for murder. What do you suppose Neal will do if the sheriff proves Theo killed Owen's girl?" Emmit perched on the edge of the La-Z-Boy next to his brother, arms dangling off his knees.

"If Theo killed Stephanie, on purpose or accidentally, Neal will fall apart. He'll lose his farm, and that will put him over the edge," Vern said. "We could be in for a load of trouble with or without *The Crossing* stirring everybody up."

"I'd like to sue Ralph and *The Crossing*."

"You can't. He always publishes under the op-ed portion. Opinion of the editor, opinion page, letters to the editor. The page where he gets to spout nonsense in the hopes someone will read it and believe him."

"What I ought to do is buy the damn paper and shut it down." Emmit flopped back into the recliner. "I'm going to make an enormous campaign contribution to Sheriff Laurent, that's for sure. Can you imagine what a mess the quad-counties would be if Greene were elected?"

"Are you trying to give me nightmares?" Vern asked. "I've got enough of them, thank you very much."

"Sorry. You seem to be feeling pretty good today."

"This mess with Dylan has me wondering."

"What have you done?" Emmit's eyebrows shot up.

"Just got some quotes for the bumper on my truck."

"What for? You're not gonna fix it."

"True, but I did discover the vehicles with front-end damage and who owns those vehicles." Vern arched one eyebrow at his brother. "In all four counties."

"You think the driver of the last vehicle you saw at the water tower killed Owen's girl?"

"Either directly or indirectly. Doesn't make a difference in my book."

"What are you going to do with the list? Knock on the door and ask if someone in the house gave Stephanie a ride and oh, by the way, did you hit her in the head and toss her in the snow?"

"I haven't decided yet."

"Give the list to the sheriff. Maybe she can spook someone into a confession. She's charging Theo and Dylan with disturbing the peace for their fight at Beaumon's and recommending community service. Dylan agreed. Don't know about Theo. Beaumon's fired his ass. So did Caleb. Theo's got no income."

"Shit. What'd you think those two will do next?" Vern asked.

* * *

Vern dreamed that night.

He couldn't breathe. The rushing river forced all of the air out of his lungs. His head was above water, and one hand clenched a tree branch. He clung to the side of the riverbank, searching for his wife's car, the water pulling at his body.

Where was she?

The skid marks started just before the bridge, and he had followed on foot. The tire tracks slid down the muddy embankment into the Turtle River. Twigs and branches snapped against Vern's face as rain pelted his cheeks and stung his eyes.

Fifty feet away, he spotted the roof of his wife's Buick. He took a deep breath and released the branch, letting the current carry him to his wife.

He didn't know how to swim.

River water filled his mouth and ears, and his clothes dragged him down. His hand skidded over the roof of the car. There was nothing to grab on to. As he started to slide past the Buick, he ducked under the water and grabbed the door handle. With one arm hanging on, he tipped his face up to the rain and spat out a mouthful of dirty water.

He ducked under again and tried to wrestle the car door open. Locked. He pounded on the window. The car automatically locked when it was put into drive and now all the circuits had shorted out. He'd have to smash a window. He surfaced, inhaled hugely, and went under again. He kicked at the window with his steel-toed boots. Nothing.

Hanging onto the door handle, he stuck his face up to the black sky again. The rain had picked up, and whitecaps swirled around the half-sunk Buick. Lightning lit up a nearby cornfield. Vern slid his hand along the roof of the car and down to the back-door handle and pulled himself along. Front-door handle to the back-door handle to the rim over the tire to the bumper. He dragged his water-soaked body onto the riverbank, crawled to the nearest tree, slumping against the trunk, and wrapped his arms around his knees.

Drawing in a huge breath, he let go of his knees and groped the riverbed trees, his hands searching under filthy, wet leaves. He needed a large rock to smash the windshield or the window.

The Buick was caught against the roots of a fallen tree, the water cascading over and around the vehicle. The river churned black and cold, the current whipping branches and twigs by at a hurried pace. The trunks of the trees at the bank were washed clean, their massive roots exposed as lightning lit up the dark sky. Vern grabbed a fist-sized rock and plunged into the fast-moving river. Back the way he came.

*   *   *

Vern awoke. Drenched in sweat. Legs tangled with blankets. He rolled onto his back and stared at the ceiling until his fists released the damp sheets and his breathing slowed. He hadn't dreamed about the day his wife died for three or four years. Why now? What had triggered the old nightmare?

CHAPTER THIRTY-SEVEN

"JOELLE LAURENT?" JIM Cotter closed the door to the second-floor office he used at the village hall and took his cell phone off speaker. No one needed to overhear this conversation.

"Yeah. Who's this and whad'ya want?"

"I'm an attorney in Field's Crossing, Indiana, where your sister is up for reelection. We're reviewing her background more extensively."

"Saint Jhonni screwed up? It was only a matter of time. What'd she do? Screw one of her deputies?"

"I'm not at liberty to speak. Is there anything you would like to comment on or feel the public has a right to know?" Jim held his breath. It was essential Greene win the election for sheriff so he could continue his embezzling scheme from the village. He'd underestimated Laurent and now he needed to distract her from the investigation long enough for public opinion to change. Sheriff Jhonni Laurent was well liked in the quad-county area. He needed to discredit her so she lost her job. Immediately.

"That's a pretty open-ended question. What's in it for me?" Joelle asked.

"Are you implying there's something in her past that's relevant to the election in March? Because it would be your civic duty to inform me."

"Civic duty? What a crock. Jury duty is civic duty."

"Withholding information is a punishable crime," Cotter said.

"So now you're threatening me? What an asshole. Giving up a kid for adoption thirty years ago isn't a crime. It wasn't a crime back then, and it isn't a crime now. Go soak your head in a toilet."

CHAPTER THIRTY-EIGHT

JIM COTTER OPENED the outer door to the Skillet and closed it before opening the inside door. The heavy snow crossed Lake Erie, picked up more moisture, and was now dumping another two feet on Buffalo, New York. After that, the weather system was heading toward Boston, Massachusetts. Indiana had been spared this time. He pulled off his ear warmers and smoothed his comb-over. He had been outside less than a minute, but still, the top of his almost-bald head was cold.

All of the regulars were here. The gossipy old men who met at the Skillet every day spread rumors faster than the women at the Cutting Edge hair salon. He chose a table near the back of the restaurant and ordered a BLT on toasted white, little mayo, chips, and coffee. Black. He blew on his hands. The adrenaline rush wasn't quite over.

Art and Dutch were the two regulars guaranteed to be in the Skillet late into the morning and arguing about something. Subtlety wasn't required with the old guys. Half of them couldn't hear, and the other half couldn't see. But they could think. And calculate. They had been doing it since their fathers had taught them how to operate a successful farming business. That was what farming had become. A business. The days of guessing what crop to plant in what field had been replaced by chemistry and testing nutrients in the soil. Farmers were accountants, chemists, organizers, planners. Projecting the price per bushel or the price per pound for crops or livestock. What was tax deductible, what was not. How to structure their farms and who owned what to maximize profit. These were smart old men. The only thing they hadn't conquered was the weather. Bitch about it, yes. Control it, no.

"The blizzard and the heavy snow we got is putting too much moisture into the ground," Art said. "We won't be able to plow or plant or get into the fields until late April."

"Rainfall was down a little last year," Dutch said. "We're gonna be fine, and there's always mud in the spring."

"I hate getting stuck in the mud."

Lunch was ending, and Karen wheeled out a cart with three gray plastic tubs and began cleaning and wiping down the red-and-white checkered tablecloths.

"When was the last time you got stuck in the mud?" Jim finished eating and picked up his coffee and joined Art and Dutch at their table. He needed to make the old guys question Laurent's competence and play up her lack of experience. The biggest problem was Greene was truly unfit for the job of sheriff.

"I ain't been stuck in years," Art said. "You seen the tires on those new tractors? They're taller than me."

"That's expensive machinery," Jim said.

"Over two hundred thousand," Dutch said. "I don't know how anyone makes a profit being a farmer."

Jim laughed. "You old coot. Between you and the Martins, it's a toss-up who's got more money stashed away."

"Emmit took top dog when Vern quit farming," Art said. "Wish they'd stop in more often. They've always got a story to tell."

"I'm guessing all of the Martins are going to lay low for a while," Jim said. "At least until the sheriff completes her investigation, if she ever does. Stephanie was the smartest girl at Field's Crossing High School. She worked part-time at the village hall, and I can tell you she wouldn't have attempted anything so stupid as to try and walk two miles to get gas right before a blizzard hit."

"I read that in the paper, but only a fool believes what's written in *The Crossing*," Art said.

"Are you sayin' Dylan left her out at the water tower knowin' she'd run out of gas?" Dutch asked. "I find that very hard to believe. No one, not even mean old Neal, would let someone walk two miles to get gas in that kind of weather."

"And two miles back," Art said.

"That's what Dylan claims," Jim said. "She told him she was pregnant on Wednesday afternoon, and he left before she did. And he was pissed."

"The Martins would have done the right thing," Dutch said. "The two kids may not have gotten married, but that's Emmit's grandchild."

"Not anymore," Jim said.

"How can the sheriff prove anything?" Art asked.

"Vern saw his nephew leave before Stephanie," Jim said. "But I can probably get that conversation thrown out. The problem for Dylan is Theo saw him leaving and claims Dylan clipped his side mirror and was driving like a crazy man. The other problem for the Martin family is Vern shoveled a path from his back door to Stephanie's pickup truck," Jim said.

"How do you know all of this?" Art asked.

"Deputy Greene pulled me aside. He's afraid Laurent's turning a blind eye until after the election," Jim said.

"Theo claims Dylan was the last one to see Stephanie alive and he knowingly left her at the water tower with no gas in her vehicle?" Art said. "And Vern was the first one to discover the victim's vehicle?"

"When was the last time Theo or Neal told the truth?" Dutch snorted.

"So, you're saying the sheriff thinks Vern or Dylan is guilty of involuntary manslaughter based on Theo's testimony, but she's not going to do anything until after she gets reelected?" Art asked. "Did I get that right?"

"You summed it up well," Jim said. "Are you sure you don't want to be a lawyer?"

"Go to hell," Art said.

"I hear there's a special place in hell for lawyers," Jim said.

CHAPTER THIRTY-NINE

"I'VE LOOKED AT these numbers until I can't see straight." Duke raised his gray muzzle at the sound of Glen's voice and thumped his tail on the gray carpet of Laurent's office.

"What do they tell you?" Laurent had asked the former sheriff to review financial data on several suspects and their families. Glen Atkins and Duke showed up promptly at nine.

"Let's start with Emmit and Jane Martin," Glen said. "They own three thousand acres in the quad-county area. Fifty percent of that acreage is paid in full, including the farmhouse. Their outstanding debt to Farmers Bank is less than one million dollars. The debt consists of land and vehicle purchases, including farm equipment. If Emmit farms until he's seventy, he'll be debt free. At that point, he'll either sell the land or lease it or leave it to his kids. But financially, Emmit and Jane are set for life. They can spend their winters in Florida and the rest of the year here. I have no idea what retirement looks like to them."

"They may take a trip or two, but they'll never leave. Just like you."

"Wish I had their financial resources." Glen dropped a folder onto the chair next to him and opened another one. "Caleb rents a house on Magnolia and makes fifty thousand dollars a year as highway commissioner for the quad-counties. His salary covers his rent and utilities, and he's taking online classes at Ball State in horticultural design.

He's taken out student loans for his degree and started to pay them off before they become due."

"I'm getting the picture the Martin family doesn't like to be in debt," Laurent said. "Next?"

"Morgan Martin-Shaw and Karl Shaw have the most debt, and it's considerable. Remember, Morgan and Caleb are twins. I never knew veterinary school was so expensive. Around here, it's more than cats and dogs. Morgan took extra classes in treating farm animals, and that subspecialty cost an extra fifty thousand."

"What's their total debt?"

"Half a million dollars," Glen said.

"For vet school?"

"School plus mortgage."

"And the bank approved it?"

"Doctors, dentists, lawyers, veterinarians, people with known high-income occupations can get loans the rest of the general population can't. The bank ties the loan to the firm or the practice's accounts receivables," Glen said.

"But she doesn't own the practice."

"Morgan and the old vet have signed a letter of intent. The old vet plans to retire in ten years, at which time she'll buy him out. The buy-out will take another ten years."

"In twenty years, Morgan and Karl will be debt free."

"The only expenses they'll have will be upgrades, new equipment, vehicles. Maybe they'll move or build a house, but essentially, they'll be fine," Glen said.

"Dylan?"

"Nothing. Doesn't owe or own a thing. Has no credit rating. I would've been shocked to find something. I'm sure Emmit will pay for college, so Dylan will graduate with a degree and a clean slate." Glen dropped another folder on the chair.

"Far better than some. I've been reading horror stories where kids are graduating from college owing eighty to one hundred thousand dollars. They can't afford to live on their own with that kind of debt, so they're moving back in with mom and dad."

"The amount of school debt is eventually going to affect the housing market," Glen said.

"I think it already has." Laurent leaned back in her chair and sipped her hot tea. "I see no financial motive for any member of the Martin family to kill Stephanie. What about tarnishing the golden image?"

"The Martins might have been embarrassed for a while, but the child would have been cherished by both families. Dylan is the only one with a motive to kill Stephanie. But I don't think he did. He's more like Emmit than he wants to admit. Life means something. Life has value. Life has purpose." Glen crossed one leg over the other. "I came across Dylan when he was learning to drive a tractor. A deer jumped out and ran into the tractor on East Road. The boy wasn't hurt, but the deer was still alive. Broken legs. I shot it. Dylan cried the whole time. He's got a soft heart inside the teenage rebellion. He'll go to college and come home a changed man. I can't see him killing his girlfriend, accidentally or not. If the rumors are true, he got another girl pregnant and helped her to take care of it. Even if Stephanie wanted to keep the child, he had time to talk her into getting rid of it. Wear her down. No reason to kill her."

"Dylan said in his interview he doesn't want to be a farmer, but if he changes his mind, he'll have lots of paid-off acreage. Caleb can't farm because of his allergies, and Morgan's a vet so Dylan gets the farm." Laurent finished her hot tea and tossed the tea bag into the wastebasket.

"Dylan's gonna be a farmer. He just doesn't know it yet. He'll go to college, major in agriculture, and realize he really does love farming. He doesn't know anything else. It's comfortable. He'll come back home." The former sheriff took off his reading glasses and twirled them by the stem. "I tried to find something on Vern. The man is off the grid financially. He owns nothing but his beat-up old pickup and the cabin and the two acres it sits on. No debt whatsoever. IRS reports little to no income for the last ten years. I talked with John Cook, and he claims Vern pays for everything in cash. Doesn't own a credit or debit card."

"He's old school. I bet Emmit hands him five one-hundred-dollar bills every month and he spends two of them on gas and groceries and hides the other three under his mattress. When I interviewed him, there were seven propane tanks in the mudroom and rows of canned goods, along with bags of pellets for his woodburning stove." With a sigh, Laurent pointed at the rest of the folders in Glen's lap. "Next."

"Pick your poison."

"Tillmans."

"Sad news all around." Glen folded his hands on top of the pile in his lap. "Some background first. Neal's wife left him fifteen years ago when Theo was about ten. Natasha leaving exacerbated an already tough situation. I never had a domestic disturbance call out there, but it wouldn't surprise me if that's why Natasha left. But, leaving Theo with his dad." He shook his head. "Theo was in and out of trouble, nothing serious, and he always paid the fine, served the community sentence, whatever was handed out. But Neal went downhill fast. Drinking and gambling. He and Theo live in that run-down farmhouse because neither can afford to get out. Theo makes a little over twenty thousand a year at Beaumon's and apparently eats it or smokes it and puts gas in that junker he drives. And he just got fired."

"He doesn't help out with bills?" Laurent raised an eyebrow.

"Mortgage is eight months past due, and all utilities are in arrears. As you know, from November through March thirty-first, the utility companies can't shut off power or gas. On April 1, the Tillmans won't have electricity or gas, which means no refrigerator or freezer, washer/dryer, stove, microwave, lights. Nothing. They can put gas in their vehicles, but they'll have to go to the library or someplace else to recharge their cell phones, assuming they're paying that bill. If they use a generator, they can keep the water pump going so they can shower and use the toilet."

"In less than two months, life is going to become very difficult for them. What do they gain by killing Stephanie?"

"Revenge, satisfaction, one last hurrah. The pleasure of getting away with it," Glen said.

"Are they that angry they would risk jail? I find that hard to believe."

"Neal's about as bitter as a man can get. He thinks life has handed him a raw deal and the world owes him. He's worked all his life, owes hundreds of thousands of dollars, and it's only going to get worse."

"Maybe jail is a better alternative. From that perspective, I understand intent and motive."

"Last thing about the Tillmans. Neal's old man didn't pay off the farm the way Emmit and Vern's dad did. Tillman inherited acreage with debt, and he's always resented the Martins for that," Glen said.

"How is that Emmit or Vern's fault?"

"That's what a twisted mind thinks. Years, even decades of resentment and anger built up."

"Is the windmill agreement going to solve Tillman's financial problems?"

"Temporarily, yes, and if he stays out of the casino. There's enough left over after paying off the casino to catch up on the mortgage and utilities. But the resentment factor in the community, no. He'll be hated now more than ever, as will Theo."

"This isn't Theo's fault."

"Sins of the father shall be visited upon the sons." Glen quoted the Bible.

"Have you left the best for last or the worst for last?"

Dak knocked and poked his head inside. "Sorry to interrupt. Bad news. Starr was found at the bottom of the basement stairs at village hall. Looks like a broken neck."

CHAPTER FORTY

MIKE GREENE CLOSED all of the blinds in Laurent's office before settling behind her desk and opening the first window on the bottom of her computer screen. Laurent had run out of the office after Dak told her the news about Starr and failed to shut down her computer. Budget stuff. Next window. Scheduling. Vacation requests. Overtime pay. He hated paperwork, but if he was going to be the new sheriff, he'd have to get used to it. In fact, he might learn to enjoy it.

He wanted her gone. He had been stunned when she won. Barely won. A few hundred votes in each county and he would have been sitting in this office, not in the squad room with everyone else. He wanted to throw her music stand out the window and kill her plants. Riding around in the SUV like it was hers. God, he hated Laurent. She had the nerve to call him in three times and bitch about some nitpicky bullshit. So what if he didn't get his reports in on time? Nothing happened in this little POS town anyway. And he didn't dare bitch about her to the other deputies. She had them snowballed. Some of them actually thought she was doing a good job. What idiots. Wait until he was in charge. Then they'd see what a piece of crap Laurent was.

On Laurent's first day of work, he called in sick and tried to convince a few other deputies to go along with him. Their own private protest. No one stayed home or supported him. No one had been willing to piss off the new sheriff or miss a day's pay because he lost the election. He was going to enjoy denying their vacation requests and messing with their schedules.

Next window. Stephanie Gattison's file was password protected. Next window. Bob Kane's file was also password protected. He leaned back and studied her desk. No one used pen and paper anymore, but he knew Laurent did. She kept a stack of yellow legal pads in the credenza behind her desk. Greene opened the middle drawer. Bingo. He extracted a yellow pad of paper with two names written on the top and a line down the middle with intersecting arrows. The way he read the paper told him Laurent thought there was a connection between Stephanie and Bob. He squinted at the arrows and snorted. Laurent didn't know what she was doing. Every arrow was coincidental. He shoved the pad back into the drawer.

Where would she keep her password file?

CHAPTER FORTY-ONE

LAURENT HATED THE smell of hospitals. She'd held her aunt's hand during chemo and when she took her last breath. When she thought about her aunt, the smell was in her nose even if she was nowhere near a hospital. "I'm going to sit and do some paperwork while Starr sleeps."

"Of course, Sheriff. Can I get you something to drink?" The nurses' station was less than ten feet from Starr's ICU room.

"I fixed myself some tea." Laurent held up her Yeti before slipping behind the curtain. She hesitated at the end of the bed.

Starr's neck was encased in a cervical collar, her left wrist in a cast. The left side of her face was dark-purple. An IV pole with a large bag of saline solution and another smaller bag of antibiotics hung on Starr's right side and fed into her forearm while a group of wires taped together snuck out from under the covers and were attached to the cardiac monitor. A pulse oximeter was clipped to her right index finger, which lay on top of the blankets.

Laurent pushed the curtain aside. "May I ask a few questions?"

"Shoot." The nurse stuck her hand under the automatic hand sanitizer machine. "Dr. Creighton has a medical release form Ms. Walters signed several years ago naming you as someone the hospital can talk to, and his office faxed it over this morning."

"I remember. Never thought it'd be of any use. Why the cardiac monitor?"

"She's morbidly obese and over fifty. She has a broken neck and broken wrist, along with severe contusions on both legs and arms and abdomen. It's really a precaution because we don't know how her body will respond to the shock of falling down a set of concrete stairs."

"How long will she be asleep?"

"I've just given her the painkiller. She should sleep for the next few hours and she'll be disoriented when she wakes up. Her body needs time to recuperate."

"How long will she be on painkillers?" Laurent asked.

"A few weeks."

"And the cervical collar?"

"Six weeks, possibly more. It will depend on how quickly she heals."

"When do you think she can go home?"

"It'll be a few days. We need to stabilize the neck area before we release her. She'll need help at home for a month or so."

Laurent nodded and slipped back into Starr's room. "Hello, my friend. I'm going to review some financial crap, and I thought you might like some company. Listen to me complain. Speak up if I sound like I'm lost or missing something. You're so much better at interpreting numbers than I am. Glen helped me with some of it and he said, no more, I'm going blind." Laurent's eyes filled with tears as she pulled the uncomfortable chair near the end of the bed, grabbed the food tray, lowered it, and opened her briefcase. And sneezed.

"Glen sorted all this paperwork. Most of it came from Farmers Bank, but he also pulled IRS records, credit card statements, car payment information, and mortgage information. One pile is for the Martin family. One pile is for the Tillmans, and he left me the biggest pile. Jim Cotter. Business and personal. Which one is going to be easier?" Laurent looked at her sleeping friend. "That's what I thought. Neither. Personal folder first."

"Here's what I've got. Today is February twentieth. Cotter's last mortgage payment was posted in August of last year. That puts him six months behind. Roughly, thirty-six thousand dollars. Utilities haven't been paid since November. Between electric, gas, and trash pickup, Cotter owes another thousand dollars. Must cost a lot to heat that mansion he lives in." Laurent pulled out a separate sheet of paper and started a column with the amount owed and the number of months behind. Not very accountant-like, but it worked for her.

"Car payments. He owes on the BMW Roadster—that can't be right. No car is worth two hundred thousand dollars." She clicked the pen. "Monthly payment is thirty-three hundred dollars, and he hasn't made a payment in the last year. Another forty thousand dollars. And look, BMW is threatening to repossess. I bet that ticked him off. He loves that car. Only one in the quad-counties."

She glanced at her tally sheet. Seventy-seven thousand dollars between mortgage, utilities, and the car. A shudder ran from her shoulders to her toes. "How does he sleep at night?"

Next page. "A two thousand nineteen Ford F-450. Ninety-six thousand and change. Jim put down five thousand dollars. Monthly payment is fifteen hundred, and he's current. Of course, he's only had the truck for two months. He shouldn't be behind. Forty-eight hundred a month for vehicles, plus gas and maintenance. Any repairs on luxury vehicles is expensive. Wonder what his insurance deductible is."

"Credit cards. American Express, Visa, Mastercard, Discover, Neiman Marcus, Bloomingdales, Home Depot, Beaumon's Hardware and Lumber. He owes over one hundred thousand dollars to credit card companies. Unbelievable." Laurent peered at Starr. "Good thing you can't see this. It'd give you a heart attack."

"He's only making the minimum payment on his credit cards, except for Beaumon's, the pharmacy, and the grocery store. All local. He doesn't want anyone to know he's in debt. Who does he think he's kidding?"

"Last few pages. The IRS. Please, please, please, pay your taxes." Laurent continued reading. "The IRS is placing a lien on his property. What a dumb shit. I wonder if the IRS notified Farmers Bank and told them they were now the second lienholder, not the first. I bet Bob knew. Jim was his best friend. Did he bring it up the last time they were fishing? What'd you think Jim did? I confirmed his visit to the currency exchange, and I assumed it was business, but now, I'm not so sure." Laurent pushed the food tray away. "I'm afraid to look at his business expenses."

An hour later, Laurent read her tally sheet. The business expenses weren't as bad as she'd feared because Jim closed his office and used the village offices for his legal practice. She wondered if Starr or anyone at the village had been aware of this or if they had gotten used to seeing him around. She was guessing he wasn't paying any rent to the village.

Over two hundred thousand dollars were past due, the IRS placed a lien on his property, and BMW was threatening to repossess his car. Jim needed money. Where was he going to get it? The income he claimed on his tax returns had decreased steadily, and the most recent return showed income of less than three hundred thousand dollars. What had happened to Jim and his law practice and did the crushing amount of debt drive him to murder?

Laurent brushed away the thought, got to her feet, and stretched. Bob and Jim were best friends and had been for a long time. There had to be another explanation. Jim had no staff, no secretary, and did his own billing, but the most recent accounts receivables she could find in the bank's records were from November 2018. Did he forget to bill his clients in December and January? No way. Lawyers kept timesheets within arm's reach on their desks or had a window open on the bottom of their computers. A two-minute phone call was billed at the quarter-hour rate. He must have a big payout coming soon and treated himself to a couple of months off. That was why there was no A/R for the last two months. Or business was slow during the holidays.

Laurent shoved all her paperwork into her briefcase. She paused next to Starr's hospital bed. "I got another request from Randi. I realize now what a chicken I was the other night, but I think you're right. Meet her, see what she wants, and go from there. I'm afraid of what people might think if they knew I gave up a daughter thirty years ago. You know this community. A bit judgmental, a lot traditional. Of course, I could drive down there and then no one in the quad-counties would find out. What'd you think? Anyway, you better wake up soon. I'm going to need that accountant brain of yours to help me put all these pieces together. I know how much you like jigsaw puzzles."

CHAPTER FORTY-TWO

"I'VE GOT YOUR DNA results. The tissue under the victim's finger-nails matches Theo M. Tillman, one of the voluntary DNA samples you sent. We don't have a match for the other sample, but we'll keep both on file." The head of Indiana's CSU was on speakerphone in Laurent's SUV.

"I was expecting this." Laurent parked the SUV in the grocery store parking lot, crumpled *The Crossing*, and threw it onto the floor. Ralph's most recent infuriating innuendos would have to wait.

"We also confirmed the pregnancy test, but we didn't scan for a paternity match," Whitmore said.

"Dylan Martin has admitted to being the father."

"The victim scratched the Tillman suspect, but the Martin suspect got her pregnant," Whitmore said. "Alibis?"

"Flimsy for both suspects."

"I've spent hours poring over the photos you sent. I'm assuming the victim was unconscious when she froze to death?" Whitmore asked.

"The autopsy report can't declare the state of consciousness, but her heart stopped beating before severe frostbite set in. Because we found her in a burrowed state, Dr. Creighton thinks the body took over and tried to live. She had no defensive wounds and didn't try to claw her way out of the snowbank, so we think she was unconscious."

"Almost like going to sleep and not waking up."

"Except for the dents in the head. I confiscated hammers from both suspects and sent them to your lab. Did you find anything?"

"The results came in an hour ago. All negative. No human hair or DNA on any of them. When I ran the specs for the dents through our database, we came up with everything on your list. Hammers are a perfect fit with that size and depth."

"That leaves me the boot tread."

"It's a shoe tread."

"Who goes out in a blizzard without boots?" Laurent asked.

"Thom Browne wingtips, size thirteen, recently polished. Find him. He might have been the last person to see your victim alive."

After hanging up with the head of CSU, Laurent googled the shoe. Who spent six hundred dollars on a pair of shoes?

She exited the grocery store parking lot and turned north on Field Street, her fingers tapping on the steering wheel. Expensive shoes. Size thirteen. A tall man. A wealthy man. Banker, lawyer, dentist, doctor. Men who sat behind a desk all day. The more she thought about the shoe, the more professions came to mind. Who would Stephanie have come into contact with? Her teachers and Dr. Yoshida, the principal. Brent Kessel, store manager. Jim Cotter. A customer at Beaumon's. Someone at the village. Laurent shook her head. Not the principal. He was too short. Would Vern wear shoes in a blizzard without boots? No way. Would Vern wear expensive shoes? She snorted to herself. Again, no. Dylan? Teenagers wore tennis shoes without boots, and on the farm, he'd have a pair of boots by the back door. Theo? She was pretty sure she remembered seeing holes in his sneakers. Laurent sighed. The shoe tread eliminated her prime suspects for Stephanie's murder. *Damn.*

She turned into the Skillet parking lot, parked behind the building, and waited. Art's and Dutch's pickups sat side by side, a light dusting of snow covering the roofs and windshields. The two old farmers left the Skillet between eleven and eleven thirty every morning. And there they were. She hopped out of her SUV and strolled toward the two friends, stopping at the driver's door of Art's pickup.

"What can we do for you, Sheriff? Here's a list of the people we know who ice fish." Art pulled a folded piece of paper out of his pocket and handed it to her.

"Don't read anything into my question, but who in the quad-county area wears expensive shoes? The type you have to polish and shine."

"Lots of guys," Dutch said. "But they only wear them to church."

"Who wears them on an everyday basis, and where do you buy shoe polish?"

"You have to order shoe polish from Brent at Beaumon's," Art said. "But all of the professional men—doctors, lawyers, bankers, the dentist, the orthodontist, village trustees, principals, teachers, and pharmacists."

Laurent glanced at the list, folded it, and stuck it in her pocket.

"Jim was in for breakfast, and he was talkin' smack about you," Dutch said.

"Talking smack about me? Did your grandson teach you that?" Laurent raised her eyebrows. Slang sounded weird coming from a senior citizen.

"I kinda like it. Feels like a slap in the face."

"What's he saying?"

"That you're not gonna arrest anyone until after you get reelected and you're doing it on purpose. Me and Art were the only ones around and neither of us believe it."

"Why's he spreading this rumor?"

"Maybe he wants Greene elected."

* * *

"What in the hell do you think you're doing?" Laurent filled the doorway to her office and glared at Greene.

His hand gripped the mouse on her desk. "My computer is slow and I wanted to finish this report before I clocked out." He jumped to his feet.

"Use Ingram's computer. He's still out with a cold." Laurent stepped back to let her deputy leave her office. Slamming the door, she rounded the desk and bumped her knee on the slightly open desk drawer.

What had Greene accessed? She had left her email open, along with the current duty roster and schedule and the one she was working on for April. The budget and approved invoices program was also open. She had password protected Stephanie's and Bob's files. Only Dr. Creighton, herself, Dak, and Glen were aware of the results and implications. Henry might be able to guess, but he was a tight-lipped funeral director.

Nothing on her computer raised any flags. Clicking the mouse, she opened her browser history and noted the web addresses Greene attempted to access. *Snoopy little bastard.* Laurent printed out the history with the recorded time and date stamps, and slid it into a folder. Evidence. Greene was smart to use her office computer. Any trace would lead directly back to her.

She leaned back and stared at the ceiling. After running out of the office, she had forgotten to shut down her computer. Anyone in the department could have accessed it, but it looked like Greene was the only one who had. She pulled out the browser list and smoothed it on her desk. Whoever had sat here accessed her reelection website, Farmers Bank, Facebook, and a few other sites, all relating to her. Why?

Laurent kicked the underside of her desk. Ralph called earlier in the day asking for a comment before he ran a story. Now she knew why. Glen had warned her, but she never thought one of her own deputies would stoop so low as to try and hack into her campaign fund. There were no cameras in the detective's squad room or her office, and, short of dusting her mouse for fingerprints, she couldn't prove Greene had accessed her account. The trace would show the request had come from her office computer.

Laurent drummed her fingers on her desk before picking up the phone. "Naomi, put a trace on Greene's computer, password, and login. I want to know all of the websites he visits using the office computers."

"Do you want a GPS trace on his vehicle also?" Naomi Jackson ran the entire IT department for the sheriff's office. Her office was on the lower level of the building, and the middle-aged IT woman claimed she liked the peace and quiet, especially when the prisoner cells were empty, as they usually were. She also loved new technology.

"Yes. From January first of this year to present day."

"Any reason why?"

"I think he's leaking information."

"Small-town politics suck, don't they? What fired up this request?"

"Ralph from *The Crossing* called and asked for a statement from me regarding the audit from the State Election Board," Laurent said. "The board called me only one-half hour earlier so either someone blabbed today or someone read my email. When I got back from the bank, I found Greene behind my desk."

"I'm sending you today's list of websites Greene accessed from your computer while you were gone. You might want to get a copy of the video security cameras from the hospital to coordinate with your time out of the office. You can't be in two places at one time," Naomi said. "Your computer doesn't have remote access. You have to be at your desk in order to use it."

"Excellent suggestion."

"Why is the election board auditing your account?"

"I asked myself the same question. After the last election, I had less than one hundred dollars in the account, so I left it. It has earned about ten cents in interest," Laurent said.

"And you have all your paid invoices from the last campaign?"

"Electronic file on my laptop and a paper copy at home."

"I don't understand what he's trying to achieve, but I'll start the search and keep the file down here with me."

Laurent hung up the phone and leaned back. What was Greene looking for? Dirt. Anything to incriminate her. Anything to get himself elected sheriff. She was glad she kept all of her personal and campaign information at home. There was no way she could be accused of using taxpayer dollars for her own personal benefit or gain. Ralph's search for campaign violations at her summer concerts must have come up empty. Greene was desperate. No deputy would use her office to file a report. Just wouldn't happen. *But then, Greene has no respect for me or anyone else in this department, except maybe Dak, and that could be because Dak is a fitness fanatic.* She slapped her desk. How do you fire someone who has been here longer than you? The union would fight her every step of the way. Was it worth it? Right now, yes.

Laurent rose and walked to the window. Dusk was falling and lights were clicking on behind curtained windows and blinds. She leaned her forehead against the cold windowpane. Why was Jim Cotter bad-mouthing her? What did he gain with Greene in charge?

CHAPTER FORTY-THREE

"She caught me."

Greene and Ralph stood smoking outside Bubba's Steakhouse. The sun had set, and the overhead streetlights reflected on the mounds of snow. The two men tossed their cigarettes into a snowbank before entering the restaurant and sliding into a booth.

"What the fuck?" Ralph glared at his best friend.

"I was sitting at her desk using her computer trying to get into her campaign fund when she walked in," Greene said.

"What'd you say?"

"I lied. Said my computer was slow and I was trying to finish up a report before going home."

"Did she buy it?"

"Of course. All of us complain about the slow internet in the office. She always says there's no money in the budget for upgrades. That's the first thing I'll change when I get elected. But, guess what I found?" Greene slid a piece of paper across the white tablecloth.

"Are you shitting me?" Ralph's angry eyebrows shot up to his receding hairline.

"She's so stupid. No one prints out their passwords and stores it in a file marked passwords."

"Did you try any of these?"

"I didn't have time. She might have the logins and passwords automatically connected, especially the bank. I think you should try to get access from a public computer like the library. We don't want anything traced back to our personal computers." Greene took a swig of his beer and wiped his mouth on his sleeve. "What'd she say when you asked for a comment?"

"She went all noble and said the election board was within their rights to check. I bet she's in her office or at home frantically moving money."

"Better if she does it at the office. Getting paid for work and using that time to work on her campaign is a big no-no. We've got her." The two men clinked beer bottles.

"Is this her garage code? Who has to write that down?" Ralph asked. "Is Laurent getting dementia?"

"You can't allege dementia based on this piece of paper. We're not supposed to have it."

Ralph folded the paper and stuck it in his wallet. "I'm not stupid, but if this is her code . . ." He winked.

"Are you thinking of breaking and entering?"

"Just entering."

* * *

One thing Ralph had learned from living in and reporting on small towns was no one liked change. Especially the older generation. Anyone fifty and over struggled with technology. Ralph wondered how many times he had heard the complaint "It was fine. Why'd they have to change it?" or "No one thinks like that. What do you mean it's intuitive?" He wasn't a hacker, but, with a password or user name and basic information, he could dig up dirt on whoever he chose.

Tonight, he chose Sheriff Jhonni Laurent.

A copy of the handwritten piece of paper with Laurent's passwords and user IDs lay on the table next to one of the library's four public computers. Ralph typed in Laurent's campaign website address. It was a simple one-page site with three headings and a picture of a much-younger Laurent. He clicked on "Education and Accomplishments" and scrolled through. Nothing interesting or noteworthy. He clicked on the next heading, "Goals," and found campaign rhetoric. The last heading was the one he was interested in. "Contributions and Donations." He clicked on it.

The page was a standard payment/billing page. Name and address. Billing information. Disclaimer at the bottom. He printed it out. Online payments weren't going to work. The donations he sought were in cash.

Ralph rested his elbows on the table. Did he dare look into Laurent's bank account? Her password and user name stared at him from the paper next to the desk.

Farmersbank.com.

User ID.

Password.

How many laws was he breaking? And did it matter? He'd never get caught, and if he did, the new sheriff, Greene, would let him slide.

He inhaled and hit ENTER.

CHAPTER FORTY-FOUR

OPINION/EDITORIAL PAGE
INVESTIGATION INTO SHERIFF'S CAMPAIGN FUNDS

February 22, 2019
Field's Crossing, Indiana
by Ralph Howard

> *Citing an anonymous source, the Indiana Election Board is auditing Sheriff Jhonni Laurent's campaign fund presently held by Farmers Bank. An election official made an unannounced visit to the bank this week. Laurent doesn't have a campaign office, and when asked if he'll search Laurent's home, the official declined to comment.*
>
> *The timing of this audit is bad for Laurent. She's running against longtime and favored Deputy Sheriff Mike Greene, and the election is eleven days away. With her campaign manager, Starr Walters, in the hospital with a neck injury, Laurent must face the election board and their questions without support.*
>
> *Will she stay in the race or bow out?*

The ethical thing to do is to bow out until the State Board of Elections sorts out this mess. Will the state have the audit completed before the election? Probably not. The citizens of the quad-county area shouldn't be saddled with a potentially dishonest public official, let alone the sheriff whose main job is to enforce the law. How difficult will it be to remove her? Will the citizens have to pay for a special election?

What is the state going to find? Is it a matter of illegal accounting methods or a question of campaign contributions? Are the same people making contributions over and over? What is the maximum amount an individual may contribute to a candidate's campaign? Has anyone exceeded that amount? How many contributions are in cash? How many are anonymous? It will be the state's task to find answers to all of these questions and levy fines.

Laurent has issued a statement saying the state is well within their right to examine her campaign fund and she's certain she's in complete compliance. She claims she can produce any paperwork requested by the board.

In the interests of fairness to the citizens of the quad-county area, and while the result of the audit is in question, Laurent should remove herself from the ballot and save the voters from potential dishonesty and certain uncertainty.

CHAPTER FORTY-FIVE

LAURENT SLAMMED HER office door, rattling the blinds. She wasn't used to dirty campaign tricks or politics. She accessed her account online and the balance was the same as last month. Ninety-four dollars and thirty-two cents. Where were these "illegal donations" Ralph claimed were in her account? No one had contributed a single dollar in the last four years. Laurent printed out the last three months of bank statements, blacked out her vital information, and scanned the documents. She was debating whether or not to post her account statements on her campaign website. She didn't want to disturb Starr with the question, even though she knew when her friend read the latest edition of *The Crossing*, she'd be spitting mad.

Laurent didn't know how to fight the blatant lies and innuendos claimed by *The Crossing*. Four years ago, Ralph and Greene hadn't attempted to discredit her because they both thought Greene was going to win the election. Since then, Greene had been less than an ideal employee, and Ralph had been outright rude and mean, his reporting stopping just short of slander.

Laurent didn't want to get into a "shouting" match with either her opponent or the media, but how did you fight the media when they were biased? By publishing the truth. The problem with living in a small town was that citizens from the older generation tended to believe whatever was in print was true. The internet was wrong.

How could she let the residents of the quad-county area know she wasn't a cheater or a liar? She pillowed her arms, laid her forehead on her wrist, and closed her eyes. What was she going to do? Murders, reelection, and a request to meet from her daughter. It was too much at one time. She'd have to count on the intelligence of the farming community and their ability to perceive lies and deceit from truthfulness. She needed to trust the residents of the quad-counties to be able to discern the best candidate for the job of sheriff.

The best method was word-of-mouth. Despite distances, the farming community was tight-knit. Laurent sat up and blew her nose before opening the file cabinet and extracting a map of the quad-county area. She'd have to find time, even with a murder investigation, to make her rounds. Stop in at all of her usual haunts and spend time with residents. The best way to counteract *The Crossing*'s allegations was time, not money.

CHAPTER FORTY-SIX

HE WASN'T A thief. He wasn't going to take anything. Just walk around and look. Ralph's cell phone vibrated.

"Laurent in office. Two hours. Will advise upon change."

He closed the text from Greene.

Ralph exited out of Webster Park onto the Five-and-Twenty. Ten minutes later, he turned into Laurent's driveway and put the rented Chevy Envoy into park. His heart was pounding, and sweat ran down his back. He surveyed the house. No exterior cameras, no motion detectors, and no sign advertising a security system. He tugged on a black ski mask and baseball hat, and slipped through the snow to the garage. Fingers shaking, he manually keyed in the garage code.

The door opened.

Sprinting back to the rental, he slipped in the snow and landed on one knee, ripping a hole in his jeans. He parked inside the garage, and sat swearing and pounding the steering wheel. Ralph clicked on his flashlight and dropped it. Reaching down, he bumped his head on the steering wheel. He wiped his sweaty palms on his jeans before pulling on his gloves. His pulse jumped in his temple. *God, I'm nervous.*

The garage smelled old and musty and the side window was cracked. The recycling bin and a regular garbage can sat next to the door leading to the house. The rest of the garage held a bench with a few tools, gardening tools, rakes, a couple of shovels, three different sized ladders, a Fat Tire bicycle, and a small air compressor. He had all of this in his garage, except for the bike. Touching a button on the wall, he closed the garage door. *Don't want anyone driving by to see a strange vehicle in the sheriff's garage.*

Ralph shone his flashlight on the connecting door. No keypad. Opening the door, he stepped into the mudroom. Same old stuff. Washer, dryer, hooks, and a few shelves. He paused at the edge of the kitchen. The slight smell of burnt toast lingered, along with the smell of an orange. A few crumbs remained on the countertop. Walking through the kitchen, he glanced to the left. Closed French doors. He turned the doorknob. Locked. Ralph peered inside. The walls were lined with bookcases filled with scores and music and books. Framed art hung from every square inch. What he was looking for wouldn't be in there.

Stepping into the living room, he stood in the middle of the room. The furniture sat on a large area rug, and sunlight streamed in through a three-sided bay window. One recliner looked well worn, a blanket thrown over the back, and the end table was piled with a stack of books and magazines. The flat screen on the far wall was flanked on both sides by overflowing bookcases.

Nothing. Except the faint smell of a cigar.

Laurent led a relatively private life, but everyone had a secret. The sheriff was no exception.

He walked past the downstairs bath and climbed the stairs to the second floor. A bedroom on each side of the hallway, another bathroom, and at the end of the hallway lay the master bedroom. The spare bedrooms were sparse. Bed, dresser, lamp, desk, ceiling fan, and empty closets.

Taking a deep breath, he opened the door to Laurent's bedroom. The overwhelming odor of cigar smoke assaulted his nostrils. He coughed. The ashtray next to the bed held a half-smoked cigar and a little ash. A bottle of hand cream stood next to the ashtray.

The room was large, almost as though two bedrooms had been combined into one big one. The bedroom was located at the front of the house over the first-floor screened-in porch. A large picture window overlooked the snow-covered gardens, and dark curtains hung on both sides. The bed was made, the floor carpeted, the closet door closed. A corner section of the bedroom was dedicated as an office. Desk and computer. Filing cabinet.

Bingo.

Ralph pulled out the chair and flipped through the file cabinet. Alphabetical. Credit card bills, insurance, utilities. The top drawer told him nothing other than Laurent paid her bills on time and carried no debt, other than the mortgage on the property.

Opening the bottom drawer, he held his breath. Campaign information and donor lists. He pulled out his phone and started snapping pictures. Half an hour later, he closed the drawer. It would take a while to decipher all of the photos and information he had taken pictures of, but he was sure Laurent's secret was in this drawer.

He closed the file cabinet and moved the chair back. Anything else? Ralph opened the closet door, peered in, and shut it again. The woman was a neatnick. Uniforms on one side, street clothes on the other, and organized by color. Last piece of furniture. Nightstand. Ignoring the ashtray, he opened the drawer and flipped through a few gardening magazines and noted the earmarked articles on "vertical farming" and "hydroponic gardening." Was the woman planning on revolutionizing the farming industry? He lifted the magazines out and shuffled through a few envelopes. He snapped a picture and slid out a letter.

"Gotcha."

CHAPTER FORTY-SEVEN

"I THINK HE'S giving the finger to the rest of us farmers. Neal signed the agreement with Renewable Energy to pay off his gambling debt. That's what I heard. Going to a casino and gambling away your farm. No self-control, no taking responsibility, always blaming the other guy." Emmit snorted. "Piece of shit."

"I get it. You don't like Neal and, by signing this agreement, he's screwed every farmer around. If you remember, last spring a guy from Renewable Farm Energy stopped by the house. They'd like my north field because of the access to the interstate. That's my best field, but they're not getting a thing," Owen said.

Vern relaxed in the chair and sipped his coffee. Old friends were the best. Even sad old friends. He and Emmit were meeting Art and Dutch and Owen at ten thirty in the morning for coffee at the Skillet after Owen and Theresa were finished at the funeral home. Hearing Emmit espouse his familiar hatred of windmill farms and Art and Dutch arguing over anything and everything soothed him. He had missed this.

"Have you talked to anybody else about this?" Emmit asked.

"No, but I asked the guy and he pulled out a list of all the farmers in the quad-county area and had them ranked according to size and location. You and I are at the top of the list because we own the most acres and we're closest to the highway."

"How long of a stretch do they need?" Emmit tucked a wad of Red Man's chewing tobacco in the side of his mouth and slid the red, white, and black bag into his pocket.

"I didn't ask. Why don't you just buy out Neal?" Owen asked.

"Remember what happened last time I tried? He shot out both rear tires on my pickup. Drove off and left me standing there. I had to call Jane to come and get me and send a tow truck. Asshole wouldn't pay for the new tires. What do you suppose his response will be this time, especially since Renewable gave him money up front?"

"I'm going to play devil's advocate. Don't take my head off." Owen held up a hand. "Part of my problem is I don't understand how wind makes electricity."

"It's the opposite of a fan. The wind turns the blades, which spins a shaft, which connects to a generator and makes electricity. The first documented windmills and water wheels were invented in Persia between 500 and 900 BC for pumping water and grinding grain," Vern said.

"Vern, you're spending way too much time by yourself," Art said.

"What happens when one breaks?" Emmit asked. "Do we have to have a road next to them so the repair guy can get there? What if one of those big arms stops rotating or falls off and they have to put on a new one? That'll take a damn semi. Who has to maintain the roads? You know they're going to stick the taxpayer with that one."

"The energy supplied by a wind farm reduces the environmental impact from fossil fuel sources," Owen said. "We're messing up this planet with our gas-powered machines and plastic and batteries and stuff. Those products are never going to disintegrate, and even if they do, how will the earth absorb them? What'll that do to our farmland?

"I saw a picture of a barge stacked with flattened rusty old vehicles. The barge goes into the middle of the ocean and dumps all those old pieces of junk right into the water. Whad'ya suppose that's going to do to all the fishes? Eventually, it's going to work its way back to the water supply. My last point is this—farmers are going to have to produce more as the world's population increases and that's going to get harder and harder if we keep spoiling the earth." Owen picked up his coffee cup. "Now my devil's hat is off."

"You're an environmentalist at heart, aren't you?" Dutch asked.

"I don't believe for one stinking minute those windmills are going to generate enough electricity for this whole county," Emmit said. "When they bury those transmission lines, they're going to break the drain tile. Who pays for that? What if they fix it and it's wrong? Dig up our cornfields to bury pipes with wires in them? What's that going to do to our yield? It sure as hell ain't going up."

"Even if it stays the same or goes down a little," Art said, "the money you receive for leasing the land doesn't offset any loss in bushels per acre, and it ruins the farmland. It would take years for the soil to get back to the way it used to be."

"My point exactly," Emmit said. "What about all the fuel trucks supplying diesel to the cranes to build the damn things? How is that reducing emissions?"

The bell above the door to the Skillet rattled, and Theresa Gattison and Jane Martin walked in.

"Done kibitzing?" Jane asked.

"We don't kibitz. We talk, discuss, argue, you know," Dutch said.

Emmit shrugged into his coat and yanked on his baseball hat. "I think Neal signed this agreement to piss me off."

"He wins that round," Owen said. "How long before the two of you bury the hatchet?"

"We'll probably go to our grave hating each other, and neither one will remember why."

Vern touched his brother on the sleeve. "Just a sec. Ralph dropped by the cabin the other day and accused me and you of buying Dylan's freedom with campaign contributions to Sheriff Laurent."

"That sonofabitch. I'm going to write Laurent a big fat check, and then I'm going to sue *The Crossing*."

"For what?"

"Impugning my integrity and false accusations against Dylan. I've had it with that little asshole saying anything he wants and getting away with it."

CHAPTER FORTY-EIGHT

LAURENT SWITCHED HER intermittent wipers up one notch. Light snow had fallen during the day as she drove throughout the quad-counties, but her anxiety over the election eased. Everyone expected biased reporting from *The Crossing*. The newspaper was the butt of jokes throughout Towson, Rogers, Little, and Alexander Counties. She relaxed into the heated seat and drove with one hand on the bottom of the steering wheel of her little red truck. She had bought the used 2013 Chevy Colorado two years ago to haul shrubs, small trees, and mulch when she had started her perennial gardens and was looking forward to planting spring and summer annuals. Laurent was ready for winter to be over but knew Mother Nature wouldn't let go easily.

Turning into her driveway, she noticed the new-fallen snow sparkled under the overhead streetlamp at the end of her driveway and two sets of fresh tire tracks led in and out of her garage. She wasn't expecting any packages. Who had pulled in and left? She pressed the garage door opener. Snow-filled tire tracks and footprints lay on the garage floor.

Someone had been in her garage. Her house.

Was that someone still here? Laurent pulled out her cell phone and called the dispatch operator. The footprints led to and from the keypad on the side of the garage door. Who had her garage code? She dialed Glen. "Did you stop by my place today?"

"No, why?"

"Someone was here while I was at work. There are tire tracks and footprints in the garage."

"Who has your code?"

"Me, you, Starr, dispatch," Laurent said.

"What did dispatch say?"

"They haven't given it out and both dispatchers aren't even sure they know where it is."

"Have you checked inside yet?"

"I was about to."

"Wait for me. I'll be there in ten. Don't shoot anyone."

Half an hour later, Glen and Laurent stood in her kitchen. "Anything missing?"

"He rifled through the filing cabinet in my bedroom. There's nothing but bills and old campaign stuff in there."

"Music room?" Glen asked.

"Locked. Whoever it was didn't get in there or didn't want to get in there."

"Do you think this has anything to do with either Bob's or Stephanie's murder, or is it personal? Who have you been talking to? Piss anyone off lately?"

"I talk to everybody. You know that. This makes no sense. Who would dare to break in and search my house?" Laurent sank into a kitchen chair.

"The bigger question might be—what were they looking for?"

After Glen left, Laurent threw the dead bolts on the garage door, back door, and front door and switched into old jeans and an even older T-shirt. The thought of someone in her house . . . She shuddered. There'd be no sleeping tonight until she scrubbed every surface. She felt dirty. Violated. What had he touched? Did he use her bathroom? She pulled on gloves and a mask and started with the downstairs bathroom. Every light in the farmhouse was on and she opened the French doors to her music room and turned the volume up, classical music pouring through the in-home speaker system.

As she scrubbed, an image of a masked intruder circled through her mind. Over and over. She wanted to see his face. Bash it in. Exhaling, she leaned back on her heels and glared at the bathroom floor. Should she wash it again? Goddamn it. He had violated her sanctuary. How long would it be before she felt comfortable again? Safe in her own home? She had never been the victim of this type of crime and didn't like it. Not one bit. While she had been glad-handing and seeking votes, someone had stolen her peace of mind. That someone would pay.

She gasped. Springing to her feet, she flew up the stairs and yanked open the drawer on her nightstand. Did he find the letters? Laurent stared at the jumble in the drawer. The envelopes were still under the magazines. Did he pull the letters out of the envelopes and read them? With trembling fingers, she picked up the pile and examined the two requests. The return address was stamped directly in the upper left-hand corner, her address in the middle of the envelope. It didn't take a genius to figure it out. She flopped onto her bed and stared at the ceiling. Whoever the intruder was, she'd know in a day or two. He wouldn't get any information out of the adoption agency, but he could search her past. Thirty years was a long time, but hospitals kept records. She had arrived with the baby, but after that ... The police report. You didn't have to be a genius to figure out what happened next.

CHAPTER FORTY-NINE

THE CALL HAD been brief. "Five a.m. Your office."

Laurent closed the door behind her and faced the two men at her desk.

"I am relieving you of duty, pending investigation. Glen Atkins will act as interim sheriff. Badge and gun on the desk."

"How long?" She choked out the two words.

The state's attorney's brusque words hit her like a sledgehammer, driving out all the air in her lungs. She couldn't talk. Her chest was caught in a vise and breathing was painful.

"Election fraud, illegal contributions. These accusations are serious. There's no way of telling."

"The accusations are bullshit," Glen snapped. "Be quick about it. I'm retired and I want to stay that way." He placed Laurent's gun and badge in a desk drawer, slammed it shut, and pointed at the state's attorney. "Get to work."

Blinking back tears, Laurent ran down the front stairs of the sheriff's office and paused, looking up and down County Street. The overhead streetlights were still on as the sun had not yet risen. Even the Skillet wasn't open yet.

Laurent kicked a pile of snow and stomped south on County Street. Shock turned into anger. *Goddamn Ralph!* She never thought he'd stoop so low as to file a complaint with the election board. Or did Greene file the complaint? Laurent imagined the faces of both men and gave them the finger, a short, jerky uppercut in midair, not caring who saw her.

What was she going to do?

Her face burned and her throat tightened as humiliation swept through her. It was Saturday morning and too late for today's edition of *The Crossing*, but Sunday's headlines would be brutal. Thinking about it hurt. Laurent crossed Woodruff Street and continued stalking down County Street. At the rate she was marching, she'd reach Bees Creek Road . . .

What about the Gattisons?

She'd let them down. She failed the entire community. Laurent hunched her shoulders and let the tears flow. Putting her hands on her knees, she bent over, the pain blasting through her as she cried more than breathed. Sobbing in the middle of the sidewalk in the ice-cold air of February in Indiana. A minute passed. Another.

Finally, she sucked in air. And slowly stood. Her nose ran. Her cheeks were drenched in tears. Her throat closed, every breath painful.

Today would not be her last day as sheriff. She wasn't going without a fight. Ralph and Greene be damned. On Monday morning, the first thing she was going to do was get a copy of the complaint. But right now, she was going to visit the Gattisons and Shelby Kane. She'd find out who killed their family members, with or without the badge.

CHAPTER FIFTY

OPINION/EDITORIAL PAGE
SHERIFF LAURENT RELIEVED OF DUTY
RETIRED GLEN ATKINS APPOINTED AS INTERIM
SHERIFF

February 24, 2019
Field's Crossing, Indiana
by Ralph Howard

In a stunning and swift decision by the Indiana Election Board, a recommendation to place Sheriff Jhonni Laurent on suspended duty was accepted by the Indiana State Police. The suspension is effective immediately. Retired Sheriff Glen Atkins has been appointed as interim sheriff for the quad-county area.

The residents of the quad-counties should applaud the decision by the election board to rid the citizens of the grossly incompetent Sheriff Laurent. Since taking over four years ago, her ineptness has manifested itself in all areas, and now, campaign fraud.

Cheating to win an election. Fortunately for the citizens of the quad-county area, the election is next week and, after Deputy Mike Greene is elected, the bungling sheriff's department will be in capable hands.

CHAPTER FIFTY-ONE

He was going to get away with it. Two deaths. A clerk with a broken neck. He tossed the Sunday newspaper on the floor and relaxed back in his leather chair. He wouldn't have to run this time and could continue embezzling, living his luxurious lifestyle. Laurent wouldn't be able to figure it out and anything Starr Walters claimed after she regained consciousness would be unreliable, the babbling of a confused, middle-aged woman.

He had retrieved the box of papers Stephanie was scanning into the archives and shredded them, one at a time, in his paper shredder at home. He then accessed the village's archives and deleted the folder with the scanned-in documents. His embezzlement scheme was covered and the only one who might have been able to figure it out was lying unconscious in a hospital bed in another county. If she wasn't back to work within a month, he'd recommend a replacement. Starr could begin receiving her lifetime pension, and he could continue stealing from the town. He wondered who he should recruit as Starr's replacement. It would have to be someone who'd lived in Field's Crossing for a long time and would trust him implicitly. Not question anything he did. How he moved money. What bills he paid and when he paid them.

His phone call to the state's attorney suggesting an investigation produced the expected result, and the continued bashing in *The Crossing* all but insured Greene would win the election next week. And next Monday, the day before the election, *The Crossing* would run the article about Laurent's illegitimate daughter, the proverbial straw that broke the camel's back.

He was safe. Stronger than ever.

CHAPTER FIFTY-TWO

LAURENT CLOSED THE French doors to her music room and tuned her cello. Early morning was her favorite time to practice, and she rose while it was still dark outside. The shock of Saturday's suspension hadn't faded. Not one bit.

The depths to which her deputy would go to get elected astonished her. She had completely misjudged his hatred of her. It was one thing to imply she didn't know what she was doing and stab her in the back via *The Crossing*. It was entirely another thing to file a complaint with the election board.

She had driven to the Gattison farm on Saturday afternoon and been unable to contain the tears as she told them about her suspension. Owen and Theresa Gattison cried with her. Each caught up in their own misery. Same with Shelby Kane. Then she had driven home, strapped on her cross-country skis, and skied around Turtle Lake. Twice. Finally exhausted enough to sleep.

Watching the strings on her cello resonate, Laurent finished tuning and settled into her chair. The sheet music on the stand was open to the passage she was currently working on. She warmed up. Scales. Arpeggios. Fast, slow. Faster, softer. Slow, loud. After warming up, she lifted her head and concentrated on the music in front of her.

On the table on her right lay a pen and a yellow legal pad, the top page blank.

She practiced twenty measures at a time. And then repeated it. As many as ten times until it was perfect and she could close her eyes and play it from memory. Then she backtracked to the opening of the movement and played it from the beginning. Perfectly. Ten times. When she was sure she had her part down pat, she put on headphones and played along with the recording. Occasionally, she stopped and wrote herself a note on the legal pad.

Three hours later, she was making too many mistakes and knew it was time to quit. Laurent wiped down her cello and bow and returned them to the case. Her music room had become hot and stuffy, and as she opened the French doors, she inhaled the fresher, cooler air.

She wasn't ready to look at her notes, so she dropped the yellow pad on the end table next to her recliner in the living room and wandered into the kitchen to make tea. Laurent poured the hot water from the kettle into the pot, cut up an entire lemon, and dropped the Lipton teabag into her cup. Lifting a spoon from the silverware drawer and a bowl of Cinnamon Toast Crunch with no milk, she carried her breakfast into the living room. She needed some caffeine after her morning practice session.

Laurent sank into her recliner and tore off the top sheet of the yellow pad and titled the next page PUTTING IT ALL TOGETHER. All of the evidence she and Dr. Creighton sent to CSU had resulted in a big, fat zero. Except for the shoe tread. None of the boots or shoes from either the Martin family or the Tillman family fit the image she snapped on her phone.

After visiting the Gattisons and before the residents of the quad-counties knew about her suspension, Laurent had contacted all of the retail shoe and boot stores in the four counties. She had spoken with department managers, asking about men who bought expensive footwear. No one in the four counties sold Thom Browne shoes. They all referred her to Dave Roberts, an exclusive men's shoe store in downtown Indianapolis.

And that was where she found him. Stephanie's job at the village of Field's Crossing had killed her, which explained why there were two files marked "capital." One ended in 'al' and the other ended with 'ol.' Bob Kane's knowledge as a banker had killed him. An hour later, she showered and drove to Columbia Hospital.

*   *   *

"That bastard. I'm making some calls." Starr pointed a long, manicured fingernail at Laurent.

The results of the MRI on Starr's neck showed two broken vertebrae but no damage to the spinal cord. Dr. Creighton prescribed a low-dose painkiller and a cervical collar for the next six weeks. Laurent helped Starr put on several bracelets and matching fuzzy socks.

"Where are my earrings?"

Laurent looked at her best friend. "Maybe you should skip those until the collar's off. They won't hang right, and that'll bug you."

"What are you gonna do about that fuckin' asshole?"

"I'm obtaining evidence to prove it was him."

"Jhonni, you're too softhearted for small-town politics. I'm not. I'm a loudmouthed bitch."

"You're not a bitch, and you're gonna have a swarm of nurses in here if you don't calm down. Your face is red, and that beeping noise just got faster."

It was early Monday afternoon as Laurent perched on the edge of Starr's hospital bed. A Styrofoam cup of ice sat on the bed tray, along with broth and an unopened cup of orange Jell-O. Upon visiting Starr in the hospital and explaining the invasion of her home and the complaint filed against her, Starr's heartbeat had shot up. She was pissed.

"I'm still making some calls. That asshole's not getting away with this."

"Is it possible to embezzle from Field's Crossing? How would it work?"

"Anything's possible. Give me a minute. Goddamn pillows. The food's for shit, too."

Laurent stood and repositioned the pillows behind Starr's back and neck.

"Field's Crossing uses a closed-loop system," Starr said. "There are a few full-time employees, like me, but the town uses an old method of government. A mayor and four council members. Each member has a specific area. Public property. Public health and safety. Finance. Streets and public improvements. The mayor and the four council members are all part-time and get paid a pittance."

"Jim Cotter is the trustee in charge of finance?"

"Jim was appointed to head up the finance department after the previous council member moved south. He also handles the town's legal issues, and he keeps getting reelected. Every two years.

"If your idea is correct, Jim would have to create a bank account resembling one of the town's accounts. On the Town of Field's Crossing's Finance account, he's the primary account holder, but he's also the secondary account holder as legal counsel.

"As finance manager, he balances the checkbook, writes checks, makes deposits, and requests funds. I assume he balances the checkbook online, but I never check. It's not my job. No one really oversees the council members or the mayor. You know how small towns trust everybody, but if you're right, I'm guessing he would have the financial statements sent to a personal PO box he controls. Most small towns and villages deposit the money collected from tax revenues, fees, federal grants, etcetera into the Indiana Fund, where Indiana municipalities earn interest. The Town of Field's Crossing or, in this case, Jim Cotter can transfer money into other accounts, corporate, motor fund, capital development, and so forth. After that he can create false invoices and write checks to pay the false invoices.

"The other possibility is to write checks to the treasurer, which would then end up in an account he created as Field's Crossing treasurer and move money from there. Or he created another account making himself the only signer, which he would then be able to send into yet another account for himself. There are at least two levels, possibly three, over which he has complete control."

"Didn't anyone ask where the money was?"

"Jim often told the mayor and council members the state of Indiana was late in paying municipalities, sometimes as long as a year."

"But what happens when we elect someone new?"

"I'm guessing he explained all of it to them and, after a few months, they trusted him and forgot. They'd have no reason to question what looked like another town account."

"How much do you think Jim has embezzled?"

"Let me at him. I'll beat it out of him." Starr winced. "Goddamn it. I can't even shake my head. Everything hurts."

"Have you seen yourself lately?"

"Shut up."

"When's the next payment to Field's Crossing?"

"Should be next week."

"Don't laugh too hard at my accounting method, but here's my list of payments Jim owes on. Would the next payment cover all of this?" Laurent handed the yellow pad to Starr.

"You're right about one thing—your method isn't very accountant-like, but I get it. Next week's payment to Field's Crossing would cover all of this and then some." Starr held the legal pad in front of her face.

"So, my theory is possible?" Laurent stuck her pen in her pocket. The idea that multiple layers were needed to cover up Jim's embezzling scheme had popped into her mind as she was practicing this morning. The plan was complex and intricate, just like great classical music, but ultimately simple in its design and deception. "How do I prove all of this?"

"Bank records. Match up the deposit from the state to the exact same amount into one or two accounts with only his name on them, and you've got embezzlement." Starr sipped ice water from the Styrofoam cup. "That asshole. What tipped you off?"

"Boots and shoes. And Art and Dutch."

"How in the hell could those two old geezers help? What could they possibly know?"

"It's not what they know but what they told me," Laurent said. "They claimed Jim was, as Dutch said—talking smack about me. I couldn't figure out why until I saw Jim's name on the complaint from the election board. He wants to get rid of me. Why?"

"Because he needs a deaf, dumb, and blind sheriff." Starr pointed at Laurent. "Creighton won't let me outta here for a few more days, but I've got a phone. And a mouth. Leave the election to me. Go. Catch that bastard."

CHAPTER FIFTY-THREE

"WHAT DO YOU need? Where are you?" Glen answered on one ring.

"I'm on the lower level with Naomi. I need a recorded conversation with Starr explaining the closed-loop accounting system used by Field's Crossing and how someone can embezzle money," Laurent said. "Once you get that, I'll need a records subpoena for Farmers Bank, specifically Jim Cotter's accounts, and another records subpoena for the state treasurer's office and a third one for the village of Field's Crossing. What account or accounts was the money deposited into, who is a signer, and who dispersed the funds and where did the funds wind up."

"Cotter? Lawyer? Town treasurer? Trustee Jim Cotter? Are you sure about this? We don't need him to slap a lawsuit on us for illegal search and seizure and God knows what else."

"When I asked Starr what Stephanie was doing for the village, she said she was scanning in some old files. Then she remembered Stephanie asking about a particular account. The spelling was slightly off. Capital "al" versus capitol "ol." She was going to check but forgot in the aftermath. When she finally remembered, she went looking for the last box of information Stephanie had been scanning in and couldn't find it. When she looked at the archive file on the laptop where all the documents were being scanned into, she couldn't find anything there either. After that, she called the bank and asked for a list of all of Field's Crossing's accounts, including account numbers and signers. There was one account she couldn't access and the signers were Field's Crossing's finance manager or Field's Crossing's Legal Counsel."

"Jim Cotter."

"The last person to use the laptop wasn't Stephanie. It was Jim. Starr thinks he might have erased a folder, so I'm leaving the laptop with Naomi. Apparently, even though you erase something, it really isn't gone. Don't ask. I didn't get it either. I'm speculating about motive, but I'm guessing Jim enjoyed his life of luxury and got way overextended."

"That it?"

"Get a subpoena for the dry cleaner in town. Confiscate Jim's winter coat," she said. "And the auto body shop. Jim's Beemer."

"I'll have everything in the next twenty-four hours."

After hanging up with Glen, Laurent read the next item on her legal pad. "Naomi, would you access the DMV for me?"

"What name?"

"Jim Cotter."

Laurent read over Naomi's shoulder. Jim owned two vehicles. A BMW Roadster and a 2019 Ford F-450. She recalled Vern's comment about four vehicles at the water tower. He said the last vehicle was a car. Not a pickup. Not a Jeep. Not a clunker. Laurent scrolled through her cell phone.

"Cook's Auto Body Shop."

"Sheriff Laurent. Two questions. Do you have any surveillance cameras?"

"Nothing inside, but one camera outside on all four walls. The whole thing erases itself on the first of the month."

"I'm getting a subpoena for your surveillance tapes. Dak will be by later this afternoon. Please don't touch anything."

"Will do. What's your other question?"

"Do you have any vehicles in your shop with front-end damage?"

"I've got two vehicles I'm doing work on. Jim Cotter's BMW and Bob Kane's Caddy."

"What did Cotter say when he brought the BMW in?"

"Said he got stuck in a snowbank right when the blizzard hit. Couldn't see a thing. Whiteout conditions. That's what he gets for driving a luxury vehicle on a day like that," Cook said.

"Did he say where he was when he damaged his car?"

"I didn't ask. It's a common problem with a big snow."

"How long before you're done with repairs?" she asked.

"Still waiting for the damn parts. BMW is so slow. They want the owner to drive the vehicle to one of their certified repair centers or authorized dealers. I told Jim his bumper would fall off before he got there. He called them, but they're still giving me a hassle. Who's going to pay for the shipping? I told them to drive the parts here or, better yet, I'll drive over and pick them up."

"The BMW is still in your shop?" Laurent had barely glanced at the other vehicles at the auto body shop the night of the break-in. She'd been focused on the intruder and the red Jeep.

"It's going to take up space for at least another week," Cook said. "I should charge a parking fee. Never buy a BMW or a Porsche."

Laurent snorted. As if that were an option. Next item. A ball peen hammer. After the records subpoena, she'd get a search warrant for Jim's vehicles and property. The smell in Jim's garage had made her sneeze, but it wasn't until she talked to Starr that Laurent remembered the disinfectant. Granted, it was circumstantial but added a layer of comfort to Laurent's certainty. She was close to solving the murders of Stephanie and Bob.

Bank records. That was what Starr said.

Laurent picked up her phone.

"Farmers Bank. Donna speaking. How may I help you?"

"Sheriff Laurent. Got a question for you—would Bob have known or had access to money moving between the state of Indiana and the village of Field's Crossing?"

"Of course. Those are usually huge sums of money. He'd know what was coming in and out and where it went."

"Once the money was transferred to Field's Crossing, then what?" Laurent asked.

"Then it becomes the village's job to pay their bills. Field's Crossing does hold all of its accounts with us, so Bob would always be able to track it if he wanted to."

"Did he ever question the payments Field's Crossing made?"

"No. That would be overstepping. Who the village pays, when, and the dollar amount aren't the bank's business. Talk to their finance manager. I think it's Jim Cotter."

"Thanks." Laurent laid her phone on Naomi's desk and sat back. Jim Cotter killed Stephanie because she discovered a box of secret bank records and mentioned it to her boss, Starr.

Jim killed Bob, his best friend, because Bob had access to all of Jim's accounts and questioned him about it. Maybe he demanded Jim bring his accounts current. It would take the bank at least a month to replace Bob, and by then, Jim would have stolen the next payment from the state to the village of Field's Crossing and paid off his debt. Bob's replacement would never know.

The next item on her list. She dialed Theresa Gattison's number and spoke briefly with her. Jim's phone records showed two calls to the Gattison house on the day Stephanie died. One at two fifteen. Theresa remembered Jim calling and asking about Stephanie. He claimed he wanted to make sure she didn't go into work. With the shock of losing her daughter, she'd forgotten. She was positive that was the only call from Jim that afternoon. They lost phone reception at four.

The last item on her yellow legal pad. Caleb. She dialed his cell phone number.

"How long did it take to pile the snow up at Webster Park?" she asked.

"We had at least two mounds of snow before seven a.m."

"The first trucks dumped the snow in the dark?"

"The village shuts off the overhead lighting in Webster Park during the winter, so it was pitch dark when the trucks dumped the first few loads."

Laurent hung up. None of the drivers would have been able to see the body, especially since the victim was wearing a white winter coat. She closed her eyes and envisioned the scene on Saturday morning. Pull the body out of the snow. Toss it into the bed of the pickup. Drive to Webster Park. Lay the body next to the mountain of snow. Shovel some snow on top. Drive away. The plows did the rest. Opening her eyes, she looked at Naomi.

"You nailed him, Sheriff."

CHAPTER FIFTY-FOUR

"Do you wish to file charges?"

Laurent stood at her kitchen sink peeling an orange. Her cell phone lay on the counter next to her, speakerphone engaged.

Laurent, the state's attorney, and an election board official were on a three-way call regarding the false accounts and donations made by Deputy Sheriff Mike Greene. It took election officials less than a day to follow the computer fraud and check her campaign account at Farmers Bank and all other banks in the quad-county area. Ninety-four dollars and thirty-two cents. Exactly. The false donations listed on her website were linked to closed bank accounts and closed credit cards all under the name of Mike Greene or his wife.

"I'll let you know. Greene will answer to me." She pulled the orange slices apart, dropped them into a Tupperware container, along with a bunch of grapes, and snapped the lid shut.

"Thank you for your cooperation," the election official said. "Clearing the path for us to do our job brought a quick resolution."

"You are hereby reinstated immediately and with no loss of pay," the state's attorney said. "I'll assist you in filing charges against your deputy."

Laurent touched END on her phone. She was back in charge. Time to wrap up the murders.

* * *

"Where do you want to start?" Glen was waiting for her in her office.

"I'd like to kick the shit out of Greene, but that's going to have to wait. Right now, I'm afraid I'll say something I regret." Laurent yanked off her gloves.

"I warned you, but even I didn't think he'd stoop so low. He could lose his job. I'm betting Ralph had something to do with this mess." Glen patted his pocket. "I've got all of your search warrants and Creighton's issued Bob's death certificate. The manner of death is homicide. Where to?"

"Jay Cook's Auto Body Shop."

Stephanie's cell phone was found under the passenger front seat of the BMW.

Farmers Bank. Two boxes waited for them.

The cleaned coat was wrapped in plastic, along with the drop-off ticket.

"Good job, Jhonni." Glen stepped down from the SUV onto the black asphalt next to his pickup. "Let me know if you need help executing the warrants for Jim's place. I look forward to Ralph eating his words in the next edition of *The Crossing*."

CHAPTER FIFTY-FIVE

"Stop blubbering. Sheriff Laurent told me to pick you up and charge you with the murder of Stephanie Gattison." Greene snapped on leg cuffs, cutting into Theo's ankles.

He yanked out his desk chair and pulled the keyboard closer. Laurent should have arrested Theo herself and completed the paperwork. Not him. Her suspension lasted forty-eight hours, and all allegations were proven false. Ralph had assured him the suspension would last until after the election. At least her reinstatement wasn't public knowledge. Yet.

"Name."

"Theo Tillman."

"Middle initial."

"M. Why does the sheriff think I killed her? I didn't."

"Address," Greene snapped.

"I want a lawyer."

"You don't get a lawyer until we process you." Greene glared at the fat young man.

"I want one before then."

"Shut up and answer the question. You're not entitled to a lawyer until you're officially charged and processed. Not before."

"You didn't read me my rights," Theo whined.

"Yes, I did, and I'll do it again down in fingerprinting. Address."
Theo shut up.

Greene opened Theo's wallet and typed the information into the online arrest record.

Unshackling him from the floor, Greene held him by the elbow. He then led him down the stairs and re-shackled him at the fingerprinting area. After Theo wiped the black ink off his fingertips, Greene shoved him into a cell and slammed the door.

"What about my lawyer?"

*   *   *

"Laurent wants him to sit for an hour before she interrogates him." After fingerprinting Theo and locking him in the county jail, Greene stopped in the men's restroom and called Ralph.

"What does she have on the kid?" Ralph asked.

"DNA under the girl's fingernails, a security video showing an argument at Beaumon's between the two of them, and a witness who saw Theo's junker at the water tower at the same time as the victim's. There's a lot of evidence against him. Mostly circumstantial. Jim will bail him out in no time, assuming Neal can come up with the money."

"I always thought the kid was lazy, but I never pegged him for a killer."

"Something must have snapped. He couldn't stop shaking while I was processing him," Greene said.

"Or the arrest is buying time for the sheriff to figure out who really killed the girl. She lost the confidence of the voters when she was suspended, and now she's trying to get it back by arresting someone. Anyone. Even the wrong person. She wants to win so bad next week, she's willing to make a false arrest. I'll make that tomorrow's headline. Keep up the pressure. There's no way, with all this bad publicity, anyone in their right mind will vote for that bitch."

*　*　*

"What's your reason for arresting Theo Tillman?" Glen sat in front of Laurent's desk, papers spilling onto the floor, reading glasses perched on the end of his nose. He'd matched up money received from the state to money transferred to Jim's accounts.

"He threw a wrench at me. But really, I don't want Greene to know what I'm up to. I've got enough evidence to arrest Theo for the murder of Stephanie, even though I'm sure he didn't do it. I think it was Theo who broke into the auto body shop and planted the hammer in Dylan's Jeep, so I've got him for breaking and entering and assault with a deadly weapon, and if I see anything on social media or hear any chatter at the Skillet before I question Theo, I'll know who spilled the beans."

"What did you tell Greene?"

"That I had more than probable cause to arrest him."

"Even though the hammers at the Tillman farm were clean?" Glen asked.

"He doesn't know that. And I've got skin under Stephanie's fingernails."

"The video shows she scratched him."

"I'm betting Theo doesn't remember, and I password protected the video. Greene doesn't know it either. I want the grapevine to start so the real killer relaxes and thinks I screwed up. I'm killing time for the DA to issue the arrest warrant. I'll go talk to Theo in an hour or so and change the charge to assault and breaking and entering. That'll give

Greene enough time to call Ralph and concoct some story for tomorrow's headlines."

"Setting a trap." Glen chuckled. "I love it."

"What goes around comes around."

CHAPTER FIFTY-SIX

JIM FLICKED ON the garage light and pressed the automatic door opener. One bay of his three-car garage sat empty. Jay Cook had picked up the parts for his BMW and he was planning on checking on his car. He loved his new Ford F-450—but pickups were common in farm country—unlike his expensive sports car.

Backing out, he waited for the garage door to close completely. Animals, raccoons, squirrels, and especially skunks were known to hibernate in or near warmer places. Under decks and in attics, barns, and sheds. Most farmers kept a dog or two plus a few cats to keep the vermin out, but Jim paid an exterminator every three months.

He crossed Turtle Lake Road and drove through the residential neighborhood of Field's Crossing. Snow was piled high on the sides of driveways, black and gray where the snow met the street. He hated the dirty look of snow. And it was piled everywhere.

His phone rang. The screen on his dashboard read "Laurent." He declined the call and wondered what she wanted. He enjoyed the Sunday edition of *The Crossing*, reading every word of Laurent's suspension. Every biased word. The suspension was better than the illegitimate daughter, but Ralph still had that information in his back pocket. Who knew when he'd use it.

Jim thought about the state's payment to Field's Crossing next week. He was planning to take the money and pay off all his creditors, except the mortgage, and leave. He briefly considered staying, training a new village manager, but knew he was pressing his luck. Whoever replaced Bob at Farmers Bank might not overlook his lack of income. It wasn't the first time he'd had to flee to escape his financial situation.

Jim turned into Cook's Auto Body Shop and honked. A side door opened and a head popped out.

"Afternoon, Mr. Cotter. The bumper was delivered late yesterday," Jay Cook said. "I'll have your vehicle ready in two hours."

"Can you have someone drive it out to my place? I'm meeting with a client all afternoon."

"Do you want us to park it in your garage?" Cook asked.

"Leave it out. I'll park it when I get home."

"When you were here the other day, did you take the gas can out of your trunk? I was going through the inventory, and that's the only thing the car came in with that isn't there now."

Jim nodded. He didn't know Cook inventoried the cars in his garage. It was definitely time to leave Field's Crossing.

"I'll drop the bill on the passenger seat," Cook said.

"The insurance company should be paying for this."

"I tried to send the claim through and it was denied. I called them and they told me the policy had been canceled for nonpayment of premiums."

"I'm paid up. Leave the bill in the car. I'll deal with the insurance company. Money-grubbing assholes." When Jim left next week, he could only drive one vehicle. The BMW. The new Ford was a pleasure, but a BMW spoke of wealth. And he had decided to head south to warmer weather. All of the bells and whistles he ordered on the pickup would be useless.

His phone buzzed. Text message from Laurent. *I'd like to talk to you.* He deleted it.

His last stop of the day was the dry cleaner.

CHAPTER FIFTY-SEVEN

LAURENT STARTED HER search for Jim Cotter. He wasn't answering his phone. He wasn't at the village hall. He wasn't at the Skillet. He wasn't at the cigar lounge. Laurent drove to his home on Turtle Lake Road and stopped at the end of the half-mile driveway. The single black asphalt lane was clear of snow and ice, the remaining water glistening in the late afternoon sun. The temperature had climbed to forty degrees at noon and was now beginning to drop. The digital temperature in Laurent's SUV read thirty-six, and night was falling. Any moisture left on the roads would be ice in the next hour.

Jim's house sat on a small bluff; the rear of the property surrounded by woods leading to Turtle Lake. To the right of the house, the land fell away to reveal a small pond, frozen over. Two snow-covered Adirondack chairs perched at the edge of the water. A three-car garage with overhead lighting sat on the left side of the house, the heated circular driveway free of snow and ice.

"Dispatch. Be advised. I am at twenty-five N thirty-six Turtle Lake Road, approaching residence. No vehicles in sight."

"Ten-four."

Laurent eased her foot off the brake and crept down the lane. No exterior lighting was activated. She circled to the front porch and parked alongside it, facing Turtle Lake Road. She left the engine running and wondered why her calls and texts to Jim earlier in the day had gone unanswered. Her secretary checked the courthouse and Jim had no matters before any court today. His pickup had been spotted at the Skillet early in the morning and his BMW Roadster was still awaiting repair in the auto body shop.

Laurent slid out of the police SUV. As she mounted the shoveled front steps of Jim's house, dusk descended upon Field's Crossing. She switched on her Maglite and knocked. Light snow drifted through the cold air as the next round of precipitation began to fall. In the bright light of her flashlight, the snow swirled and sparkled like glitter.

No answer.

Opening the screen door, Laurent banged on the glass in the front door and peered in. A night-light glowed in the hallway, the rooms on either side dark.

The back door slammed.

Laurent trotted down the steps and jogged to the back of the house.

Jim was in full snow camo gear, backpack strapped on, shotgun loosely gripped in his right hand, marching toward the forest in his backyard.

"Jim. I need to talk to you."

"Come and get me." He disappeared into the woods.

"Dispatch. Suspect is fleeing on foot, east toward Turtle Lake. Suspect is armed. Set up roadblocks at Turtle Lake bridge, the Five-and-Twenty, Turtle Lake Road, East Road, and Bees Creek Road. I am in pursuit."

"Ten-four. What assistance do you require?"

"Send in two officers from the north end of Turtle Lake and two from the south. I will advise if suspect tries to cross the lake."

"Ten-four. Be careful, Sheriff."

Laurent didn't answer. She returned to her SUV and pulled an orange vest with fluorescent green striping over her head and turned the engine off, securing the keys in a zippered leg pocket. She slid hand and foot warmers and two mini-flashlights into the deep side pockets of her coat. Extra batteries went into another leg pocket. She turned the volume down on the radio at her shoulder.

Half an hour until complete darkness.

The snow was big, fat, and fluffy.

Cotter had a three-minute head start.

Laurent paused at the edge of the woods and turned back to face the rear of Jim's home. The house was dark and, as she watched, the cloud covering the moon drifted away, the shadow of the house casting its outline on the pristine snow. With a final look at the darkened house, Laurent plunged into the forest, clicked on her Maglite, and looked down. The deer path was well traveled, trampled down. She snapped a picture of the boot print before following Jim's imprint on the path.

Would he follow the deer trail all the way to the lake?

* * *

Vern pulled out of his brother's driveway, turned left on the Five-and-Twenty, and pulled onto Turtle Lake bridge. He tapped the steering wheel with his fingers and peered into the falling darkness. A light flickered in the barren forest across Turtle Lake. Throwing the ancient pickup into park, he turned off the engine, grabbed the shotgun behind the driver's seat, and trudged down to the edge of the frozen water.

He wasn't going to wait. Ever again. If that little voice in his head told him to go and look, by God, he was going to. He hadn't listened to that niggling voice and Owen's girl had died. He should have walked over while both vehicles were still there.

And now he was going to find out what idiot was traipsing in the woods as the sun was going down and more snow was on the way. The sheriff didn't need to find another body.

*   *   *

In ten steps, the woods closed behind Laurent. The wind was light and snow plopped from tangled overhead branches, where a few dry brown leaves clung fiercely, the last to fall. Off to the left, rabbit tracks disappeared into a fallen log. Laurent brushed against a thornbark tree, a small barb piercing her jacket. Stepping back, she freed her arm, listening for Jim's footsteps over the thudding in her chest.

Crunch. Jim was ahead of her and still on the deer trail.

A few birds fluttered high above, and the snow thickened. As the sun set and the winds died down, the snow would freeze and crust over again. Wherever Jim was heading, Laurent knew he wanted to get there before she could track him in the snow. Once the snow turned icy, she would hear every step.

Jim had chosen his time well. Laurent needed a flashlight to follow. Jim would be able to see her and stay ahead of her. She had no idea which direction he was heading, but if he stashed an escape vehicle in the culvert by the bridge or at the abandoned campground or on the other side of Turtle Lake, he'd drive straight into a roadblock. But if he had access to a snowmobile somewhere in the woods, he might get away.

Laurent quickened her step. Her gaze darted left and right, and she almost missed where Jim detoured off the deer path. He was heading south toward the abandoned campground, Emmit's empty cornfields, and open farmland, barren of houses.

Laurent spoke quietly into the radio clipped to her shoulder. "Suspect is heading south. Maintain radio silence." Jim had enough of a head start. He could see her coming. He didn't need to hear her coming.

A branch snapped.

Laurent slipped behind a large oak tree and dropped to one knee. The sound was directly ahead.

Another snap.

Why was he making so much noise?

She slid behind another tree. Bark shattered in her face, a sliver slicing into her cheek, drawing blood. *Shit.* She had forgotten he was a crack shot.

"Trying to hide behind a tree?" Jim shouted.

"Just wanted to talk to you. Why'd you run?" She pulled out her Glock.

"Don't play coy with me. You're smarter than that. I've got alerts on all my accounts. Starr never would have snooped at the bank unless you told her to. I knew someone was watching me. You were the logical conclusion."

"Why'd you kill Stephanie?"

"Who says I did?" Jim yelled.

"The ball peen hammer I confiscated from the pegboard in your garage and I found her cell phone in your car." Laurent crouched behind the tree. *Keep him talking. Get a bearing on his location.*

"Snoopy little bitch. She found my secret account."

"Was she alive when you buried her at the park?"

"I didn't check."

"Caleb saw a Ford F-450 early that morning when he was plowing out his secretary. I checked with Ford. You're the only customer who bought that new truck in the quad-county area. How much did it set you back?" She paused. "I know about the embezzling."

Tree bark shattered over her head as the next bullet embedded itself into the oak tree. Laurent pulled off her ear warmers. No crunching of hard-packed snow. Jim was walking in the deep stuff with a heavy backpack. *That'll slow him down, but he won't make a sound.* She pulled out her phone and activated the built-in tape recorder and returned the phone to her pocket, securing the Velcro tightly.

The snow was up to her knees. If he was heading south, that put her parallel to him, but behind him. Instead of pushing through the deep snow, Laurent decided to high-step it. Ten steps at a time.

She picked her next tree. Ten steps.

Safe. Slight panting.

Next tree. Fifteen more steps. Breathing heavier. Next tree.

Laurent paused after fifty feet and peered to her left, both hands wrapped around her weapon. Where'd he go? Nothing. But no shot in the dark either.

Next tree.

The bullet hit her in the chest.

*   *   *

Hearing the first shot, Vern jumped behind a tree. He'd forgotten his deer hunting vest and was about to turn back when he heard noise. Was that the sheriff's voice? Who was the other guy?

Another shot.

What the hell is going on? Why is the sheriff yelling at this guy?

Keeping to the edge of the lake, Vern dashed from tree to tree, jumping over snow-covered roots. The snow around the lakeshore was deeper than it was in the middle of the forest. His long underwear was tucked inside the calf-high fleece-lined rubber boots, and his jeans covered the boots. His worn Carhartt jacket was zipped up. He flipped up the collar, pulled out a headband, and snugged it over his ears before settling his baseball cap back on.

Another shot.

The man laughed.

*   *   *

Laurent stared up through the branches, not breathing. The force spun her halfway around, and her head was buried in the snow, the cold seeping into her ears, fat flakes landing on her face. She inhaled and clamped down on the pain, but not before a groan passed through her lips. *Oh my God. That hurt.* But the bullet-resistant vest helped. And she hadn't lost her gun in the deep snow.

"Did I hurt you? Too fucking bad." Jim laughed. "The next shot is going through your eye. Do you have a preference?" His voice floated around her.

I've gotta move. She gasped and rolled over onto her hands and knees.

"How'd you figure it out?" Jim's voice was coming from a different direction.

Laurent pushed to one knee, left hand on the tree. "I followed the money. Some of your former employers were less than complimentary and, even though they didn't accuse you of embezzling from them, they did mention excessive fees, questionable accounting practices, and missing money. You've embezzled before. Why wouldn't you do it again? And you didn't quite kill Starr."

"I heard she was unconscious."

"You heard wrong. We had a long talk two days ago. On my day off. Thanks for arranging that. Why'd you file the complaint with the election board?" Laurent pulled herself up and leaned against the shattered tree, catching her breath. She needed to keep moving.

"To get you out of office."

"That didn't work too well." Where was he? He was close enough to carry on a shouting conversation, but he wasn't in front of her anymore. With the thick falling snow blinding her, she couldn't see ten feet in front of her. Which meant he couldn't either.

"I had a nice chat with your sister."

"How'd you find her?"

"Her parole officer. I don't think she likes you," Jim said. "*The Crossing's* going to publish the information about your abandoned daughter right before Election Day."

"Guess I can't blame that one on Ralph." She'd cross that bridge later. *Which direction? He'll expect me to move forward. Follow his trail.*

"You've got no one to blame but yourself. I sent the information to Ralph anonymously, but I can't wait to read the column he writes," Jim said.

"You're staying in Field's Crossing?"

"No, but only one of us is leaving the forest alive."

*   *   *

Vern bared his teeth and a low growl escaped from his throat. Jim killed Owen's girl. Left her out in the snow to freeze to death. Death was too good for him.

He skirted the end of Turtle Lake and now he dug deep into the forest. Laurent and Jim were close to the frozen lake. He'd approach from a different direction. Slipping from tree to tree, Vern was grateful he didn't have his orange deer hunting vest on. There were three marksmen out in the falling snow and darkness. Two were shooting at each other. Neither one knew he was there. He had the advantage.

To his left, a flashlight clicked off and the sound of tearing Velcro filled the quiet forest.

*   *   *

Laurent tore off the outer fluorescent vest, wincing at the sound of Velcro. Jim would know what she was doing.

"You should have started with that. I could see you a mile away with those bright yellow stripes. You've been a sitting duck for the last half hour. And if you take your vest off, I'll claim self-defense. Your days of being sheriff are over."

Laurent dropped the vest in the snow, ran to the next tree, and peered around the edge. She clicked off her flashlight and slid it into a pocket in her pant leg. The odds were more even now. Dark-blue jacket, black pants.

"Back to my original question—why'd you kill Stephanie?"

"She was scanning in documents from my hidden account."

"Do you really think she would have understood? I flipped through a bunch of those boxes, and it all looked the same to me. Why'd she have to die?"

"After she told Starr, what choice did I have?"

Laurent was quiet. If Stephanie had been a little less conscientious, she might still be alive, but Jim would still be embezzling. "How'd you know where to find her?"

"That was the hardest part," he said. "I drove all over Field's Crossing that Wednesday after school, looking for her pickup. The water tower was my last stop. I was already working on Plan B when I found her stuck in a ditch along the gravel road. Ungrateful brat. She had the nerve to make fun of me for driving my BMW. She'd have frozen to death before the storm passed."

"She still froze to death." Bent over, Laurent slid from tree to tree. Jim's voice was louder, closer.

"That's when the idea popped into my head. All I had to do was hit her hard enough over the head so she didn't wake up and dump her outside. So, I did."

"I noticed the bleach smell in your garage."

Jim snorted. "I had to clean the floor after I dragged her across it and tossed her outside. The blizzard did the rest. I threw her into the back of my truck and dumped her in Webster Park. The tires on my truck cut through the snow like it was water. I love that truck."

Where was he? The snow was falling faster and thicker. White flakes clung to her eyelashes before melting and sliding down her cheeks. Jim's voice sounded as though he was to her left. Had he reached Turtle Lake? Would he try to cross it? *No. Then he'd be out in the open. He's gonna try and slide on the edge of the ice.*

"Let's change the subject. I thought Bob was your best friend. Why'd you kill him?"

"That was hard, but Bob was asking too many questions. He knew I was late on my mortgage and credit cards and the BMW dealer was coming to repossess my car and the IRS had notified Farmers Bank they were the second lienholder. I kept all of my accounts at Farmers Bank. I should have spread them out and used several different banks, then no one would have made the connection. A mistake I won't make again."

Laurent crouched behind a tree fifty feet from the edge of Turtle Lake. Snow clouds covered the early night sky. Would Jim attempt to cross the frozen lake? Or shoot her first? "Walk me through the ice tent scenario."

"It was easy. He leaned over to get a beer out of the cooler, and I bopped him on the head. I held his face under water until he died, and then I pulled him back. I wanted it to look like he had fallen into a diabetic coma and drowned all on his own."

"You almost got away with it. You left a boot print on Bob's back and a shoe print next to Stephanie's pickup at the water tower. Once I tracked who owned both pairs of footwear, you were easy to pinpoint. You have expensive taste."

A branch snapped. Jim was approaching from her left. Fat, fluffy snowflakes obscured her vision.

"I didn't give you enough credit. Bob knew business had been slow and I had no accounts receivables to speak of. My mistake was in telling him I had a big payout coming. He wanted to know the case number or the client."

"Since you didn't have any money coming in from your private practice, I'm assuming you were planning to embezzle the next deposit from Field's Crossing's account." She crouched low and slid out from behind a tree.

The bullet hit her in the upper arm, the Glock dropping from her hand and disappearing into the snow. She grabbed her arm, blood oozing through her gloved fingers, tears leaking out of the corners of her eyes. Pitching forward, she twisted at the last second onto her back. Gritting her teeth, she reached over and packed the open wound with snow. "Shit, that hurts."

* * *

Vern peeked out from behind a tree and watched Jim shoot Laurent in the arm. He raised his shotgun. Too late. The camouflaged shooter disappeared into the thickening snow.

Where was Laurent? How badly was she hurt? Should he follow Jim or stop and help the sheriff? Vern shook his head. Jim killed his own best friend. What kind of a man did that? The sheriff would be fine. He hoped. He really didn't want someone else dying right in front of him.

And then he heard her speak.

*   *   *

Lying on her back in the snow, Laurent touched her radio with a bloodied, gloved finger. "Officer down. Repeat. Officer down."

"What's your twenty?"

"East of Turtle Lake somewhere in the woods. Suspect has fired four bullets. Proceed with extreme caution. He doesn't care who he shoots."

"Ambulance will be coming from Turtle Lake bridge."

"Activate the GPS on my phone. I'll proceed on foot when I can." Laurent lay flat on her back on the ice-cold ground, snow blanketing her. Sweeping her left arm like a snow angel, she found her Glock and shoved it into her holster. She'd need her left arm to get up. She crunched her stomach muscles, sat up, and rolled onto her knees. Staggering to her feet, she picked up her right hand, placed it in her pocket, and pulled her Glock out with her left hand. She tried to pull the tattered ends of her parka over the wound.

Where was Jim? She needed to keep him in range until backup arrived. Stephanie and Bob's murderer wasn't going to get away. She raised her voice. "Jim, your aim's a little off."

"Bitch."

Jim was close. Did he really want to kill her?

"You tried to blame Neal for Bob's death. Good idea. I ran around for two days before I realized Neal was a smoke screen. Did you suggest he contact Renewable?" She leaned against a tree. She had never fired a weapon with her left hand.

"That idiot did it on his own," Jim said. "People will forget me and what I've done because Neal's bringing windmills to Field's Crossing. He'll be hated long after I'm gone."

"You've been planning to run away."

"It wasn't until I stopped to pick up my winter coat and found you'd confiscated it. Any evidence you obtained from the auto body shop, the bank, the village, the dry cleaner, anywhere, I'll have it thrown out in court."

"If you're so sure you can beat all these charges, why in the hell are we out in the freezing cold and snow screaming at each other?"

*   *   *

Vern listened as Laurent spoke on her radio. She sounded coherent to him. Probably in shock. He squinted into the forest. Laurent leaned against a tree, gun in her left hand, bloody snow oozing down her right sleeve. The three shooters were in a triangle. Jim was to his right, Laurent to his left. In the middle of the forest, he spotted the black barrel of Jim's shotgun, rising, aiming. Without thinking, Vern raised his shotgun and hit the branch above Jim, showering the shooter with snow.

*   *   *

Laurent fired into the cascade of snow.

The air filled with Jim's scream and the ground shook as he hit the snow-packed forest floor. She spun around, left arm extended, finger on the trigger.

"You make sure that sonofabitch spends the rest of his life behind bars."

CHAPTER FIFTY-EIGHT

"RETIRE OR GET fired. Your choice." Laurent's right arm was in a sling and she had swallowed four ibuprofen before coming into work.

"What are you talking about?" Deputy Sheriff Mike Greene sat up straight in the chair.

"The charges are as follows: leaking classified information to the press, attempted computer fraud, illegal tampering and use of office equipment, conspiracy to commit election fraud, and aiding and abetting an illegal breaking and entering," Laurent said. "These are the major charges. After that, I will add in dereliction of duty and impeding progress on a murder case."

"On what grounds?"

"I sent emails from Bob's browser for you to analyze and you said there was nothing there. When I looked at the emails, it was obvious Bob was auditing Jim. You're a detective. You should have picked up on that."

"Bob was dead before we had access to those emails. Figuring out Jim was the killer wouldn't have saved Bob's life."

"It would have saved me from getting shot. Twice."

Greene was sweating. His face was red, and half-moon circles grew under each arm. Laurent stood behind her desk and flipped open a manila folder.

"Let's start with tampering and misuse of office equipment and conspiracy to commit election fraud. On February nineteen, twentieth, and twenty-first, two thousand nineteen, you attempted to access my campaign fund via Farmers Bank from a computer in this office. You also sent anonymous donations from empty or closed bank accounts and closed credit cards. IT was able to trace the illegal donations back to closed accounts in your name. You wanted it to look as though I were accepting illegal contributions."

"You can't prove that."

"Not only can I prove it, I can prove attempts on my personal savings and checking accounts from the same bank. Since the day I found you sitting behind my desk, IT has tracked your password and login. I have a list of every website you've been in and every website you've attempted to access."

"That's illegal."

"Not at all. As head of this department, one of my duties is to ensure the integrity of all communications and equipment assigned to the sheriff's office. Naomi in IT had no problem with this directive, and the state's attorney informed me I was well within my rights and responsibilities to look into this matter."

"You can't single me out. I'll challenge you in court on this." Greene's knuckles turned white as he gripped the arms of the chair.

"The state's attorney said the same thing, so I put a trace on everyone in the department. Your activity is the only questionable activity."

"You're in over your head. Be careful who you're messing with."

Laurent opened another file. "Shall I continue? Here's a picture of you and and Ralph having dinner at Bubba's Steakhouse in Columbia."

"It's not illegal to eat dinner with a friend, even if he is a reporter."

"What's illegal is using personal information, not your own, for nefarious gain. This next picture shows you handing Ralph a piece of paper."

"Again, not illegal."

"Here's a series of photos showing Ralph receiving the paper, reading it, and putting it in his pocket. The last picture is a close-up of what's written on the paper." Her left hand bunched into a fist. "You copied my passwords and gave them to the media. Do you know what the state's attorney wants to do to you?"

"None of the passwords worked."

"Except for one." She stared at the sweating deputy. "My garage code. Which leads me to the most serious charge. You helped Ralph break into my home."

"He did that on his own. I had nothing to do with it. You can't prove a thing."

"I thought you might say that, so I contacted the state's attorney, and they put a trace on Ralph's cell phone. Your text to him immediately before and after the break-in is in their hands."

"Circumstantial bullshit. You're afraid of losing the election, so you trumped up some fake charges. I'm going to have your badge." Greene shoved his chair into the closed office door, rattling the blinds.

A discreet knock and Dak poked his head inside Laurent's office. "Everything okay here?"

"No, it's not okay. This bitch is threatening to bring me up on false charges so she can win next week. The press is going to crucify you."

"Everything's fine, Dak. Thanks for asking." Laurent glared at Greene. "Sit down. I'm glad you're going down fighting. I'll add insulting and abusive language directed at a superior to the list of charges."

"You're not a superior officer. You're an insult to this department and have been ever since you were elected. You wouldn't have gotten elected if it hadn't been for Glen Atkins. He was supposed to endorse me. Not you."

"Which way do you want to go? Retire or fire?"

"I'll see you in court."

"You are hereby suspended without pay. Badge and gun on my desk."

* * *

The hardest part about having her right arm in a sling was putting the SUV into gear. Park, reverse, drive. How simple. Laurent finally gave up, eased her arm out of the sling, and turned the key. Pain shot from her fingertips to her ears. Jim's bullet had torn through flesh and nicked the bone. The orthopedic surgeon who removed it told her she'd have pain for the next six months. The bruising on her chest would be long gone before the pain in her arm disappeared.

She crept down the lane to Vern's cabin and stopped fifty feet away from his front door. Before she could put the SUV into park, the cabin door flew open and Vern strode out. No coat, no hat, no gloves, boot laces untied.

"Unlock the door. Let me help you."

"I'm not an invalid."

"Of course you're not. Now, unlock the damn door."

Laurent pushed the unlock button.

"You took your sling off."

"I could barely turn the key, let alone put the car in gear, with my left hand."

"You're not working, are you?"

"Desk duty only. For two months." She turned sideways in her seat, holding her right arm next to her body.

Vern grasped her left elbow. "One foot at a time."

"I can get in and out of a car."

"I see the pain on your face. As soon as we get inside, the sling goes back on."

"Vern, relax. I'm fine."

"I thought he was going to kill you," he whispered. "Right in front of me, and there was nothing I could do to stop him."

"You saved my life. I drove out here to say thank you." Slowly, arm throbbing, she extended her right hand. "Thank you."

Gently, he squeezed her hand. "Come, sit a spell."

CHAPTER FIFTY-NINE

"What's going to happen to Jim?" Jane Martin asked.

After Stephanie's funeral, Laurent changed into street clothes and picked up Starr, who insisted on being at the voter registration drive, even in a wheelchair. She and Starr looked like the walking wounded when they entered the high school gymnasium. They joined Theresa Gattison and Jane Martin along the back wall of the gym. The two women held Styrofoam coffee cups.

"He's admitted to killing Stephanie and Bob and attempting to kill Starr," Laurent said. "He'll never leave prison."

"Why'd he do it?"

"He never wanted to be poor again."

"How much did he embezzle from Field's Crossing?" Jane asked.

"With the state's attorney's help, I'll be able to figure it out. It looks as though that asshole's been embezzling for the last ten years. I'll have to think of my own personal revenge. Asshole pushed me down the stairs." Starr bared her teeth.

"Can the village recover any of it?" Theresa asked.

"Field's Crossing will have to work to get any of it back. The state will claim we should have had better oversight, not put all the money into one person's control, and we'll need to change our accounting methods and system. The state will oversee Field's Crossing for a few years until they're satisfied we've got it under control and this can't happen again," Starr said.

"What about his personal estate?" Theresa asked.

"Since he wasn't married and had no kids, siblings, or parents alive and he didn't have a will, it'll all go to the state of Indiana. The state will sell everything. It looks as though most of the money will go to back taxes." Laurent adjusted her sling.

"I don't understand why," Jane said. "We all go through financial uncertainties."

"Jim was raised by his aunt and uncle in Greensburg," Laurent said. "It wasn't a good relationship. He left the day he graduated from high school and never went back. I spoke with two of his former employers, and, while they didn't admit it out loud, they implied Jim had embezzled from them also."

"But he was a lawyer. He knew the consequences."

"There are things about Jim we may never understand," Laurent said. "How's the voter registration drive going?"

"We've signed up ninety-seven new registered voters, and not all of them are high schoolers. Did you know Shelby has lived here all her life and never voted? She's going to vote for you on Tuesday, put the farmhouse on the market, and move to Tampa with her sister. And Dylan and Caleb have been dragging all the millennials in to register," Jane said.

"Owen and I are going to bust our butts in the next few days to make sure you get reelected," Theresa said. "Starr's got us all lined up with phone numbers and what she calls 'talking points.'"

"Me and Emmit and Vern are doing the same," Jane said. "*The Crossing* has gotten away with publishing crap for too long. We're all tired of it. It's time to fight back."

"Jhonni, here's a loaf of bread to take home with you tonight. Sheriff Atkins was right in supporting you four years ago. I wish you well in the upcoming election, although I don't think you'll have any competition. What's gonna happen to Mike Greene?" Shelby asked.

"I can't discuss his case."

"Are you going to press charges against him or his buddy Ralph?"

"*The Crossing* will publish a full retraction of all nonverified information about my campaign funding and a verified account of the murder investigations. Both of these articles will be approved and confirmed by the state's attorney's office before publication," Laurent said. "Those were the conditions I placed on Ralph and his newspaper. They will run on the front page. Every registered voter will receive a copy, and all merchants in the quad-county area will have extra newspapers, free to everyone. *The Crossing* will pick up the cost of publication and distribution, and every newspaper must be distributed by Monday at noon."

"Just in time for the election. Ralph's going to hate you now more than ever," Jane said.

"Ralph has lost all credibility in the quad-county area," Theresa said. "I hope he goes bankrupt."

*　　*　　*

As the backhoe had cut through the frozen tundra, the casket of the high school senior waited, heavy on the gurney, to be lowered into the ground, Laurent had stood at attention, her eyes staring over the crowd of mourners, hearing the girl's killer screaming on the forest floor, her shot exploding his kneecap. She hadn't been thinking about the upcoming mandatory administrative leave or Stephanie's funeral or Bob's dead body or the attempted murder of her best friend.

She had said yes.

Her daughter was driving north to Field's Crossing and meeting her at the voter registration drive at the high school today. Laurent's stomach muscles were rigid, her left hand constantly sliding in and out of her pocket, her right in the sling. What would her daughter think?

Across the gym, Laurent saw a young woman hesitate in the doorway. Her breath caught.

BOOK CLUB
DISCUSSION QUESTIONS

1. Did you think that there was a single killer of the two murder victims in this small Indiana community? Why or why not?

2. How did you feel about the political instability of Jhonni Laurent's job? The impact of sexism or ageism? The extent of the collusion of Deputy Mike Greene and reporter Ralph Howard to influence the election? How important was the support of the former sheriff Glen Atkins? And the old-timers at the Skillet?

3. Discuss the extent of inaccurate reporting by the media. Do you think the following statement is accurate? "The problem living in a small town is that citizens from the older generation tend to believe *whatever is in print is true; whereas the internet is wrong.*"

4. How had the Grandad Martin and Grandad Tillman feud set up the Emmit and Neal dispute that set up the murders in this rural Indiana community?

5. In *Bones Under the Ice*, only one of the three Martin children may continue farming. What happens if none of the children

from a farm family want to become a farmer? How often do you think that happens?

6. Sheriff Jhonni Laurent has buried her feelings about the daughter she gave up for adoption as well as her destroyed musical career. What do you think of her decisions and reactions?

7. How important to Jhonni Laurent was her one and only female friend, Starr?

8. In today's age of transparency, would putting a child up for adoption thirty years ago influence your vote? Would it make a difference if the adoption was disclosed by the press vs. self-disclosed? Would you expect a different response from rural community voters than big-city voters?

9. Has your opinion changed about windmill farms? Do you think there will be eventual benefits of wind energy that outweigh the initial costs and soil disruption?

10. Did *Bones Under the Ice* unfold the way you expected? If not, what surprised you?

11. Are there any lingering questions from the book that you're still thinking about?